TRIAD ONE

Short Stories by JAMES GORDON
Poems by ELIZABETH BERRIDGE
A Novel by GWYN THOMAS

TRIAD TWO

edited by Jack Aistrop

This Very Sun by EDITH HEAL

States of Mind by JOHN ATKINS

The Gibsons of Glasgow by DOROTHY K. HAYNES

LONDON 1947
DENNIS DOBSON LTD

FIRST PUBLISHED IN 1947 BY
DENNIS DOBSON LIMITED
LONDON

All characters in this book are fictitious

PRINTED IN GREAT BRITAIN
BY WHITEHILL (PRINTERS) LTD
BIRMINGHAM 9

607/R

A NOTE FOR WRITERS AND
SUCH READERS WHO CARE TO READ IT

TRIAD TWO contains two short novels and a collection of stories and poems by a writer who writes poetry and prose and has no preference for either form.

The aims of the *TRIAD* series, as expressed in *TRIAD ONE*, are to publish work, both prose and verse, by writers who, for technical reasons, find their finished work either too long or too short to meet the requirements of publishers and editors. The volume of correspondence from writers, following the announcements of *TRIAD ONE*, confirms our belief that the series will provide an outlet for worthwhile work which might otherwise remain unpublished.

JACK AISTROP

THE WRITERS

Edith Heal

HAS been writing publicity, advertising and newspaper copy since she graduated from the University of Chicago in 1925. In the last twenty years, her typewriter has travelled with her from Chicago to Canada to France to Arizona—and finally to New York City where she now lives. Her first book, written soon after she left college, was a '165,000 word *Robin Hood*—at a penny a word'. She has written juveniles and had stories in various American publications.

John Atkins

BORN in Surrey, 1916. Worked as a Mass Observer; became Assistant Editor of Tribune and inaugurated its Literary Section of which he ultimately became editor. Rejoined Mass Observation as Public Relations Officer but was called up in 1944; released under Class B in 1945. Is now teaching. Has published poetry and prose in many collections and magazines, a collection of poems 'Experiences of England' and 'The Diary of William Carpenter' (fiction) which has been broadcast. Now edits 'New Saxon Review', a magazine devoted to the publication of good class work in the English tradition and points of view which do not normally find expression'.

Dorothy K. Haynes

HAS contributed to 'English Story', 'Modern Reading', etc. Her first novel is about to appear from Methuens and she is already at work on another, 'The Gibsons of Glasgow' having been written in between. During the same period, she also managed to get married, and to continue to give English lessons to Allied troops stationed near her home in Lanark. Headed the list of women applicants in this year's Tom Gallon Trust Award and was only beaten in the competition by a very short head. Is too modest to write biographical notes herself.

CONTENTS

EDITH HEAL

    This Very Sun   9

JOHN ATKINS

    The Dead House   85

    The Eviction   96

    Music Hath Power   110

    Names   133

    Rules of Action   134

    On Returning to Poetry   135

    Inquest   136

    My Future Life   137

DOROTHY K. HAYNES

    The Gibsons of Glasgow   139

THIS VERY SUN

CHAPTER ONE

EVERYTHING leads up to everything, the fat man thought, staring in panic at the unfamiliar scene. An editor wanted resort pictures for the January issue, so a man and his camera got off at a desert town in July.

'I'm doing it again,' the fat man said, wondering helplessly why he must always be wondering where he was. For a long time now he had felt homeless in his fat body, though it moved around with him quite easily, boarding trains, getting off at the right station, travelling from there to here like any other man. But it must be constantly reassured, this fat frightened body, so that his mind was never at rest because it was constantly recalling, repeating, to explain what was happening by what had gone before.

The white wall of the station was like a cinema screen waiting for the projector. Nobody met the train except a corpse in a box and its attendants. The fat man's hand, brushing against the mahogany box, felt wood, warmed by the sun. Heat came up from the cement platform attacking his legs. Walking made moisture behind the knees. After a while the legs seemed heavy. Then later, they seemed to float away. His hand jerked back from the burning metal of the cab, and he found he was breathing quickly to keep the hot dry air out of his lungs. Off there, in the air-cooled train, the mahogany box would be losing its warmth and breathing deep again.

'110 by noon,' the cab driver said.

And the fat man saw a child's drawing of the wind with cheeks puffed out like bellows blowing white waves of heat over the town.

The mountains can wait to be admired, he thought as he closed his eyes against the sun. But he could still see their scalloped rim around the saucer of the town, as he could see the postcard clouds that the camera would reproduce as cotton, cream puff or snow. And if the lens came closer, as nothing at all. He savoured the pleasure of making a cloud become nothing at all. The feeling lasted all the way to the hotel.

The dark hole of the hotel lobby had an early morning emptiness. He expected bamboo and linen slip covers. Instead there was plush and brocade and flecks of gilt on the pillars. A frail skeleton on the plush lounge turned into an old lady in print silk cuddling a bottle of mineral oil. He remembered the mahogany box at the station. Resort town? Hell. The town was sick. And he saw again the deceptive beauty of a hill in Athens, a white dune in Morocco, all the beautiful, beautiful places harbouring the dead.

It was a shock to come back to the lobby of the hotel, grieving as he was for all the far-off disappointing places. Wherever he went, the weight of sorrow, like the weight of his body, went with him.

The clerk at the desk had brown eyes as mournful as a woman's. He would not like the signature Perry K. But there was no need to explain to a hotel clerk why he had changed his name from Peter Kapek to Perry K. The fat man had made his explanations to old Peter Kapek a long time ago.

'It's because I'm going to be famous, father, like an artist, and I gotta feel like an artist instead of myself. Artists sign special ways, like I'm going to sign my photographs Perry K.'

And whether old Peter Kapek understood why young Peter Kapek had to go around signing his pictures Perry K, nobody ever knew, because old Peter Kapek was a fat healthy lusty old man who laughed more than he talked, as he laughed at this notion of his son's.

'Sure, sure, Peter,' he said, and continued to call the boy Peter, the way all the other fat healthy lusty members of the Kapek tribe did.

Only Marta knew how Perry K originated.

'Take off your clothes, Marta, and lie down in the sand. Not like that—on your stomach, Marta, with your face and all of you hidden.'

'What do you want to take my picture naked for with all of me hidden?' Marta laughed, her fifteen-year-old body pleased with attention.

'Never mind,' young Peter Kapek said, frowning, 'just lie down in the sand as if you were all buried except the back of you.'

Still laughing, Marta burrowed into the sand, her legs spread fanwise, her arms limp at her sides, and her young cousin Peter photographed the sweet lines of her long legs and the buttocks as chaste as a boy's. When it came time to send the picture to the prize contest, he could not sign it Peter Kapek. The lusty big-bosomed women of his family would be disturbed at naked purity. Nervously, he had signed Perry K. No one saw the picture of Marta because is didn't win a prize. But he had kept the name, wiping out its association with guilt by his boyish justification: 'Artists sign special ways . . .' Only now, half a lifetime away, the guilt stirred as an ignorant clerk looked at him suspiciously.

'Perry K?' The clerk's voice soared, seeking and imploring. Together, his voice and his mournful brown eyes tried to delve, with sudden hostility, into the life of a man who denies his surname.

'Perry K. That's all,' the fat man said, reaching for his wallet so the hand of the clerk would move for the key and the still figure of the wary bell-boy would spring into action. 'And give me some change.' As he spread money on the counter he saw greed in the clerk's eyes.

'Certainly, Mr K.'

'This way, Mr K.'

Without so much as a please and thank you, the fat man saw his identity slip away.

Going up in the elevator he tried to live up to Mr K. He stood, big and silent as Mr K would stand, accepting the deference of the bell-boy. He became Mr K, traveller; Mr K, on government business; Mr K, tipping well but not too well for bags covered with steamship labels. The bell-boy went away, taking Mr K with him, and Perry K, a fat slob of a man in baggy clothes, looked around with bewildered eyes.

Any other man, after a long train trip, would fall into the welcome bed, the fat man thought wistfully, as his big homeless body stood in panic in the unfamiliar room.

Blame the editor, his mind kept saying, blame the editor for the panic and the homelessness.

'God, but he's a slave driver,' the fat man said bitterly, thinking of the editor and forgetting all about the fat boy who had twirled a schoolroom globe and dreamed of planes, trains, ships, anything that would take him farther and faster than his fat legs could carry him.

Assignments in Spain, Greece, Africa. Bleak and lonely trek from battlefield to battlefield. 'Curse him,' the fat man said, still blaming the editor instead of a forgotten fat boy trying to escape the weight of his flesh.

'Cibola,' the pillow case read. Who was the woman who spent her days practising Palmer Method handwriting on pillow slips when she might be stitching rick-rack on her aprons and lace on her gowns? Who was this driven woman at an electric machine, threading brown thread through intricate cogs and wheels that she might watch the needle spell out Cibola? What is Cibola? thought the fat man as his eyes posed the picture of a woman's hands carefully guiding the pillow case to and fro.

'Try the Cibola,' the editor had said. 'It's a first class

hotel on the desert, which means rotten room service in New York.'

Each year the editor spent a winter vacation at the Cibola. 'A man needs to get away from it all,' the editor was fond of saying. 'A man owes himself a vacation in times like these, and out there in God's country I feel closer to God.' So each year the editor consorted with God at the Cibola, because he never seemed to meet up with God in New York. But like a lot of other people who came to the desert to get away from it all, the editor brought it all with him. The only change in his à la carte, bottle-fed existence was his comforting illusion that Heaven hung lower out here so a busy man could get at least an annual peek in.

Perry K spent the winters photographing the dead. The Greek dead. The Czechoslovakian dead. Growing heap of highly international dead.

The shiver that went through his big body reminded him of the bottle of brandy in the suitcase. He dug in the dirty laundry and drank from the bottle. After the nausea went away, he picked up the phone.

'Call me every hour on the hour,' he said to the operator.

'Huh?'

'You heard me,' he said.

'All day?' The voice went irritable.

'All day. And don't ring me for anything else. A man named Burd will call. Tell him I'll meet him in the bar at eight.'

So. Something for everybody to think about. The operator could think about the lunatic who had just checked in. And the lunatic could think about the sound of the operator's voice breaking into the loneliness every hour on the hour. And Mr Burd could think about waiting around all day for a meeting with Perry K.

And what would Mr Burd say to a photographer with a tremor in his hand? And who was Mr Burd to have anything to do with a photographer with a tremor in his hand?

'There's a guy named Burd who can do your legwork,' the editor had said. 'Funny fellow. Kept us up all night talking about his novel. Bad novel. But he knows the town. I'll write him to make the arrangements. All you'll have to do is shoot.'

'Shoot,' the fat man said. He said it as a reverie and as an oath, as his mind saw the morbid picture of the camera shooting what the gun has shot. The murdered man gets his picture taken. So does the suicide. So does the striker caught in the way of a gun. And the soldier, the fine brave soldier, and all the fine brave soldiers. The fat man cried because it was hot and because he had photographed the dead. He cried and rejoiced at the tears that hung on his short thick lashes, wet evidence of his grief for the dead.

'How real this is, this tear-wet grief,' the fat man said, delicately prolonging it, seeking new stimulus for it. His small darting eyes found the camera, resting against the seven-drawer chiffonier, draped and mysterious in its shroud.

He remembered again what the doctor had said: 'No, I wouldn't throw your camera away. That isn't the way to forget. Go on a vacation. Get some shots of pretty girls. Life isn't all death, you know.'

Maybe not. If Burd lined up girls, pretty girls in the sun, girls smiling into the sun, the camera might let him sleep. Holding tight to the bottle of brandy, Perry K lowered himself on the bed like a kid with a teddy bear.

CHAPTER TWO

PUSHED back like this, against pillows soft and spineless, Archibald Burd might have been any length, any stature and any manner of man. It was easy enough, lying here in bed, to remember when he had been Archibald Burd, six feet four in his stockinged feet, looking down at women, loving little women.

There weren't so many women now. The accident of arthritis is apt to jockey a man out of his natural role of pursuer. It's damn difficult to get places when you have to rest between lamp-posts.

Still, there were women. There was Justine, waking up in the other room, staying with him God knows why in her half of the piano crate. Soon she would fix a breakfast tray, putting sugar in a glass jigger and balancing the egg on a napkin ring, and saying goddamn because the bread was mouldy again. Later she would tie a bandanna around her head to keep her thick warm hair from getting dusty when she swept the room. Her clean face would peer into corners and she would fish out the socks from under the bed and if it were Saturday she would bring in the soap chips and a pail and get down on her knees and scrub. She had beautiful hands. Perhaps her mother had beautiful hands. But she didn't live up to her hands. The way nobody out west lives up to his mother.

Sure there were women. There was Bangs, blonde, whom he kept for a memory. He kept her for a memory after he had looked at himself in the mirror and decided she wouldn't like the frame behind the empty pockets. The frame and the empty pockets represented his returns on a seven-year investment in blood transfusions, traction that didn't work, wax treatments, fever cabinets and serums that had gone down the drain. Now the germs had stopped boiling and gone to live in his bones. He was a fine fossil of a man at thirty, with a back ankylosed to stone.

Bangs was slated for a memory when he thought of how an arthritic makes love, with his shoulders sunk against the pillow, his head resting against the wall, and his limbs carefully arranged as arthritis made them. 'I'm ready, my darling.' You didn't say that to a woman you could love. You saved it for the bitches because the bitches didn't care.

The memory was better than the girl he had met at the party anyhow. For a long time he hadn't looked at her. Then when he did, he saw that her eyes were all pupil and her pale hair touched her eyebrows. He had known she was afraid of the healthy men in the room and had let him take her home because he had an arc for a back and the stooped walk of the men in her anthropology book. And he knew that she had kissed him for not kissing her.

He had kept making the trip home with her ever since. You'd think he might have tried to see her again. But he could do a better job of pursuing alone in bed. The gal didn't have a chance. There she was. Female and young and nameless. A guy gets tired of tagging names on pure pleasure. The privacy was good, too. He could lie back with his eyes half closed and think of the motionless perfection of her lying in his arms. He could keep the precious silence. No disturbing touch of her hand on his bare shoulder, no feather touch of her eyelashes on his cheek. No fragrance of woman to distract the slow beautiful pyramiding of thought that began, as always, with the first sight of her and ended exquisitely with the feeling of her mouth moving under his. Sure, it was better this way. You can't trust the promise of passion. You can't trust the tricky quickness of your heart and the shaking of your limbs. Keep it, instead, my boy. Keep it, academically, like the professor hoarding specimens. You, Bangs, are hoarded for all my short appointed time. He shut his eyes against the image of her and whistled softly to himself.

'Good, you must have slept,' Justine said, her woman's mind joyfully seizing the clue of the whistle to trace back the lonely hours of the hot night that must have been blanked out by sleep or why should he wake up whistling? But had he slept? Her mind came back to the suspicious now, and she thought of his whistling as a man's trick to lead her deliberately away from the question he did not want her to ask.

'You did sleep, didn't you, darling?'

The tenderness he felt as he saw her with the heavy tray in her arms flamed into anger. Why couldn't she see that his sleep was his own private affair, as personal as any other function of his body, and whether he passed out on nembutal was none of her goddamn business. Did he bother her with questions about her life in the other room? Did he push his face into her bed and charge her with questions as to why her light flashed on at two in the morning and did she have a good time with her last lover?

He helped her settle the tray and pulled her down on the bed beside him.

'Hello, pretty,' he said.

This was routine; the way to stop questions, the way to let questions go unanswered, the way to seal her beautiful lips against the confessions waiting to be said, the way to protect the men who stalked the complex corridors of her mind, waiting their turn to be introduced to him, the way to protect himself against the emotions of anger and love and the milk of human kindness. He felt sorry for her when she looked like this, fear-ridden and mystified. He was sorry he had nothing to give her in return for the proudly, lovingly offered breakfast tray.

Now that he had kissed her he could go on with his breakfast, and she could go on with her sweeping and the emptying of last night's ash trays.

'Pilot your course among the chairs and the tables, Justine, but don't try to dust out my mind. Rearrange the vases and the lamps but don't try my heart a new way. A boy and his mother part company when she begins to take charge of more than his underwear. Did you know that, Justine?'

He heard her close the windows and pull the blinds against

the heat of another Arizona day. He heard the sharp slap of
the fly swatter. Twice, before she got the fly. This was
routine, too, like the breakfast kiss. He looked forward to
the emptiness she would leave behind her when she put on
her clean nurse's uniform and went off to the foothills where
medical attention is delivered daily, as a matter of course,
like the milk and the cream.

'Hurry, Justine, because when you are not here you will
get the love and tenderness you deserve. Burd, the man, will
be grateful to the woman who moved him out of the
boarding house with the stink in the bathroom, the roaches
in the kitchen, and the asthmatic wheezes and discreet throat
clearings. Hell, yes, there was plenty to be grateful for when
she wasn't moving in on his privacy and looking bewildered
when he threw her out.

'Shall we have a drink tonight?' she said.

That meant pay day. Justine's pay day. Justine hurrying
home after eight-hour duty for a quick shower and a clean
dress. A dress for him, his favourite yellow jersey dress that
made her look like a dancer so he could be proud of drinking
with a dancer while the whole town wondered what Justine
saw in him.

There she stood, waiting for his answer, waiting for him
to be pleased with her plan for that night so that she could
go off to work happy early in the morning.

So, he should hand out happiness like a lollipop. For a
moment he thought of saying, 'To hell with a drink at your
expense,' just to see the light go out of her eyes. Kick over
your birthday cake, Burd, and make your mother cry. Tear
up a woman's plans before she has a chance to build something enduring from them. Her meccano set is always
ready. She will even build nests out of driftwood and expect
them to be there when she comes home. Poor bird. Poor
blown bird.

'Drinks? Sure,' he said, thinking of between pay days

when they couldn't buy drinks, thinking of the small brave spurt of recklessness that brought them together on pay days.

'Good-bye, darling,' she said, on her way now to the car with the satin-smooth tyres parked in the sun. Unpaid for car, uninsured car.

He loved her a little as he listened to the bent fan fighting its way through the radiator, and he imagined her smiling because he had been a good boy.

CHAPTER THREE

IT WAS such an old car it had to be coaxed, with a quick pull at the choke and your foot quick on the gas to surprise the engine in the middle of a cough. It was a car that took both your hands and both your feet to drive, Justine thought, as everything started at once with a rush so that she had to use the brakes to slow up the car that had so miraculously gone on going.

'And it all has nothing to do with me,' she thought while she worked hard with her hands and her feet, trusting them not at all, because this throbbing noisy power seemed so much a thing of itself.

'And you'd think I'd never driven before,' she said, patronizing her fears, whereas it made no difference, she knew, how often or how long she had driven. Nothing could change her intuitive suspicion that a car went along on its own superior power. She had not even tried to warn the driver the time the cab had hit a street car. What could a warning do against the will of the ongoing motor? The driver, she remembered, had been killed. It must have been because he had rebelled at the power of the engine. She who had nothing but respect for it had bounced helplessly on the back seat and come out unscathed. Like men, she thought irrelevantly. If you went to bed with them willingly, you were never hurt. Sex was power. Noisy, throbbing, driving power. It was better to submit, half-awake, acquiescent, like a drugged butterfly on a pin. Sometimes sex was an experiment, a page from a book, a diagram of a muscle here, a tendon there, a swimming centre of sensation. And sometimes it was sacred, though Burd spat at the vows of marriage. Once it was being together, as warmed by another's thought as by his body. 'That must have been love,' she thought, wondering why she couldn't leave Burd for it.

Leave Burd. Run away, her instinct told her. Run away from the spite of his bitterness. But the other, the love, the sleepy fusion of mind and body, that too was dangerous. Keep away from it, her instinct told her. You can lose your strength in it, the languid comfort of it . . .

'It's all making me a bitch,' she thought bitterly, 'and not at all what my father planned for me.'

The postman on Route 5 cursed women who wove on the road and recognized the nurse who shared a rural delivery box with Archibald Burd. He wondered if she shared more than a rural delivery box as he drove up to the house with separate entrances divided by a tired pomegranate hedge. Did the hedge go on, inside, as a wall dividing the house, with a door, perhaps, that could open and close between the two establishments?

He rummaged in his bag and pulled out a collection of bills for Justine Bradley and an airmail special for Archibald Burd. He grinned at the postmark five days old. The envelope was covered with pencilled notations. Cibola Hotel. Not here. Try 2020 Stone. Not here. Try Box 40, Route 5. Home at last. He honked his horn in honour of the special delivery and waited until the door opened and the tall stooped man came out. Then he stepped hard on the accelerator and drove off with a wave of his hand. It was too damned hot to listen to a speech about the lousy postal system.

Bills, thought Archibald Burd, because it is the first of the month. Bills for Justine to worry about. He tried to remember when he had stopped worrying about bills. It must have been when the doctors told him that bets on his life expectancy were about as sensible as nickels in a slot machine. After that, he had begun to live the arthritic's pace, cramming two years of affection into two weeks because you might be flat on your back in two years, and spending every nickel that came your way because there might as well be debts as well as daisies on your grave. Why die in elegant solvency when you had never been solvent when you were alive? He reached for the bills and his whole body felt the impact of the letter with the airmail special addressed to Archibald Burd.

He stood in the sun and ripped open the envelope. Type swam in the light and moved into meaning.

'The damn fool editor,' he said, and his heart shook with the excitement of a man who has put something over, as he read and re-read the words of the man he had met in the Cibola bar and had bluffed, by God, had bluffed into thinking Archibald Burd was a writer.

'We'll pay you two hundred dollars for captions ... you know the stuff ... society girls in the cactus ... get in touch with Perry K at the Cibola on the first ... he'll want models ... photogenic girls ... curves ... bathing suits ... how's the novel?'

For a moment the transformation was real. He was no longer Burd bluffing. Burd cashing in on a conversation across a bottle. Burd, the arthritic, talking an editor into thinking he was a writer. Success and the sun baked out the pain and the bluffing and he stood there straight and strong, free of ankylosed bone and failure, remembering his mother's pride in the long length of him and the professor who liked his writing. Oh promising young man who had become Archibald Burd with an assignment from an editor who would pay two hundred dollars.

He stood there, straight and strong, until the sun was hot on his head and the novel was nothing more than it ever was, a stillborn, bar-born conversation.

'But why a novel about arthritis?' the editor had said.

Look at the lungers. Hadn't they made literature? Done up in style on their magic mountains. Posturing around with their camaraderie of illness. Filling the whole world with the enormity of a little spot on the chest.

Yes, the editor agreed, quite a number of books had been written about lungers.

'And who are the lungers to get to be classics? What if they do flap a broken wing—it doesn't show. They can lean on their pneumo, their phrenics, their thoracoplastics—we're the guys who have to use a cane.'

That was it, the editor said. There was something heroic about the hidden wound. There was nothing mysterious about a cane.

'So it's mystery you want?'

He felt again the stuttering excitement of trying to explain the mystery of arthritis. 'Don't you know . . . haven't you heard . . .'

No one knew anything about arthritis. Not even the doctors.

'The layman says we're paying the fiddler or suffering the sins of the fathers. The layman is nuts. Sure it might have been a venereal disease. But it could just as well have been a strep bowel or an abscessed tooth or a diseased tonsil. Even the therapy is guesswork. Let's try diet, the medical men say. And now that we've tried diet, let's try surgery. And now that we've tried surgery, let's go back to diet. And in between there is all the other stuff. Serums and splints and even pure gold in your veins. Mystery? Hell, man. Now what do you think of my novel?'

'It hasn't got a happy ending.'

The editor was right. There was no future in a novel about

arthritis. Who wants to read about babes with their fingers curling and their hips jutting out of style? Who wants to hear the long tale of passing the hat to the relatives and carting specimens to the laboratory? There was no future in that either. He gave up the novel because it was too much like peeing in bottles.

Just the same, he'd hooked an editor. The letter said so. But the letter was late and today was the first and Perry K was waiting for him unless everybody was fooling. His knees jerked with impatience as he plunged for the house and the telephone.

'Yes, he's registered,' the Cibola said. 'He left a message to meet him in the bar at eight.'

'Until eight tonight,' thought Archibald Burd. 'Until eight tonight to line up girls for a photographer named Perry K.'

What girls? Society girls fled the summer sun. Besides he didn't know any. And they wouldn't know him, if there were any. He was suddenly aware of a profound lack of girls. Beautiful, effective, generous presence of girls. He felt a sick despair as he thought of how he was going to miss the editor's offer, of how he was going to have to say 'Sorry' because he didn't know any girls. This was the way a man missed an opportunity. Golden opportunity. He watched it tarnish as he racked his brain . . .

The only girls he knew were Justine and Minna's vagrants. Minna's vagrants? Why not? Some of Minna's vagrants were very pretty, and very photogenic too. He felt a wave of laughter, the reeling triumph of a boy introducing a whore to his mother. The idea of a whore posing as a society girl appealed to him. When is a whore a society girl? When Archibald Burd makes her one. Maybe it worked better the other way. When is a society girl the other? There were a lot more possibilities in a society girl as the other. There were practically no possibilities in the other as a society girl.

'This,' said Archibald Burd, 'is pure snobbery. A pretty girl, a photogenic girl, deserves to have her picture taken whether she is the one or the other.'

Still riding the wave of laughter, he called Minna.

'Business,' he said.

'Come to breakfast. Nobody's up yet.'

'What time?'

'This afternoon. Late,' Minna said.

Burd picked up the phone again. Opportunity made his hand shake. Two hundred dollars made his hand shake. A man didn't expect opportunity in July. A man didn't expect two hundred dollars any time on the desert.

'Yes,' Justine said, as she waited for the bad news over the telephone. And what did he mean he had a job? And what did he mean he wouldn't be home tonight? The sequence flashed in her mind. The dangerous night. Burd out in it. Her terror until he was safe at home again, exhausted, in need of her.

'Shall I meet you—later, I mean?' she said.

No, no, Justine, he thought. Leave me alone with opportunity. Don't interrupt miracles, Justine. Two hundred dollars is a miracle. A job as a writer is a miracle. You didn't know I wanted to be a writer, did you, Justine? You thought it was the conversation of a sick man, amusing himself with thinking up ways to amuse himself. You didn't know I read the other guys in bindings and that I think I can do better than the other guys in bindings . . .

'I'll stay in town,' he said briefly, hanging up on the mystery of how he could stay in town with fifty cents in his pocket.

It was a long wait to late afternoon and Minna. He moved to the bookcase. The bottle of gin was still behind the volume of Shakespeare.

'To Burd's miracle,' he said as he drank deep from the

bottle. 'And to the other guys,' he said, looking at the books in the bindings.

'Not you,' he said to Somerset Maugham.

That, for Somerset Maugham, and he made a rude gesture. There was only one character in Somerset Maugham. Mildred, the green-faced little bitch whom the author did not even succeed in making a bitch. She only showed up because she repeated the same twelve sentences all through the book. And people only remembered her because she was Bette Davis in the movies.

'Not you,' he said to Thomas Wolfe. Spilling words and adolescence.

'Maybe you,' he said to Faulkner.

He had a feeling, a shamefaced feeling, that maybe Faulkner was one of the guys in bindings he ought to drink to. He had ditched *Light In August* after 161 pages. It was too damn much exercise to read any further. In 161 pages, he had travelled a long way. First a gal arrived in town. The next chapter told about a man named Xmas who came to town too, but that was three years before. Just when he was getting interested in Xmas, he had to stop and read about Joe Brown and Bunch. And just when he was beginning to figure the whole thing tied up with the gal, he had to go back twenty-five years and find out what happened to the pastor's wife. Then the story started with the first chapter again, but this time it told about a house that was on fire when the gal arrived and how Xmas was feeling three days before the fire. Just when he had grasped the plot for the second time and figured out that Xmas probably killed the old lady who lived in the house and Joe Brown probably was the one who set fire to it, he was back on a chapter which opened when Xmas was three years old, eating tooth-paste in the orphanage. Oh yes, and Xmas was part negro and Joe Brown was probably going to turn out to be Lucus Bunch. Life was too short to finish *Light In August*.

Half-boldly, half-shyly, he began to think about his own writing. Not the novel on arthritis that was never going to be written. But the story of Odra, the young lesbian with white hair. She ought to make a short story collection. He fumbled in the desk and found the yellow dime store paper with the pale typing on it. Odra was sluggish. She was still in the horizontal position were he had left her months before. She hadn't wanted to be born. She hadn't wanted to live in a studio next to a church. She had balked at seducing her victim. And maybe Odra was right. Maybe a story glorifying a lesbian was hush hush. The editor would know. But he hadn't told the editor about Odra. He was keeping Odra for a surprise.

Carefully, he replaced the yellow dime store paper in the drawer, remembering that surprises must always be kept hidden. He went to sleep, after that, with the alarm clock set for three o'clock so he could catch the bus for Minna's.

CHAPTER FOUR

'CALM yourself and make yourself at home,' Minna said.

He took off his coat, which was one way of making yourself at home at Minna's. He hadn't realized he was excited. But now he knew he was fairly intoxicated with excitement. The bus driver must have noticed it. 'Hi, Burd, where's the parade?' the bus driver had said. And remembering the walk from the bus to Minna's, he was conscious of his sense of hurry and elation and of how he had wanted to call out, 'Hello Pioneer Paint, Hello Pioneer Hardware, Hello Pioneer Lumber,' as he passed the pompous mansions in the old part of town.

Minna's house was a flamboyant study in pink stucco, ill-fitting grillwork and coloured window panes. The porte-cochère hung over the driveway in derelict splendour. The owner of the house was dead and his son was in the state asylum. The rent was paid to the estate and there was nobody to care what went on behind the high hedge of oleander that fenced Minna in.

'Good lord, Burd, can't you tell my World's Fair chair from the others?' Minna said, as the chair Burd sat on tinkled a music box tune.

Minna's furniture had been shipped from Chicago. It dated back to Carrie Watson. As Minna did. The traditions of her house were as ornamental as the furniture. Her girls were called Mitzi, Trixie. Minna believed in atmosphere. Just as she believed in black net hosiery and garters that snapped.

And Burd felt the atmosphere. Sitting there, his fingers tracing urns and cupids in the carvings of the chair, he was lost in the magic, caught in the spell. There was a suggestion of Christmas morning in the immense length of dining room. The heavy curtains were a Christmas colour. Candles burned in the icy chandelier. And Minna herself, wearing black satin in July, might have been the dowager at the Christmas celebration. The air, thank God, was cool and damp, as the air-cooler purred in the distance.

It was all marvellously intriguing, thought Archibald Burd. Could anything be more normal than the girls, sleepy-eyed and friendly. Yet five in the afternoon was not the breakfast hour for normal people and a bordello with Victorian furniture was not a native growth of the desert. Dream-like words floating across the table were something else to marvel at: 'I just finished paying the instalments on my typewriter,' Ruby said.

'Typewriter?' said Burd.

'She's learning the touch system,' Minna whispered. 'Any time now I expect a complaint from a guy who objects to having exercises tapped out on his vertebræ. Now—is—the—

time—for—all—good—men—to—come—to— you can imagine it!' Minna said.

'What's she learning typing for?'

'Ambition. That's what gets them,' said Minna. 'If they'd just learn to stay in their own niche.'

Ambition. Burd began to remember why he was here and the job that had to be done before he met Perry K.

'Can we go in your office, Minna? I want to talk to you.'

'What's on your mind?' said Minna, moving on mincing swollen feet across the oriental rug, and ducking head-first through the tasseled portières. She sat down at a big desk.

'Look, Minna,' Burd said. 'I've got a chance to make some money and there's money in it for you, too.'

'Money did you say, Burd? How much and what have I got to do with it?'

That was Minna, Burd thought, noticing the crack of her words as she spoke of money. God but she was a hard old bitch. As hard as boned foundations and arch supports and a lifted face could make her.

'There's money for you, Minna, if you'll let me use three of your girls tomorrow morning. It won't interfere with their work.'

'Anything outside this house interferes with their work,' Minna said. 'What's the idea?'

'All they have to do is wear bathing suits and get their pictures taken,' Burd said desperately as he saw Minna's eyes, stone-cold, staring at him.

'I still don't get it,' Minna said, and he could imagine her going through his empty pockets and lighting triumphantly on the fifty-cent piece and saying, 'Money?'

'There's a photographer here from the east. He wants models—you know, Minna, girls in bathing suits. He's got expense money. Somebody's going to get that expense money. It might as well be you.'

'Publicity,' Minna said. 'I don't go for it.'

'Not publicity for you, Minna,' he said patiently. 'Publicity for the town—see? You can help the town, Minna, and when the pictures get published all over the country, everybody will know how you helped the town.'

'I'm already a subscriber of the Sunnyside Club,' said Minna, 'twenty-five bucks a year I contribute for the publicity of the town.'

'Hell, Minna. They're just a small town Chamber of Commerce bunch. They don't know what publicity is. This is big-time stuff. It will get the tourists. It will make your business better next winter.'

'I can get along without the tourists,' Minna said. 'They're temporary. Give me the steady home-town trade any time.'

'All right, Minna,' Burd said. 'All right. Skip it.'

But he couldn't skip it. He could feel himself sweating desperation and defeat. And Minna knew it. Part of him laughed loud at the other part of him, nervous, pleading, making a life and death matter out of hiring a few whores.

'Will you do it for me, then, Minna? Will you give Burd a chance? Will you cooperate just this once so that Burd can . . .'

'Can what?' said Minna. 'How much are you going to make on this deal?'

'Two hundred dollars,' Burd said hopelessly, wondering why he couldn't lie to her. 'I'll give you a third of it. Besides the money the photographer pays the girls.'

'Half,' said Minna.

He couldn't dicker with Minna. And the money was not important. Not as important, anyhow, as the opportunity, the job, the making sure that Perry K got photographs so Archibald Burd could write captions to order, to appear in print, actually to be paid for by an editor.

'O.K. Half.'

'And don't look so sour about it,' said Minna.

When does two hundred dollars become one hundred

dollars, he thought. When Burd makes an ass of himself. Going back into the other room, he wondered if he would know a photogenic face if he saw one. His body ached with strain. Minna, on swollen feet, seemed to be dancing as he dragged after her. He wished he had a drink. He wished he could say to hell with Perry K. He wished he had more than fifty cents so he could go to bed with Ruby.

CHAPTER FIVE

WHEN Burd left Minna's, the elation was gone. He was conscious of hunger, thirst, fatigue, and the sun in spinning discs before his eyes. He dealt with these sensations briefly, knowing it would take longer to pacify the other feelings, the feelings of fear and trepidation waiting to spring at him. Hunger was normal. He had forgotten lunch. His throat, dry and a little sore, needed more gin to oil it. After more gin, it would get dry again. The ache in his knee he understood. He hoped the pain in his chest was physical. Dizziness was the sun. Why look for other causes when a hot ball of fire still hung in the sky. He could feel his stomach muscles tense as he faced the sense of loss that had followed him out of Minna's, and he was as scared as a boy with a belly ache and no green apples to explain it.

Perhaps the feeling of defeat was as simple as a joke turning sour. Perhaps he was afraid that Perry K would look at the three blondes with breasts and recognize them for what they were, three tired whores in the morning. But somehow he knew it was not as simple as that. The defeat went deeper, erasing Burd himself, along with the flicker of hope that the assignment from the editor had brought him. Everything became nothing, as he moved clumsily along the sunny pavement. One assignment did not make a man a writer. Two hundred dollars was as temporary as Minna had chosen to make it. And stripping things down even further, his whole life became as meaningless as sex in a whorehouse. Still, he'd rather have it that way. Back there, at Minna's, sex was all dressed up with no place to go, a hell of a lot better than sex in little houses, with seed destined for life, and quarrels made up in bed so everybody would wake up refreshed in the morning.

His race with his thoughts took him into the first doorway where fifty cents would buy beers.

The place was familiar, shabby, and loud with life. Burd felt exhilaration rising within him as voices hailed him and chairs were pulled out for him.

The little doctor was poised on the edge of his seat so everyone would know he was limiting himself to the quick one he allowed himself on the way home.

'Damn fool,' he said to Burd. 'What are you doing here? I told you to rest that heart.'

So now he's worried about my heart, Burd thought. Let him worry. And he became Burd the guy who had outwitted arthritis. Burd alive. Burd, the pride of the little doctor.

'Can't you ever forget the oath,' he said, and the doctor laughed, enjoying his laughter and his drink and thinking that most of the day had been lean on laughter and it was good to know a man like Burd. Brain over pain, the little doctor thought, as he saw the fine lines of illness in Burd's face dance with laughter and laughter shaking the wide breadth of shoulders bent by pain.

'Every time I got drunk I sent a box of candy to the Queen of Spain . . .'

That would be Brent telling his same old story, Burd thought.

'And every time I sent a box of candy to the Queen of Spain they put me in bed in a mental hospital. It was a long time ago but I still resent it . . .'

Keep on listening, Burd thought. Listen and don't talk. Don't tell them about the assignment from the editor. Don't tell them about Perry K. As long as you keep it secret it will begin to be real again. Like love, hidden and unspoken. Love was real until you took it out and talked about it. Then it evaporated like a bubble because a bubble must not be touched by your breath, your body . . .

'And there she stood, looking like a centrepiece . . .'

'It's never any fun to walk away from your life work.'

Keep on listening. That's one of the reasons they like you, Burd, because of your still dark listening face. And the sympathy in your eyes. And because none of them has guessed your unspoken scorn of them.

'The poor guy craves a purpose like nourishment . . .'

'And speaking of nourishment, the fish was high . . .'

That would be Shay, sleek with health and money and stupidity. God, thought Burd, it's always the healthy guys who carry their health around like a prize package. Shadow-boxing with fears, worrying whether the fish is high or the pimple is going to turn into a boil. It's better to be a seasoned arthritic than a guy waiting around for things to get worse. At least you don't have to worry about the cloud on the horizon because you won't be in on the tornado.

'That famous guy who does war pictures is in town. Perry K. He's over at the Cibola . . .'

And that, thought Burd, is that. People in this lousy little town always nosed out secrets. The way women always nosed out love. And now that Perry K was a name in a bar, Burd could talk about him.

'He's taking shots of the town. Winter resort stuff. I'm writing captions for him,' Burd said, waiting for the surprise in their eyes.

'I'll be damned . . .'

'This winter resort stuff is a joke . . . the dudes ought to see the sun when they're not around . . .'

'Captions, huh . . . do you get paid?'

'Sure I get paid.'

He wished he could stop this damn fool posturing. It was convincing enough to a bunch of bums in a bar, but it did nothing to quiet his own uncertainty. How did you go about writing captions? He could see himself searching the dictionary and the thesaurus. Sun . . . fun . . . fun in the sun. Sun stroke. Sun stroking . . . he had something there! He grinned at the picture of unabashed bodies stroked by the sun.

'I didn't know you wrote,' someone said in a voice reserved for sick beds and works of art.

'Oh, sure.' He felt like a damned rosette.

'Since when . . .?' they persisted.

He decided to finish Odra and stick her in the mail or put the paper on which she was written to some base use.

One by one they dropped the subject and after a while they drifted off. Burd was left with Shay who ordered another drink for both of them.

'There's something I've wanted to ask,' Shay said, flushing the way a man does when he isn't sure where his question is heading. 'It's about Justine . . .'

Never discuss a woman. Always protect a woman, Burd thought. So now I'm supposed to protect Justine . . . Justine who does nothing to protect love . . .

'What about Justine?'

'I've met her around,' Shay was saying. 'I was wondering if I could take her out.'

'Why don't you ask her?' said Burd.

'That part's easy,' Shay said, his good-looking face bright with masculine confidence. He stared at the blond hairs on his powerful hand. 'It's you I'm thinking about.'

'What about me?' Burd said.

'Well, I'd rather know. I'd rather know about you and Justine . . . before. . . .'

'The trouble with you is you treat your friends like relatives,' Burd said, remembering all the things relatives said that were better left silent. How much did it cost? Is that a sty in your eye? Are you going to marry the girl?

'Naturally I want to know how things are with Justine and you,' Shay went on defensively, talking against Burd's silence.

'What difference does it make? As long as you have feelings about Justine, why in hell do you have to stop and wonder what my feelings are? You and Justine are two other people. You have nothing to do with Justine and me.'

'You know that isn't true,' Shay said.

He was right, thought Burd. He was right in his stupid fumbling way. And this hysterical fury Burd felt was because he didn't want to include Justine in the picture of himself. He cherished the image of Burd alone, Burd sharply isolated and cut clean of family, religion, medicine, love and all the comforting weakening ties. He launched out in desperate defence of his proudly won loneliness. 'Whatever I say will be just so much more fuel for the sentimental complications you enjoy. To hell with you.'

'Don't let Justine come between us,' Shay said, an attempt at laughter in his voice, a man to man note of women are the ones who always make trouble.

'Justine is just a small ripple on the Biblical flood that will always lie between us. You and I are as far apart as stone and soaked biscuit. I'm tough and you're soft. I'm tough because I live with arthritis. I'm tougher than a gangster or a dictator. Their toughness is an attitude and mine is a deformity. Now torture your soggy mind with ideas of Justine and me the rest of your days. You'll never know what to believe because you haven't got the guts to stop wondering.'

He got up slowly because his anger seemed to have lodged in his spine. And with a picture of Justine's eyes in front of him, he said deliberately: 'I won't be with Justine tonight. I'm spending the evening with Perry K.'

He saw Shay's look, bright and sly.

Let them be together, Burd thought. Let complexity woo complexity in the tangled sheets. Let wedding bells ring out the jangle of confusion.

He thought of telling her, over the telephone, that Shay would be coming her way, but somewhere he had read that women only went to bed with men they wanted. It sounded logical enough.

CHAPTER SIX

THE long summer day persisted and Burd, facing the bright hot sun, felt like a man waking up in the morning, his body naked and his mind stripped of protective dreams. All his hopes were back there in the bar, stranded, along with the false exhilaration and the distorted truth. He looked at the truth and turned away, protecting himself from his own insight as a man protects his body from the sun.

The fantasies began to build themselves again as he started for the Cibola and his meeting with Perry K.

He thought of the way the old man used to do business, old Ira Burd, pulling off deals by telephone, telegraph, cable, everything big and reckless, so that even after the crash when the deluded old fool had to fly to South America, everybody still went around remembering him as the bird who gilded the dollar sign. Nerve. That was what old Ira had. And he'd bluffed his way in and out of every country in the world. Why shouldn't his son do a little bluffing? The pictorial soliloquy went on as Burd saw his long line of ancestors cheering and waving him forward, the buccaneering ones on his mother's side, and the old man's pa who had talked himself into a peerage, and that other one, way back, who sailed around the Horn and took up with a black girl because he didn't give a damn. And there was the picture of Burd himself in the days before debts and arthritis. He remembered trips to Europe, clothes from Bond Street, and further back, private schools and tutors, even a Scotch nurse who made him crush his eggshell every morning so the devils couldn't lurk inside. Hell, a man couldn't lose all that. He still crushed eggshells, years later. He began to be proud of all the money that had been spent on him. And all the money he had spent himself. He was even proud of all the money he had borrowed to spend.

The soldiers in the lobby of the Cibola hotel turned away from his painful swinging gait. 'Poor bastard.'

'There goes old Burd—still humping,' the clerk at the desk said to the girl in the cashier's window.

'I hear he's a swell guy.'

'What's he got that I haven't got?'

'Bum credit,' she giggled.

The clerk nudged her soft hip.

'What've I got—that he hasn't got?'

'Gee,' she said, shivering at the sight of Burd's body, 'you give me the creeps.'

(. . . While Burd plunged on, confident, exhilarated again, noting the clock said eight exactly, eager now for the meeting, ready to greet Perry K easily, casually, on a light note of success . . .)

The Cibola operator rang Perry K's room and said sharply: 'It's eight o'clock.'

'Page Mr Burd and tell him to come up to my room,' Perry K said.

'Mr Burrrd . . . call for Mr Burrrrd,' the flute-like voice of the bell-boy sang.

Burd turned, afraid. The voice of the bell-boy calling him

by name was the voice that had doomed the enchanted voyages of childhood. Just a few steps more . . .

'Yer t'go up to 805,' the bell-boy said.

Burd turned away from the bar, disturbed and anxious because Perry K had failed to meet him at the appointed place. Small deviations, insignificant reversals, minor postponements, they were symbols, all of them, of the broken promises that had plunged him long ago into boyish despair.

Oh God, he thought hopelessly, as he passed the house phones and saw he could not avoid Flick, on her way out of a booth, looking hot, beautiful, furious.

'That odious operator says she can't disturb him,' Flick said.

He knew she was talking about Perry K. Flick pursued names. They were always a friend of a friend. She was one of the bright transplanted people who spent their time sharing nostalgia for New York, Chicago, Paris-Before-The-War; re-living the past with extraordinary disregard for anything that might have been unpleasant about it; on the look-out constantly for anything to link them, even momentarily, with the life they had left behind. They were rootless because they could not forget the city pavements and they could not dig into the desert waste. But no one ever said to them: 'Why don't you go back?' because everyone knew that they had exchanged civilization for the sun, and even if the germs had been baked out, or their excuse for coming was dead and buried, the sun had a way of holding them though they mocked it for shining.

'Who are you so intent on disturbing now?' Burd said, trying to sound insinuating instead of curious.

She looked pleased. 'I'm just being nice—there's a man here Martin knew, a photographer. One of the Ones . . .'

So Perry K, One of the Ones, was not at home to everyone. Burd began to enjoy himself.

'Why don't you ever come around any more?' There was

a poppy juice quality about her and she knew it. 'It's horrid of you, darling. Tonight?'

'I'll come if I can,' he said, waiting for something to distract her so he could get to the elevator. Nothing ever changed at Flick's. Gargantuan draughts of conversation. Feverish people. High ceilings and graceful windows. The Matisse over the marble fireplace heightening the reality of females by its splendid distortion of female. Burst of bloom on hand-blocked curtains. Elegant lines of fine furniture. Elegant lines of Flick herself. Static. All of it.

'I'm going to Mexico with Bernie,' she said.

'That's nice.'

'It isn't nice. You know it isn't nice. We'll both be thinking of someone else.'

She meant Martin. Martin had been dead for five years but she had managed to keep him indecently alive in the bedroom as well as the drawing room. She was so unsure of herself she needed two men in bed.

She is boneless, he thought. Her highly civilized little self is like the soft forms of life that vanished without a trace when the earth was young. Too soft, too slippery, to leave their mark on the fossil record. It took at least the timorous start of a backbone to leave an impression. She will vanish, he thought, like an invertebrate lost in the mud of the proterozoic seas.

'Promise. Tonight?'

He walked away from her last question.

The tired old man in the elevator started a hopeful conversation.

'Hot,' he said.

'Looks like it might rain.'

'Miss an awful good opportunity if it doesn't,' the old man said, jerking the elevator to a stop. He left the elevator and walked down the corridor with Burd. 'Gotta get me an aspirin,' he said, 'fellah up here always gives me one.'

'Toothache?'

'No. Jaw. Jaw ain't a very well put together mechanism. Least mine ain't.'

Burd waited for the old man to shuffle off before he rapped on the door of 805.

'Come in.'

Burd saw a bed with an enormous man lying in it. The man's face was buried in the pillow.

'When in hell does it get dark in this town?' the man said.

CHAPTER SEVEN

NOTHING was going the way Burd wanted it to. Perry K stayed on the bed, hiding behind heavy-lidded eyes, and he didn't mention the assignment. Burd talked aimlessly about the town because he was shy about bringing up the editor's name or any of the reasons why he was in the fat man's room. Somebody had to say something and the fat Buddha on the bed wasn't contributing. He wasn't even listening, if the blank inattentive look on his face was real.

'It's not a bad town,' Burd said, 'not bad at all.' He felt unfaithful because he sounded off-hand about the town. It was a swell little town. A town you could trust. It didn't bite at you with sudden mists and snow and cold. He wouldn't be walking around if he lived anywhere else. It would be nice to feel about a woman the way he felt about the town. Trusting. Loving. But you couldn't tell a stranger about it. A hell of a funny idea being in love with a town.

'You ought to see our night-club,' he said, helping the conversation along by making fun of the town, the way a man would make fun of a woman, sounding light-hearted and feeling ashamed because he had betrayed the beloved for the sake of conversation with a stranger.

'The whole damned place is over-lit,' Perry K said.

'Other towns have magnolia trees. Or a river. Or handsome monuments,' Burd said. 'We've got the sun. It's a permanent fixture. Rises every morning. No fooling.' Burd laughed at the sun because he didn't want Perry K to know how he felt about it. As far as he was concerned, the sun was as good as God. But there was no sense spreading the gospel. Faith started inside a man. You couldn't go around introducing God or the sun to a man and expect him to start in worshipping.

After a while the fat man found he could look at Burd without any of the shock he had felt at the first sight of him. He saw the image of a man who would never get any better in the wire-sharp outline of the bent back, but the suggestion of death was gone. A picture was meaningless without suggestion. All the anastigmat lenses in the world could not create an emotion unless suggestion was in the picture along with the lines of truth. The pictures of the desert would need cool-looking flesh in dazzling sunlight.

'Are there any girls in town who look cool?' Perry K said.

Was he talking about the assignment or a date with a girl? Burd hesitated and plunged. 'I've got three hot-looking babes for you to photograph. A cool view of them in bathing suits ought to be something.'

'Bathing suits won't do it. The flesh must look cool,' Perry K said impatiently. Then he closed his eyes again and stopped talking.

Burd stopped talking too. What was the use. He had a feeling the fat man would say to hell with it and take the next train out. The whole project must seem pretty silly to him. It seemed pretty silly to Burd, as he sat there wondering whether to stay or go.

'I'd never get up until night if I had my way,' Perry K said.

Secretive bastard, Burd thought bitterly. He never said enough to let you know what he was thinking.

The bed creaked suddenly and the fat man rolled out of

it, swinging his legs to the floor, and rolling an empty bottle out with him.

'Someone seems to have mistaken the place for a saloon,' he said, kicking the bottle and laughing.

Laughter transformed him into a jolly stranger. A minute ago he had looked like a bewildered old man who had taken permanently to his bed. Now he was kicking around in such high spirits, Burd was embarrassed.

'Is the bar downstairs convivial? How about it, Burd? Shall we be convivial? Let's make a night of it.'

Burd looked at the bottle and wondered if the hilarity was delayed action.

'Sure, let's make a night of it.' A night of it was one way to keep him around till the pictures were taken.

'Hang on while I sing in the shower,' the fat man said, and Burd tried not to stare at yardage draped around the fat man that must have been underwear made to order.

'Let's be con-vi-vial,' Perry K sang to the tune of God Bless America.

Jesus, Burd thought, for an old man of forty he's staging quite a come-back.

There was the sound of water splashing, a tooth-brush doing a thorough job, spitting and convivial noises. Separately and all together the noises began to get on Burd's nerves. And the fat photographer got on his nerves when he came out of the bath still dripping. The shower had made designs of the hair on his legs. The flesh was a monstrous pink. It was overpowering, this flesh. It demanded underwear made to order and the damndest looking shoes, wide, half-high, laced so the front gaped open. And the suit of fine linen had a sag in the behind, waiting for the flesh to sit down in it.

Burd watched a silk handkerchief disappear in a pocket and a flashy wrist-watch slip past a white hand, to be anchored deftly around a wrist that was small in proportion to the rest of the body.

'Timing is essential in some types of photography,' Perry K said in a dreamy voice.

Burd wondered what the linked gold bracelet, suggestively wide, had to do with it.

The wallet came next. It was bulging with bills.

'Expense money. You'll have to show me how to spend it,' Perry K said softly, almost apologetically, trying to convey his innocence of what men did when they made a night of it, got tight together, painted the town red.

Burd saw for the first time that the fat man's eyes were gentian blue under the heavy lids and that his lashes were like thick fringe.

Burd remembered an old joke about three sexes; men, women and photographers. But this guy with the gentle smile was too nice to know about it.

CHAPTER EIGHT

THE bartender was a Mexican with a silky body. He was called Rollo, or little Rollo, depending on how many drinks his patrons had had. It made no difference to him what he was called except that he was supposed to smile when somebody called him little Rollo.

Rollo, along with pandering for Minna, made a point of knowing all about Minna's business dealings. Minna was doing business with Burd and Burd was doing business with the fat photographer. Rollo made their martinis double strength. Better for business.

After he served the drinks, Rollo spoke into the housephone. In a minute a bell-boy with a face like a choir boy came in the bar. Rollo flicked his head at Burd and Perry K. The bell-boy left and went to a telephone booth in the lobby. He consulted a smudged card, felt for a nickel and called a number. Flick Donahue said thank you when he told her that Perry K was in the bar. Flick was a woman who was willing to go to an effort to get what she wanted. The bell-boy left the booth and went into the dining room. He moved unobtrusively toward a table where a man sat with a girl in yellow.

'Mr Burd is in the bar now,' he said to the girl. Her eyes smiled and trusted him. She gave him an envelope and fifty cents. 'Will you see he gets this right away. It's important.' The man with her pretended not to notice.

The bell-boy went back to the bar, gave the envelope to Rollo and slipped him the fifty cents. Rollo gave him back a quarter. Rollo made a ceremony of delivering the message to Burd. He left his towel behind him and when he presented the envelope he inclined his slight body forward in a kind of half bow, intimating that Burd was an important man receiving an important message. He looked at the fat man to see if he were impressed, but Perry K was smiling at nothing in a dreamy stupor.

Justine would be the only one who would try to reach him. Bitching in, Burd called it, in his anger at her intrusion. She was like a mother dog shamelessly nursing in public, Burd thought, as the ten dollar bill fell out of the envelope. Bitch, bitch, maternal bitch, making sure that he would get fed. The words she had written on the scrap of paper made her another kind of bitch. 'Don't leave me with Shay . . . we're in the dining room.' So she was afraid of blond flesh. He tore up the note and put it in the bowl of popcorn. More popcorn.

He smiled as he thought of Shay, the hunter, jumping the barriers, heading across the moors. Justine would fool him. She would hide in the bracken, run for her very life in the ferny woods, and then when he was ready to give up the chase, she would come out and meet him, with the captured look in her eyes. Very often Justine was the first to propose bed, feeling it was inevitable, wanting to get it over with. Futile chase, my Shay, Burd thought, because Justine had never been captured in bed. Justine was a huntress in bed. She was a beautiful and enduring thing in bed. And when she had reduced a man to the level of the sheets and drugged him into the sleepy aftermath, she laughed at his sleep and satisfaction. Then it was time for her to leap up, light a cigarette, ask for a drink, tell him the complex thoughts she had been memorizing, make him feel like a fool because he was heavy with sleep and satisfaction.

With ten dollars in his pants, Burd decided to mention food. Justine had a way of rescuing him from hunger. His feelings about her would always be confused. There was so much to remember. Some of it filled him with tenderness. He remembered the day she had taken charge of his life, carrying all his stuff out of the boarding house and loading it in the car. She wore yellow shorts that day, and a faded blue shirt and huaraches on her nice narrow feet. The arches of her nice narrow feet hurt when she got through moving. Right after the excitement of moving, right after she had admitted that yes, maybe here it hurt, in the curve of her arch, they were as near being in love as they'd ever been.

'Oh darling, are you glad?'

'Sure, I'm glad.'

'Quick. Say something funny. Something loud and funny so I won't cry. People do, you know, when they're happy.'

'Why don't you, if you feel like it? Come on now, cry hard.'

So she laughed and clung to him and surprised them both when she burst out crying after all.

He held her for a long time before he said: 'Here, wipe your little nose. You've cried enough.'

'Yes,' she said, 'now you know how much I love you.'

He had wondered as far back as then why she felt the need of proving it.

It was all far away, very far away. He tried to feel free of the memory and free of now, with Justine calling out to him from another room in the hotel. He tried not to feel guilty because he wasn't going to do anything about her. And then there was no longer any need of trying to feel any way because the door of the bar opened and she came in. And without trying, he felt depressed, and sad because it had to be this way.

Shay was with her, smiling down at her. The two of them gave the appearance of a man and a girl who were having a wonderful time. They kept on coming toward him, and pretty soon he had to say, 'Hello, you two,' and introduce them.

He thought of all the ways he might introduce Justine.

'This is Justine. She doesn't know any principles but she plays by ear very well.'

'This is Justine. She thinks all men are brutes because it's easier to forgive them that way.'

'This is Justine. Say something nice to her because she is still a little girl.'

Once she had followed a man around for a year because now and then he remembered to call back: 'Come along, little darling.'

Future relationships, thought Burd, would be far less complicated if introductions were more than a name.

Perry K, with a deference for beauty, was asking her to join them.

Shay looked annoyed. 'We're on our way.'

Justine looked at Burd. He was feeling stubborn and left it up to Shay.

'We'll join you later if we can,' Shay said.

More power to him. Maybe he'd make an honest woman of her yet. Usually she had her way, walking in and out on men before they had a chance.

The loveliest thing about her is her hair, Burd thought,

as he saw it, thick and black, swinging around her defeated shoulders. Shining stuff to think about. 'Even I,' he thought to his amazement, 'would like to bury my face in it.'

'She's a beautiful unhappy girl,' Perry K said soberly, watching her walk off with Shay.

'Unhappy?'

'There was something . . .'

So he had seen her flagrant little soul instead of the grace of her body. The yellow dress was far more modest than her eyes.

'She's like most women. She doesn't know what she wants,' Burd said, hoping to end Justine by putting her in a class, by breaking the associations that brought her close to him.

Rollo looked relieved as Flick Donahue came in the bar. She had paid a dollar to catch up with Perry K. Rollo liked to see people get their money's worth. He nodded at the table where Burd sat with the fat man. Then he reached for fresh glasses. There would be another round of drinks coming up now that Flick Donahue was here.

'And how did *you* find him? I've been trying for hours.'

Flick's voice was half-accusing, but Burd was glad to see her. What the night needed was Flick. He welcomed her hair, red, with a tiger lily topping it; he welcomed the faked wit, the stolen epigrams, all the artificial gaiety she might very well provide.

'I'm Martin Donahue's wife,' Flick said to Perry K. 'He often spoke of you.'

'Martin . . .' Perry K showed a troubled memory in his face.

'He would have wanted us to meet,' Flick said, dismissing Martin and letting sadness glide away as she moved in, fragrantly close to the photographer on the leather seat.

Both men watched fascinated as the tiger lily lost its moorings and trembled in her hair.

'Symbol of purity, isn't it? A lily?' she said, appearing to pin the thing straight into her head.

'Sure,' Burd said, 'symbol of purity. Even when it roars like a tiger.'

CHAPTER NINE

THE lovely Flick went on ridiculing the lovely Flick so the fat man would laugh again and the young wistful soldiers with crew-cut hair would envy the gaiety of the corner booth in the bar.

Deftly she plucked among her memories for the outrageous, the improbable, because to her they represented the last word in honesty and it was important to her to be honest. She seemed to be under some compulsion to put everyone clear on her entire life as soon as she met them.

What fantastic exposure, thought Burd, as he listened to her triumphant naughtiness. And yet, how deceptive the bald truth could be. Why not credit her with honesty. Should she be blamed, after all, for omitting the incident behind the incident? The sad shades of the unconscious elude the best of men. And he had a feeling that if she ever stumbled on her own dark motives, she would reveal them, too.

. . . It was innocent warmth that had got her kissed by a waiter when she was twelve. And it was only the tremendous fuss that had put her in such a state that she broke out all over.

And itched until she was sixteen, Burd supposed, as her inelegant adolescence was revealed.

. . . It was innocence again that had turned her first visit to a hotel room into a seduction. 'But all nice girls are seduced the first time they go to bed,' she said practically, 'and besides I deserved it. My innocence was almost illiteracy. I thought a prostitute was a gypsy.'

. . . And how could she forget Martin? She gave them the picture of Martin making a hey-day of his death-bed, surrounding himself with talk and liquor, saying: 'Who wants to live a prolonged life,' as he treated his tuberculous kidney to another brandy.

Let everyone remember the devoted Donahues. Martin was a man that the world considered well worth grieving for. Robbed of him, she had suffered insomnia. Suffered and suffered insomnia, until someone told her to think of the womb picture. 'Now I just curl up and go off,' she said brightly, 'so much better than counting jumpy phantom sheep.'

Let everyone see the devoted Mrs Donahue bravely facing the death of Martin.

He had been a sort of secondary sun in the empty desert, Burd remembered, pulling the bored and lonely into his gaudy radius. He had endowed his bed with a physical splendour, wearing flashy robes, putting fierce energy into his talk and gesture, so that he seemed a figure of gallantry to those who enjoyed the drama of his dying. He had been a magnetic voice making not very much sound fine. And they had all listened to him. And they had basked in his glory because they had no glory of their own. As Flick was still basking.

. . . And wasn't Perry K the lucky man, though, spending all that time in Europe when scarcely anyone could get across any more? How she had adored Europe with Martin. Of course she knew there was a war but war was a movie she hadn't seen so how could she be expected to imagine Europe any way except as she remembered it?

Perry K felt the astonishment and the horror sweeping over him and he began to grope and probe again, looking at the distorted picture and wondering who this woman was with the bright jungle flower in her curls and the blind beautiful stare. Didn't she know? Didn't she know that everything was dying.

Paris, Vienna, Prague, Amsterdam, Brussels—they were dead. They were all dead. Even Rome might die. Rome could be wounded in spite of awe of the Catholic Church. Even now, for all that any of them knew, Rome might be battered and bleeding.

Her voice came back, clear and childish. No, no, nothing could change her picture. Rome was the de Russie hotel with women wearing their scarlet lips and darkened eyes for young men to stare at. Rome was a leather curtain pushed away from the door of St Peter's and the dark cavern within and gardens of candles growing in the gloom. Rome was the English graveyard with green moss and violet plants and tiny ground pine. It was Shelley's grave, very formal, with a gleaming white slab, surrounded by a stiff clipped hedge. You had to step over the hedge to read what Shakespeare said on the slab: 'Nothing of him that doth fade . . .' Keats was in a rough meadow outside with excavations going on, and did they know that Keats had written his own rebellious epitaph in the bitterness of his heart, at the malicious power of his enemies . . .

Rome was St Paul's outside the Wall, all alabaster and marble and the man peddling cameos in front shouting 'Fine and Dandy' for the American tourists. It was white swans in the pond of an old water-clock. It was the cheers at the Augusteo concerts and crumbling antiquity. It was a street carnival with booths of melancholy Pierrots and wooden houses. It was the name Frangipani on a wall, a night-club with a doorman in plumes and brass buttons, dray-carts painted with flower designs, hovels and court-yards, chicken-coops on a balcony, and didn't Burd think so?

Burd didn't.

It was the Fête de Bambinos, one Christmas, with rich little Romans wearing ermine-edged coats into the balloon-decked Excelsior. It was a bare-legged child with purple knees and a long sweater and a cottony fur like a ruff around her thin little neck. And Vino on the shops with swollen grapes hung over the doorways. And the Holy Virgin peering down from shrines like bird-cages perched on the creamy walls. And if you wanted your religion all decked out in public, why not?

Hadn't travel broadened her though, said Burd.

Rome was sausage shops, fish shops, bakeries and purple postcards of brazen women. And a baby's funeral procession walking between the street cars and the traffic, the pure white hearse drawn by white horses like a fairy stage. And why should Perry K hide his eyes? It was a sweet funeral. There had been the sound of sobbing behind drawn curtains as the row of hacks followed the hearse. In Rome the officers wore capes. And the priests wore velour hats. Plumes, coral, amber, shawls, laces, flowers and magenta suede shoes. That was Rome.

'But it isn't that way now,' Burd said.

'It's that way to me,' she said triumphantly and there was no answer he could give her.

This is worse than apathy, thought Burd. This is delusion. Reality smacked down by dreams; smacked down with a vengeance while the dreamer sleeps and smiles. Ah false false security.

And why does she speak of graves, Perry K was thinking, seeing the clipped hedge and the snowy slabs.

'There are no epitaphs any more . . . there is no time for epitaphs.'

'Who wants one?' said Burd, and he told them about the finest grave he had ever seen, the temporary and anonymous grave on a hillside in southern France where D. H. Lawrence was buried.

'There it was,' said Burd, 'no name, no hyphenated dates, no pleas or prayers.'

It was part of a hillside in Vence, part of the sunlight and the peace. All the rest of the cemetery was smothering under plaster angels. There was nothing but a cluster of periwinkle growing on the grave and a primitive slab of concrete set with coloured pebbles to represent the wings of a phœnix.

'The finest damn epitaph a man could ask for,' said Burd. 'What good are words and plaster angels to the dead?'

And why were the dead following him, Perry K thought; why couldn't he escape them? In a minute the young soldiers would put on their caps, covering their clipped shining hair, and go out of the bar on their way to join the dead. The fat man started up in terror. 'Let's get out of here,' he said.

Food, that was what they needed, said Burd.

There was cold chicken at Flick's house, cold chicken and white wine and a French salad waiting for them. 'Please,' she coaxed.

'No. We've got business to discuss.'

'Business?' said Flick.

The word meant nothing as she said it, lightly, questioningly, making any connection between Burd and a famous photographer seem remote.

He wanted to tell her how he had not let up for a single moment all day, juggling the assignment, pushing himself and the fat man toward it. He wanted to tell her that big things started with little things, so that a little job like this might lead to something pretty big. Christ, he thought, if it were really that way . . .

'Come on,' Flick said, starting after Perry K.

And Burd was glad after all that she was along to take charge.

'The fat man wants to make a night of it. How in hell do you make a night of it?'

'Somebody will think of something,' Flick said.

'Don't keep the door open, mister,' Rollo called, hurrying

with a broom to sweep back the crawling things that were moving into the bar.

Flick hid her face in her hands. 'Oh God, a cricket storm. What a lovely country.'

Perry K brushed flying pellets off his coat and moved out into the soft sweet darkness. 'How beautiful . . .'

'Yes, desert nights are all right,' said Burd. And all at once he felt sure of himself and amused at getting Minna's three little unmentionables to pose for pictures everybody would be talking about.

CHAPTER TEN

FLICK'S house was only a few blocks away. 'Shall we walk?'

Burd thought a taxi was a better idea.

Perry K said it was a fine night for walking.

So they started off on a fine night for walking with Burd dragging behind, light-headed with hunger and pain. He passed the time between lamp-posts wondering if he would reach the next one. 'Hello, lamp-post,' he said to himself whenever they passed a lighted corner. It was a game he had been playing with lamp-posts for quite a while. Once he had played another sort of game. 'Archie—you get right down or I'll tell your mother.' The nurse had worn her rusty hair in a bun and her legs were as gnarled as a walking stick. The lamp-posts stood at regular intervals in Central Park. He had shinned up and hugged them passionately for years.

He began to think about Justine because Justine would have voted for a taxi. Justine would have seen to it that he had a ride when he needed one without explanations or apologies. Maybe that was why a man finally married a woman, one particular woman, because she got to know his weaknesses and helped him to keep them from showing. With Justine around he would have gone the six blocks in a cab in spite of a fine night for walking. And everyone would be riding with him and he would be feeling as superior as ever. Maybe that was a good enough reason for marriage, to hang on to your superiority.

The conversation up front was going along all right. Perry K had come out of his anesthetic silence and Flick was offering small and secret talk. Stalking their revealing words, Burd felt like a dream censor.

'Martin would have none of the desert,' Flick said. It was nature's junk-yard. It was untidy surrealism. They had expected rolling sand. They found mud with pincushions in it instead. And all the flora and fauna were spiny and the colour of mould.

'And what is the fun of fresh air unless you are opening windows to let it in or shutting windows to keep it out? As you do in New York,' Flick said.

And the space. Miles of it. Stretching into agoraphobia. And what if she did dream of stairs. There was nothing symbolic about it. She was simply homesick for the house on 10th street.

Yes, yes, Perry K understood. 'There is a house in everyone's memory.' He had been lonely in hotels and they always seemed empty no matter how many rooms were filled. The house at Sheepshead Bay was always crowded.

'The old man made clocks. We used to say that every time he got an order for a hand-carved cuckoo clock he brought another relative to America. There were always aunts and cousins on the way.'

'Certain houses have a quality, an atmosphere, a temper . . .' Flick said, knowing she was piling on words because she did not know how to say that her heart, the very fabric of her being, all peace and security had been tattered and torn since she left the house on 10th street. And what had been so reassuring in the thin tall box with the fifty stairs winding up to the top and the doll's rooms with miniature fireplaces that wouldn't draw, and the humpy floors and the windows that opened up on somebody's wall? It was a house where she had lived as a child and where Martin had come home to live after he married her. They had torn cupboards out and built cupboards in and finally made it exactly as they wanted it. They had left the house behind but they had brought furniture, rugs, pictures, china, with them. And they had settled down in the pavements and turned their back on the desert, but the desert was still there, burning in the sun, swirling in the wind. It was so dry the river beds were smooth roads where you could gallop your horse. But a freak storm could bring a wall of water roaring down a quiet country lane.

'You can drown in Arizona,' she said, 'and you can die here without having any of the famous ailments Arizona is supposed to cure.'

'You hate it?' said Perry K.

'No. I don't hate it. I just can't figure out how to get myself and my silver and the Crown Derby back to 10th street,' she said bitterly.

And what made her think that everything would be the same back there? Burd wondered.

No, he had no brothers and sisters, Perry K said. 'There were just the cousins.' Marta was the one nearest in age. They were like sister and brother. But she had gone back to Europe, the only one of them who had left for good. She was an actress. They might have heard of her. Thin. Tall. Her face alive like inspired sculpture. 'Marta Kapek . . . she played Ibsen a lot and made some movies in Paris.'

'Marta Kapek,' Flick cried. 'Oh how wonderful she was! Martin and I tore our programmes to bits and we shouted out loud. Everyone did.'

'My father loved clocks,' Perry K said. 'He loved clocks

but distrusted watches, especially women's wrist-watches, the exquisite little watches covered with jewels outside. My father talked like a poet or a philosopher when he talked about women's watches. He said they were like a beautiful woman with a false heart-beat, and he handled them warily and with scorn. My mother's heart beat the way it should, strong and wonderfully steady, but she was big and fat.'

'My mother never understood me,' Flick said.

'I don't know whether my mother understood me or not,' Perry K said, his voice sorrowing in the darkness. 'She died when I was too little to give her anything but trouble. She died giving birth to another. And that one died, too.'

They died screaming, he thought, the sharp wailing cry of mother and child stabbing him in the night as it had on the other night in the old house with people running back and forth, whispering and hushing, and the boy Peter shut up by himself knowing nothing of death except the sounds of dying. Everyone dies screaming, he said to himself, even though they plummet soundlessly to the ground when the bullet hits them. The scream is there in the throat, in the eyes, only sometimes it is snuffed out, the frightened scream, by the quickness of death or by the comforting drugs needle-quick in the vein, paralysing the scream, shutting down on it, so it can only be seen in the eyes, in the lax muscles of the mouth, gaping open, waiting for the scream to come. Everyone must scream at the time of dying, even the man Burd back there with his hells and damns, making light of his back caught in contortions, even Burd challenging everything with Christ and Jesus would scream out for life at the time of dying. All else, love, fame, beauty, life, was two-faced and double-tongued, one way to one man, one way to another, there and not there, a dream confused with truth and truth with a dream. There was no confusion in death. It was the one unalterable reality.

'I suppose what I remember of my mother, actually, is

what the aunts told me and what the old man used to say, grieving for her. All that is mine and wholly mine is a blurred picture of her face. There is not a single detail of feature or voice or dress or movement. It is a soft-focus portrait, too badly done to be recognizable, yet, somehow, marvellously familiar . . .'

'I wish that the picture I have of my mother were not so clear,' Flick said bitterly, thinking of hopeless lengths of words that had stood between herself and her mother, thinking of baleful looks, tears, recriminations, thinking who was at fault, my mother or me, in the endless life-long arguments. 'I don't blame my father for going off and leaving us. He just left one day, walked out on his pipes and books and his wife and child. He did one decent thing at the time of the divorce when he gave the house on 10th street to me. My mother finally married again and I never enjoyed anything more than sweeping her old powder puffs and broken jewellery and worn clothes out of the house.'

And why didn't she sweep out the memory of her mother at the same time, Burd thought, instead of letting the image grow rancid? Families should be left in the dust-bin along with the broken toys of childhood. There was something horrible about a fat man grieving out loud for his mother in the night. Hell, the woman had died when he was a little boy. What made her his mother, anyhow? Did the fœtus owe love as well as the breath of life to the womb that held it? Just because a woman gave birth to him did he have to go on the rest of his life crying mother, mother, mother? And Flick with her petulant, 'My mother didn't understand me.' Why must she still be torn between guilt and wistfulness? The past was dead and the future problematical. Neither offered anything but disappointment. The only fact is the living fact, Burd thought. Myself on a summer night, moving down a street counting lamp-posts, hungry because I haven't eaten, limping because I have arthritis. Keep your nose clean, your mother told you. Keep your vision clear was better advice. He felt like shouting to the two up ahead: 'Don't go looking at the world all your life with pieces of past in front of your eyes.'

Flick's house was around the next corner.

'Past the police station,' Flick said.

The police cars were gathered like silver beetles under the bright flare in front of the courthouse. Inside was a jail with a stench that should have brought the voters in a hurry. But the bright light went on burning and nobody in town had a sense of smell.

They came to a white house, neat as a child's drawing, with a flagstone courtyard and a row of stiff orange trees. The leaves of the trees were electric green where the lamp-light shone, like a cluster of emerald scarabs.

'We took something without any plumbing and made it into this,' Flick said, and her voice was soft with pride remembering the hovel it had been and the fond dream of a house it had become. 'Burd loves the lock on the door.'

Yes, Burd loved the lock on the door, the uneven scroll of the brass plate with the mysterious keyhole. He loved it for the sublimely simple reason that it resembled the lock on a pirate's chest he had been given one sunny Christmas morning in Spain. It was a wise move to pin your loyalty to something permanent like the look of a lock that could never change. The pang of delight was permanent. Whenever he thought of the lock he could be sure of joy, distilled and pure, the joy of a ten-year-old on a Christmas morning.

The door opened into a living room with shadowy walls rising to the primitive ceiling. The smooth naked sahuaro ribs that made the inner roof were all that was left of some Mexican's memory of home. The furniture from 10th street, the imported wall-paper with silver stripes, the lamps, the rugs, had brought another world into the old abode.

'It's food I want,' said Burd.

There were voices in the back of the house. Bernie, thought Flick, Bernie in my house as if he belonged. But he would never be content to stay. Bernie was a hawk, a swooping flying exploring hawk, who perched on a cornice for a quick look around and then made off, quickly, lightly, to another part of town, another part of the world, with something new to look at.

She was finished with Bernie. She would not be swayed by a ring and a ceremony. She made her decision quickly, putting her trust in solid foundations, protective walls, and the immutable beauty of her constant house. She led the way, a glowing mistress of a passive but rewarding love.

Voices greeted them.

'Doesn't it make a nice still life,' Burd said, looking at the kitchen table cluttered with empty dishes and the chicken bare to the bone.

'There's plenty of brandy,' Flick said, and went on with the introductions, saying 'Perry K' as if she had known him a long time. 'This is Bernie and Nigel—they have last names but we never use them.'

'I've brought you a present,' Nigel said.

'Oh, how I love presents,' She took the record, tenderly. A present was an emotion waved into being. You could hold it in your hands. 'Let's play it now, right now,' she said.

It was a spiritual, a new one, new to him, anyway, Nigel said, appearing amazed, rather, that it had escaped him. His manner was academic and English. The patch of moustache improved his full lips.

'It's got plenty of boogie in it,' Bernie said, wriggling his lively little body.

They wandered into the living room and the conversation stopped when the spiritual began and they heard the husky and compelling voice of the black man plead:

'Seek, seek and ye shall find
Knock, knock and the door shall be open
Ask, ask and ye shall be given
When the love comes twinklin' down.'

'And isn't it a fine thing—faith,' said Nigel.

'It sounds so easy.'

'Listen to the next part.'

'My mothah you ou-gh-ta been there
'My mothah you ou-gh-ta been there
'My mothah you ou-gh-ta been there
When the love came twinklin' down.'

'Wouldn't one's mother have loved to be around, though,' Flick said.

'I never knew one yet that didn't want to peer.'

'Play it again.'

'Sure. Play it again.'

Burd looked at Perry K. The fat man seemed happy enough with a glass in his hand.

Bernie put the record on and Burd moved quietly out the door. Up the street old Manuel would be sitting in the kitchen. And his dutiful daughter Angela knew how to fry an egg.

CHAPTER ELEVEN

LOVE came twinkling down in the fragrant courtyard as Burd stood outside Flick's window, listening to the music and wondering how it would be to sing like a dark thrush of God's miracles. And what of the black man's faith? Did it begin in unquestioning childhood with the presence of God in a crowded room, punishing the wicked, rewarding the good, effecting cures, answering prayers? Or did it come later, in noisy terror, with a bullet-headed preacher haranguing his congregation as the Reverend Tom Timothy Jones at All Saints, Incorporated, harangued every Sunday? Intimidating, threatening, promising, goading, the Reverend Tom Timothy Jones won his people by the might of his vocal cords: 'Brothers, you are lost . . . brothers, I uster be lost.' At collection time the Reverend Tom Timothy Jones identified himself with the doubtful, pantomiming the torture of their indecision as he reached down into his pants pockets, pulling the coins out slowly, reluctantly; counting them; dividing them on the surface of his pink palm; choosing one, two, three; finally dropping them all with a triumphant ring in the collection plate, while he pointed a long black finger and counted out loud: 'Fifteen . . . sixteen . . . seventeen! Pass the plate, brethren, and don't nobody fall under seventeen cents.'

Buy your religion for seventeen cents; seventeen cents is the Sunday Special for the Reverend Jones and his congregation. Scrabble in your pockets, brothers. Have you got the price of God's love?

Love belonged to simple people. Manuel's world was filled with it. Love of God, love of the Saints, love of the family. The old adobes in the Mexican quarter were brimming with love. Manuel's voice on the Spanish hour every morning was a testimony to this tender and glowing emotion of his people. Day after day, Manuel spoke the flowery greetings of birthdays, marriage days, Saints' days and holidays on the radio. He spoke the felicitations of the son to the mother, the mother to the son, the young man to his sweetheart. All the intricate relationships of love were made audible on Manuel's programme. In exchange for grubby dollars, the sentiments soared through the ether, half-whispered, half-sung in a grave and formal third person, complying with the rules of radio that prohibited person to person messages. And it was always of love that Manuel spoke as the soft clatter of Spanish came over the air. The heart was as real as a valentine to this world of simple people, and love was what the heart felt for the beloved.

In Burd's world love led a dubious existence. Literature glorified it. Psychiatry denuded it. Man's experience nullified it.

'The Mexicans can have it,' said Burd, secure in the knowledge he was denying himself love because he didn't want it.

Thought gave way to feeling as he left the lighted courtyard, aware of the pull of darkness, his senses primitively alert as he moved into the shadowy lane that led to Manuel's house. The night murmured with invisible life. He started back as his face brushed against a drooping curtain of leaves and he hesitated for a superstitious second. Ancient forebodings stirred within him. He remembered charms and warnings. He had crossed the magic circle when he left the lighted courtyard. For all that anyone knew he had vanished in the abracadabra of the night.

What a fool he was to go off and leave the fat man. The wavering outlines of plans began to disturb him; Minna, money, arrangements for the next day, the renting of a car, the use of the club, all the items that would go on Perry K's expense account. And who was keeping vigil over Perry K's expense account? Burd made a bet with himself. 'The money won't be there when I get back.' He made another bet with himself. 'The money will be there when I get back.' He didn't really care which bet won.

The household of Manuel Rodriguez was an over-flowing collection of dogs, children, saints and old women. Nanita, the grandmother of many years, was only slightly more wrinkled and shrunken than Maria, her daughter, who had given birth to ten. Neighbours and relatives swelled the number of indistinguishable old women. The children were narrow and leggy with big heads. They looked like dolls with bisque-coloured skin and straight black bangs as shiny as glazed porcelain.

The smells of the house were of garlic, beans, chicken, cheap perfume and sweat, all at room temperature. Many voices made up the duet of Spanish and English, eternally shrill. Everywhere there were traces of the old and alien mingling with the new. The santo on the wall had traditional angels hovering on a background of clouds. Each angel wore a halo above the rigid scallops of her marcelled hair. Two worlds had blended with little conflict. A saint was still a saint, even if her hair had been dressed in a beauty parlour. The old women did not complain as long as there was a santo in the room.

Manuel, alone, bridged the two worlds in his household. He was volubly Spanish and volubly American. Away from home he wore dashing shirts and high-heeled boots and heads turned and voices whispered: 'He is on the radio.' At home he tossed his fine shirts into the laundry and sat in his underwear, a sleepy Mexican father, a lazy husband for Maria to wait on, a son for Nanita to scold because it had been weeks since he had gone to mass.

There were lights in Manuel's house and music and laughter rang out of the windows.

'Somebody's birthday, somebody's Saint's day,' thought Burd.

'It is Tony's birthday,' Manuel said, flushed with beer and the importance of fatherhood.

'He has eighteen years,' said Maria, heaping the tamales in their steaming corn husks on an enormous platter.

'Now he can be a soldier,' said Angela, the sister, rubbing her nose with discreet passion against Burd's sleeve. Love overflowing, thought Burd, as he moved away. Love overflowing everywhere in the old adobe. Tony's birthday. He heard it on all sides. Pride of Tony. Miracle of Tony reaching the age of a soldier. Rejoicing for Tony.

The air was filled with it; the tamales steaming with it.

'Where is Tony?' said Burd.

A twilight gloom filled the room. The laughter died. Smiles went away. Eyes looked down. The sadness was so complete that Nanita, Maria and Angela might have been wearing black.

'He is in the jail,' said Angela softly, her voice accepting the sad fact of authority, law, society, the police and the indiscretions of Tony.

Marvellous separateness of happiness and unhappiness, thought Burd. Their emotions had a chemical purity. The joy of Tony's birthday exquisitely distilled from the sadness of Tony in jail. One emotion to celebrate. The other to sigh for. He remembered the birth of Angela's illegitimate child. She had wanted a boy. The household was busy with prayers and charms so that Angela might give birth to a son. They rushed to meet Burd with the news: 'It was a boy,' they cried, radiant with the wonder of prayers and charms that had been answered. 'But it was born dead,' they added, putting happiness away and recalling their grief, letting laughter give way to tears.

Only a paranoiac or a child could separate emotions, laughing one minute for one, weeping one minute for the other. No wonder there was no happiness in his own world, thought Burd. Happiness could not preclude unhappiness and the intelligent fused the two. They fused many things, thought Burd. Instinct and knowledge. Desire and the lessons of the church. And they found themselves like Justine, barricaded from happiness, torn with confusion as guilt cried in one ear while passion bit at the other.

He stopped thinking and enjoyed the food. He joined the others when they sang Happy Birthday. For a little while happiness was all around him, as warm and visible as sunlight.

CHAPTER TWELVE

RECKLESSLY, Flick poured the brandy. Pour it down them, she thought bitterly. Titillate, stimulate, intoxicate. Lift their voices, oh lord, above the level of the commonplace. There was no grace, no wit, no civilization without liquid, the accomplice, golden, treacherous, to prod the flesh, stir the senses, loosen the tongue.

They sat sodden against satin stripes, ponderous on exquisite chairs. Heavy. Stupid. As somnolent as listless fur in a zoo. Their phlegmatic pipings were of money, the war, the state of their health, while her own divining intellect spun, soared, probed, seeking stimulus as a starving man reaches for food.

'Have you heard,' Flick said. Have you heard. . . . She tangled truth with the lie and the lie with truth in airy and biting observations. Have you heard . . . Delicately she suggested the wavering suspicion.

'She leaves her friends naked in the streets,' Nigel said to the fat man.

'Never give her a knife,' Bernie said.

'Not even a blunt instrument.'

Lift them, oh lord, from their lethargy. Didn't they know, didn't they know, thought Flick, that life ebbed, died, that one must seize each moment, savouring it, sucking it empty, so that it could be ground under one's hurrying feet without regret.

'You were probably the sort of little girl who burst into tears at a party,' Nigel said.

'Are you suggesting over-stimulation, darling?'

'Something of the sort,' he said, watching her deliberately pour herself another drink.

'If I wept as a child, I wept because I was bored,' she said. But damn him, damn him for making her think back. There was something horrible about the remembered tears of childhood, lonely weeping because no one shared her elation. She could see herself passionately pinning the tail on the donkey, careening madly at Blind Man's Buff, out-reaching them all as they angled for prizes in the fish-pond. She was years, eons, a lifetime ahead of the other children who stood around like sticks. She had wept (he was right) for disappointed ecstasy when the cake sagged, the candles dripped, the phonograph ran down and the party disintegrated into torn crepe paper, crumbs, greedy children and a pain in her head from the frozen mould. But she had learned her lesson. Now all one's wit and wisdom were directed toward the prolonging of pleasure—and if the others were tired, bored, stupid, drunk, she sent them home. There was always herself, her responsive little brain, her erogenous little body, to keep her company.

She is like the gleaming decanter, sparkling a thousand reflected lights, thought Nigel. She has no glow of her own.

She may be too much for me, Bernie thought, seeing the dancing energy in every line of her body. He could almost hear her nerves sing. He could imagine the constant torment. 'Dance with me, darling.' 'Sleep with me, darling.' 'Talk to me, darling.' He remembered scar tissue worn like an exquisite patch on his chest.

She is as meaningless as a figure in a dream, thought Perry K. They are all meaningless. And he thought of the only presence he could believe in.

'Where's Burd?'

Had he spoken out loud? the fat man wondered. Had he cried out the drumming refrain he heard in his ears? 'Where's Burd?' Anguished syllables of panic. How one reached for the familiar presence. He had known the arthritic only a few hours longer than the others, but the tall stooped man was part of a reasonable pattern, linking the fat man with an editor in New York and an assignment to be covered the next day. Insecure, forsaken, the fat man felt the unbearable anxiety of the child who finds himself alone on the brink of nursery stairs. How sickening the solitary plunge into the abyss, how instinctive the screaming flight back into welcoming arms. The fat man's soundless voice echoed the childish scream: 'Where's Burd?'

'Substance and sustenance,' said Burd, alternating Angela's moist kisses with the steaming tamales. His stomach was full and he was tired of enveloping love. He untwined Angela's arms and fought off a last bit of hasty passion. Up the lane, through the night, the miracle was waiting. Visitation of a fat man. Divine favour of providence. He turned his back on warmth and comfort, substance and sustenance, and plunged off into the darkness toward the alluring and deceptive outlines of fantasy.

'True—False,' said Nigel, playing an intellectual game of discernment. 'The brandy is real, but its effects are false.'

'The two go together, nevertheless,' said Flick.

The two go together . . . the fat man's loneliness transferred itself to the image of death. Beneath the voices in the room, he could hear the laboured breathing of his lungs, the rush of blood through the arteries as the desolate heart pumped. He closed his eyes to hide the tears. One died alone. One died among strangers.

'Is there a night train out of here?' he said.

'Night train? Which way?'

Any way, he wanted to shout. Any way out so that he need not die among them.

'But I thought you were taking pictures of the town to-morrow,' said Flick. And who, by the way, was going to pose for him?

He didn't know. Burd was attending to things. He had meant a train for the next night. Of course he was waiting over for the assignment. For pretty girls . . .

'Tomorrow,' Ruby said, 'I am having my picture taken. I'm supposed to have a photogenic face.'

'Tomorrow,' Lilith said, 'I'm posing for a photographer.

No, *not* in the altogether, what do you think I am?'

'Do you think cake make-up will cover up this scar?' said Ellie.

'What bit you?'

'A scorpion—don't be funny. If anything besides a bug bites me, I yell for Minna.'

Minna balanced her books, crediting an extra hundred dollars to the day, charging it to the account of poor old damn fool Burd. She wondered how much the girls would be paid and decided not to guess. It was a bad idea to count one's chicks before . . .

Tomorrow at this time I'll be in bed, Burd thought, humping up the walk to Flick's door.

'Burd,' said Perry K, jumping up eagerly.

So he had wanted to leave all this time, the unfriendly bastard. Flick watched the fat face that had been as empty as a plaster mask all evening come to life for Burd.

'There's a storm coming up,' Burd said.

'Don't go.'

There was going to be a cloudburst. The desert devils were twisting like geysers.

'But it's early . . .'

It was midnight. There was no point in getting wet.

Of course if they were tired and wanted to go to bed . . .

Flick closed the door against all of them. She leaned against it, safe on the inside. The room was hers again. She plumped a pillow, patted a sagging seat, walked empty glasses and heaping ash-trays to the kitchen and washed everything neat and clean.

The crystal ceiling light was burning in the bedroom. She turned it out, pulled down the venetian blind and switched on a small lamp. In the dim shadows she faced the full-length mirror. Slowly she began to drop her clothes. Woman disrobing, she said softly, seeing herself in a gilt frame, and for a long time she looked at the slow rise and fall of her breasts, never once lifting her eyes to meet her eyes in the mirror.

CHAPTER THIRTEEN

THE desert wind, wet as a sea wind, swept over the town. A glittering tree went down. The alien cultivation in patio gardens was torn and destroyed. Only the deathless desert plants survived.

A Mexican ancient climbed painfully out of her bed to put crosses of salt on the threshold to keep the thunder away.

'Oh God,' thought Flick, 'don't strike me dead.'

But crosses of salt and Flick's terror of noise were not enough to ward off the threatening furies.

The thunder crashed.

'The mountains skipped like rams, the little hills like lambs,' Nigel said to the lively sky.

'What's that? A nursery rhyme,' Bernie shouted above the storm.

'A biblical nursery rhyme,' said Nigel, but he was too drunk to remember the exact chapter and verse.

The house stood lonely and dark with the pomegranate hedge lashing it. The only lights were the penetrating yellow flashes of the storm. Burd hadn't come home.

'Yes,' Justine said, 'you may come in.'

The walk was a shining pool. Shay lifted her in his arms and waded through. Looking down at the water she saw the drowned eyes and submerged lips of her lovers. So that was where they went when they left her. Why should I feel unfaithful? Justine thought sadly. I belong to no one.

'Missed us that time, by God!' Shay cried, as the thunder crashed; Shay, the conqueror, defying God, providence, nature and the whole myth of man's frailty as he carried his woman through the storm.

Money talks. Money sings. Money yells out loud. Burd,

throwing the expense account around, hiring cars, tipping clerks (and tucking ten dollars in three envelopes for Ruby and Lilith and Ellie), saw the miracle begin to assume dimension and proportion. He had left the fat man at the hotel when the storm broke.

'Here. Fix things up.' Perry K had said, thrusting money into Burd's hand as the Cibola's canopy was blown from its moorings and the potted palms were plucked from the walk.

'Eight in the morning,' Burd called above the wind and the noisy rain.

And now it was all arranged, automobiles, striped umbrellas, green lawns, turquoise swimming pools, patio walls and ramadas. The loaves and the fishes were ready for delivery. The pillar of fire already aflame. Divine visitation of a fat man.

He walked in the rain, letting it beat against his face and soak him through. He was beyond caution. Somehow, all along, he had expected the photographer to drop dead or walk off, ending in some way the luck that had started that morning with the arrival of the editor's letter.

Justine's money was still in his pocket, mingling with the crumpled bills that represented the power of the press and the business acumen of publishers. Poor little Justine, trying to buy his health and love.

Sailing drunkenly along in the storm, he headed for Manuel's because that was where he always headed when he was drunk and out in the night.

Manuel moved an armful of children from one bed to another. They whimpered in their sleep, half-waking as they heard the thunder.

Burd dived for the empty bed.

'Are you drunk? Are you sick, Mr Burd? You are wet. Wet is bad for arthritis.'

'I have no arthritis,' Burd said. 'I've got a miracle instead.'

Drunk, thought Manuel, dead drunk. He did his best to

get off the wet clothes, thinking of Tony. Poor Tony. Thirty days in jail for drunken driving. Thirty days in spite of what Tony said: 'Please, Mr Judge, I plead innocence.'

All over town they wakened out of sleep to the sound of the noisy sky. And some of them laughed and made love as the cool wet air released the tension of months of hot dry summer. And some of them slept, the sick ones burdened with the necessity of sleep, reaching down in their dreams for the covers at the end of the bed because it was suddenly cool. Everywhere there were listening ears for the swish and sweep of the rain and the loud crack of thunder as the clouds came together.

Perry K sat solid and unmoved by the storm. It had none of the hidden horror of a night bombing. He sipped the amontillado he had bought from the bell-boy after the bar had closed. It was a poor imitation with a pale sting. His mind was clearing after the confusion of hours. He could feel the pin-point stabs of thought that meant his brain was awake. There were things to be done before tomorrow.

Money? He reached for his billfold, found it nearly empty and remembered giving money to Burd to take care of details.

The camera? He looked at the scuffed and battered case, marvelling as he always did how it could suffer such rough treatment and yet protect the delicate and finely balanced contents within.

There was actually little to do . . . check the shutter, load the film. The real preparations had been made long ago, through years of work and study, heartbreaking trial and error, lonely hours of exploration in laboratories and dark-rooms. The picture now was a matter of inspired timing, the click of the shutter at the exact and luminous instant. Light travelling 186,000 miles a second must be caught in its flight and made to serve a fat man. The path of the shadow must be halted at the infinitesimal inch, and the far more fleeting expression of emotion must be precisely recognized. The photographer could feel the moment when a photographer begs, prays and mutters charms as he waits for the culminating pattern of light, shade and emotion.

And if the pretty girls did not register emotion? Then he must suggest it. He thought of the crestfallen chicken, photographed on a bare expanse of checkered marble floor. The forlorn spectacle of a white hen pecking at a black marble square had hung in a salon for months portraying an idiot's futility.

He would like to photograph a nun's hands adjusting her veils as an elegant woman adjusts her hat. Did they ever remove their veils, he wondered, and was it true that they shaved their hair?

A final triumph would be the photograph of death at the split second of departing life. He had been told of figures that had hardened in their last exact convulsion when the lava flowed over Pompeii. The upright sexual organ trans-fixed . . .

His troubled thoughts wound tortuous paths through the night. The feeble call of the brain cried out. There are things to be done . . . check the camera . . . shutter . . . film . . .

The long sigh of sleep sounded in the room.

CHAPTER FOURTEEN

'GOOD-BYE, my beauties,' Minna said, 'and lord love you if you get sunburned.'

'Come along, my night-blooming cereus,' said Burd, patting Lilith into line.

He hasn't long to live, thought Minna. That's what they

say about him. Arthritis pushing the air from his lungs, arthritis squeezing the bones around his heart. Hump, trudge, hump, trudge, that was the way he walked with the three girls dancing beside him. Hair in shining scallops, white skin, engaging curves, bathing suits cut in laughing V's. Little skirts caught at slender waists. Satin mounds and satin hollows. Like flowers, thought Minna.

There were tears in her eyes. Tears in the eyes of a wicked old woman, thought Minna, punishing herself for softness. She felt the sweat in the air, the sweat of last night's storm that had troubled her dreams. She felt the cold wet drops on her upper lip, short Irish lip, lip that quivered when she laughed. How she had laughed at the city father, what a hearty laugh she had had at the sick look of him when he nipped at her with his nasty question in front of her friends.

'How's business?'

How's business, he had dared to ask in the bar of the Cibola where she sat with her lawyers (high paid lawyers, lawyers above reproach). Fixed him, she had; gave him what for with her ingratiating answer: 'Business, Maxie? Well, I wouldn't complain if everyone was as good a customer as you are.'

Red, he got. Red all over his sallow face. And how they had laughed, the lawyers above reproach and Minna who had been in business for twenty years.

She lifted her arm to wave good-bye and she heard, or perhaps she felt, the crackling movement of money. She looked down at the bills tucked in her breast, bills that had been in the envelopes that Burd gave to the girls. One was young once, and it was grief and happiness hidden there in the soft breast.

'Be off with you,' she shouted, 'and be back by noon.'

'Is this guy, this photographer guy, connected with Hollywood?' Lilith said, because of course she was only marking time with Minna. Marking time with plans in her little head. Marking time with a one, two, three of disciplined patience until the time . . .

'Is he cute?' said Ellie.

'Oh you and your cute,' Ruby said, and turning to Burd: 'She's such a kid.'

'Perry K,' Burd said to the doorman.

In a little white the doorman came back.

'You'll have to wait. He just got up.'

'No hurry,' said Burd.

No hurry any more. The end of the assignment was near enough to believe in. He could relax now, at the finish, and wonder at the strain and the fuss of the day before. To hell with one's presentiments and the insinuating misgivings that got in the way.

'Where are we going?' said Lilith.

'The club.'

'The club . . .' she sighed the happy sigh of fulfilment.

'It's too damned early for anybody to be around,' said Ellie.

'I've been there,' said Ruby.

'What?'

'When?'

'I don't believe it.'

'Once,' said Ruby.

'After dark—on the golf course?' said Ellie.

'Pig.'

'Pig yourself.'

'Oh excuse me but I can't help it,' Lilith said, pointedly apologizing for her laughter. 'Excuse me for laughing, Ruby, but it's too absurd.'

'What in hell do you think you're thinking?' Ruby cried.

'Shut up,' said Burd.

The bell-boys interrupted them, a caravan of bell-boys laden with equipment. Room was found for the blunt-nosed camera, the mahogany tripod, the box of film. Perry K came next, a fat man with sleep in his eyes and buttons winking in and out of buttonholes.

'Hi,' said Burd.

The three girls strained their ears in the awkward silence that followed.

CHAPTER FIFTEEN

I T had been going on for hours, the subtle stalking of evil in the cactus garden, the preoccupation of a fat man with species of evil shape and colour.

Or is it in my mind alone? thought Burd, hearing the voice of Lilith, the voice of a woman crying out in protest as her flesh was called upon once more: 'Oh, not again.'

'Hold it.'

Hold it. Hold it. How many times had the photographer commanded the exhausted flesh? Flesh pinned brutally against horny bark and crusty bough. Flesh caught, held, in foliage sharp with spines. Was he merely a captious artist, driving toward perfection? Was his mind innocent of symbol and suggestion?

'Hold it.'

The repetition bit at Burd's nerves like prolonged desire as he waited for the release of the shutter, waited while the fat man stalked the scene again, his eyes shifting beneath heavy lids, moving from the figure of the girl to yellow fruit, swollen and cracked, hung between leaves that were thick, blunt, and as flat as a snake's head.

'Reach for the fruit. No, cup it in your hand. Don't hide it,' the fat man said, eternally stalking, shifting the creaking tripod, settling the camera, letting his gaze rest on the reclining curves of the girl's body, the tangled pillow of hair, the sensuous upturned face, the white hand reaching for forbidden fruit. 'Good.'

Burd wiped sweat from his head and licked the salty dryness of his lips.

'Damn, damn,' Lilith said. 'You said it would be fun. Fun,' she cried, 'fun. With spines digging you in the rear and pig eyes boring into your front.'

'Shut up,' said Burd.

'I should lie down with the lizards,' she cried, unable to stop as the sick feeling of abuse rippled through her. 'I should lie there with his eyes crawling over me.'

'He'll hear you,' said Burd.

But the fat man heard nothing as he stood, lost, puzzled, in the pale green jungle that grew on the floor of the sea. 'I must get out of here,' he thought, shifting nervously under the weight of the blue waters that covered him. Swerving, side-stepping, he escaped the white-bellied monsters that reached out for him. He was breathing hard when he reached the safety of an adobe wall.

'Your turn, Ruby,' Burd said. 'Go on over to the wall. He'll tell you what to do.'

Define it, the fat man thought, remembering a long ago lesson. Define it so that anyone will know it is an adobe wall. Straw stamped into wet mud. Mud poured into moulds. Sun-baked. Rain-washed. Wind-crumbled. Search for the flaw in the wall, the weathered cavity, the worn depression. Search with the camera's eyes for the veining of straw. 'There.'

'Where?' said Ruby.

'There,' the photographer said, pointing to a blanched hollow.

Ruby draped herself cheerfully against it.

'No, oh no.'

'You mean like this?' she said, giving herself a boost to the top of the wall. Modestly she fluffed the chintz skirt of her bathing suit. The skirt and the spread of her thighs hid the section of the wall the photographer's eyes had chosen.

What was she doing here, this girl with blue veins and heavy ankles? Why was she watching him, waiting for him, posing the stiff smiling pose of a girl on a magazine cover? 'No, no.' He seized the camera, folded the tripod and hurried away.

Ruby slid off the wall. 'Beast. Pig. So he wouldn't take my picture . . . he wouldn't take it.' Her lip trembled with hurt vanity. She wanted to run away from her own clumsy body.

'Jesus. Look at the back of your legs.'

Skinned, red, hurting, Ruby burst into tears.

'What the hell,' said Burd, watching the fat man pirouette at the foot of a palm tree. 'Get over there, Ellie.'

Far back, in another time, Peter Kapek had learned to look for shadow patterns. 'Patterns,' Perry K said, searching his memory, gazing at the fronds of the palm, knife-edged, glossy, delicately entwined. Fronds crossed like swords. Static in the still air. 'Patterns,' he said. Then he saw the girl beside him. She had a thin scrawny body, a bird-like head. Bird enmeshed in fronds; girl enmeshed in shadows.

'Lie down,' he said. 'Right where you are, where the shadows twine.'

'Shadows?'

The fat man gazed above his head at the shining green swords. The girl stared at the yellow earth with no mark of a shadow. She sat down.

'Head back. Twist your neck. There. Hold it.'

He gazed through the camera. The awkward outlines of a woman met his eyes. She was sitting in a hot square of sunlight.

'Move over,' he said. 'You're sitting on it.'

The girl jumped up. 'Sitting on what?'

The fat man began to stalk. He tore the camera from the tripod. He stalked with the camera in his hands. He searched with his eyes behind the eyes of the camera.

'Hey, is anything the matter? What's wrong?' a voice said.
'The shadows,' he cried. 'I can't find the shadows.'
'Shadows?' said Burd.

Above them the fronds of the palm tree stirred. Logic stirred in the sick brain. There are no shadows without the sun. 'The sun,' Perry K cried. 'Where is the sun?'

The world was a great white light. The world was spinning, tumbling, falling away from the safe orbit of the sun. The world was plunging into thin cold air. The breath of death was over the world. When he saw the camera, he knew what he must do. Caught there (for he had seen it), trapped there in the hollow box was a hot square of sunlight, all the sunlight that remained in a world falling through space. He wrenched the tripod apart. A broken stick became a weapon in his hands, a furious weapon releasing the sunshine as it beat and smashed at the camera.

The three girls fled. They fled screaming with terror. They fled over rough hot earth, leaving their shoes behind them.

Would there be bars at his windows, locks on his door? Would there be certificates and testimonies? Would the fat man be marked with Latin words denoting the collapse of something in his head or something in his heart? These were the thoughts that moved coldly through Burd's brain as he watched the fury of the fat man spend itself on a battered camera. In a little while the violence passed. There was a wary stillness about him now (indeed he might have been dead except for the shaking of his limbs and the coursing of tears down his cheeks), and he had dwindled somehow, as if the air had been let out of his lungs and his teeth pulled out so that his face sagged and his lips hung loose. There was no bulwark of brain behind the tired eyes. There was nothing left except flabby baggage to be lugged back to the Cibola, delivered to the bell-boy, ticketed for Room 805, with a doctor on the way.

'Better come along. Leave it now. Leave it. All finished. All right. Everything all right.'

The fat man let himself be led. After a few steps he dropped the furious stick. Then he began to cry. He cried for the sun. The warmth, the beauty, the comfort of the sun. He sat quietly weeping in the car while Burd loaded the broken camera and the precious film.

They crashed, Burd thought, before the heart gave, before the germ killed and while the sore still drained. They crashed because their guts were swimming in fear and the voice of their fear called out for help. 'Take care of me . . .' They were carried off on a long stretcher and covered with a white sheet. Indecent effigies muttering gibberish, they could still be heard above the sedative, calling out as the fat man called, for a sun behind a cloud. Their eyes were bound with disbelief. They were blind and deaf with delusion. They feigned truth and defended falsehood and suffered no honest pain.

'I'll take care of things,' the little doctor said. 'You get home to bed where you belong.'

Burd shivered. 'Thank God,' he said, 'the thorns are in my bones and not my head.'

It was like robbing the dead, Burd thought as he picked up the box of films. The only thing of value plucked from the unconscious form. The bright bauble of intrinsic worth that went into the pocket of the passerby. Hell, he thought, since when have I been squeamish. The pictures belong to me.

CHAPTER SIXTEEN

LEO LEVINE, Photographer, was a sign half a block away. Leo Levine hated the desert. Leo Levine, suffering from a perpetual cold in his head, hated the sun. He came out of his dark air-cooled hole in the back of the shop when the bell rang. His nose was moist. He looked at Burd with hate.

'Rush job,' said Burd.

'Three days,' said Leo. He might have made it two days. Then again he might have made it four.

'Three hours,' said Burd.

Haste. Hurry. Leo saw himself back in Chicago in the gyp joint on State Street. One dollar . . . one photo . . . one hour.

'What the hell,' he said. There was a nice balance of pained surprise and outrage in his voice. There was a grudge, a question, an argument. I'm here, Leo seemed to be saying, because I don't have to hurry. As soon as I have to start hurrying I might as well go back to a man's world, a man's town, the town where I was born.

'Look,' said Burd, 'I'll pay you twice what the job's worth.' He brought out the last of the expense money. 'I'll pay you quick and by God you'll do the job quick because I'm in a hurry. And if you don't I'll drape my arthritis around that nozzle of yours and squeeze the last drop out of it.'

Leo remembered the time when the gangster had visited him on State Street. The gangster was in a hurry, too. But he had wanted plates smashed. There was the same smell of threat in the air. Leo smelled it. And sneezed.

'Three hours,' said Burd. 'I'll be at the Little Gem. Call me if you finish before.'

At noon the Little Gem was empty. Pat flicked flies off the bar and brooded about business. He felt like failure at noontime. He could never believe that at five o'clock business would boom, bottles gush and that there would be the clink of ice and the clink of silver and faces grinning back at themselves from the polished mirror of the bar.

'On the cuff,' Burd said. 'I'm down to bus fare.'

'On the cuff,' Pat said, looking gloomy and reaching for the bar Scotch.

'Sticky outside,' said Burd.

'You look bad.'

'It's the heat.'

'Too damn much heat.'

Burd studied the change in his pocket and put a nickel in the juke box. A sob came out.

'Corny.'

'Everybody plays it.'

'Corny just the same.'

The phone rang.

'Lilgem,' said Pat. 'Huh? Can't hear.'

Good for business when the sound of the juke box sang over the wire and the prop said huh, can't hear.

Pat waited a while and said: 'Who? Oh sure . . . wait a minute, I'll see . . .'

He deadened the phone against his chest and fondly imagined that the man at the other end of the wire was picturing a crowd in the bar.

'It's for you,' he said to Burd.

'Who is it?'

'Who's calling?' said Pat. The receiver crackled. 'It's Leo. Leo Levine. He says come on over.'

Burd looked at the clock. It was six minutes since he had left Leo. Too soon. What the hell. He drank the Scotch. 'See you later.'

'Sure.'

Hump. Drag. The thorns pierced his bones. Men died with their boots on in the good old days. Down there, away down there, Burd could hear the dying boots hit the pavement. He could feel heat through the thin soles. Heat and pain. Sill alive, he thought, walking with the heat and the pain.

Leo was smiling. This was the first time Burd had seen Leo smile. The smile made a dent under Leo's nose, a dent designed to catch the drop of moisture. Sniffling and smiling, Leo said: 'Well, well, well.'

'What?' said Burd.

'Who took them pictures?'

'An artist took them,' Burd said. 'A goddamn world-famous photographer. The kind of photographer a snotty-nosed little guy like you never heard of.'

'Well,' said Leo and he began to laugh. He laughed until his eyes watered along with his nose. 'Well, I tell you, Burd, this goddamned famous photographer whoever he is had better check up on himself because there ain't no pictures. There ain't a sign of a picture because the goddamn bastard forgot to load his film.'

'Film . . . film-holders . . .' Burd said.

'That's right,' said Leo. 'Those are mighty nice little holders but they gotta be packed with film before they can make a world famous photographer out of a man.'

Somewhere a voice joined in Leo's laughter. Somewhere a voice yelled: 'Jesus, that's good. Jesus, it's pretty. Isn't it the prettiest goddamn artistic ending.'

CHAPTER SEVENTEEN

LONELINESS was a mood. Loneliness began in a nursery crib with a puffed duck on the quilt and a voice saying good-night. Loneliness was a fat man ending in a booby hatch in a strange town. Loneliness was riding a bus with a jigger of bum liquor making your stomach raw and the bus-driver saying: 'Where ya' been? Didn't see you come home last night.'

Burd thought of Justine and of how she had tried to tell him whenever he would listen that love was the answer to loneliness. He thought about love. 'Another's warmth,' Justine called it. Another's warmth, like the warmth of the sun, if you could trust it, thought Burd, the way you trust

the sun. If you could know it was there, the way you knew
the sun was there, even when the clouds were thick and the
icy rain washed everything away. Love and Justine . . .
Justine and Burd . . . We might try it, he thought. But the
next thought came quickly. It would take a hell of a lot
of trying.

He had nothing to give her. A few years of his life. A
lousy body. He had nothing to give her except what she
wanted—another's warmth, like the warmth of the sun.

The wheels of the bus ground in the gravel and stopped
in front of the pomegranate hedge.

'Be seeing you,' the bus driver said.

Her car was there, waiting there as she must be waiting
inside. She should have been at work. Instead she was
waiting for him and he would have to see her before he had
thought things out. He walked quickly, nervously, to the
door on his side of the house. We might try . . . no, he
hadn't had time to figure it, to test it, to think how it
would be.

He pulled off his clothes and lay down on the bed. He
felt nothing but pain and weakness.

In a little while she came through the door. She had her
drowned look, as if she had been fished out of deep water.
Some of the wet still clung to her lashes and the words she
spoke had been washed in bitterness.

'Shay came,' she said. 'You stayed away and Shay came.'

Pain swirled all around. And he shut his eyes because he
could not shut his ears as Justine's voice went on and on.

THE DEAD HOUSE

ON the third day the same thing happened again. We crowded to the window, huddling together for warmth, and peered through the slit in the curtains. There she was, in the street below, barely visible in the half-light, going through her strange ritual and reciting what must have been an eerie gibberish. Although we could just see her lips moving we were too high up for her voice to reach us, and she looked so old that it was doubtful if she could manage more than a whisper or a feeble croak. For ten minutes, in the freezing cold of a January morning, she stood there, her right arm raised above her head, and her left clutching the shawl tight round her shoulders. Then she turned and went in.

We all moved away from the window and squatted by the gas stove, warming our hands. 'Mad as a hatter,' said Chambers. 'Ought to be put away.'

I looked at Brent. His pale, lean face reflected the fire like metal, and made him look more miserable than ever. 'Poor devil,' he muttered.

Cobbett suddenly got up and strode across the room. 'Do you realise how fishy all this could look?' he said. 'What do we know about her? The only time we ever see her is at half past six in the morning, when every sensible person—meaning those who aren't in the Army—is still tucked up in bed. All day long the house is shut up—no one is seen to go in, no one is seen to go out. The blinds are always drawn.'

There was a silence. No one could visualise the old girl as anything but a mental case—except Cobbett, of course, whose restless mind allowed him to visualise anything.

'Sounds like one of your spy stories, corporal,' I said.

'Of course it does,' he said, smacking his thigh. 'That's

just the point. And there's no need to look so bloody superior about it either.'

'No, corporal,' I said.

'I read in the papers the other day,' said Chambers, 'about an old man who used to tap his way round the streets with a white stick, and get people to help him across the road. He used to make up to people, and get them talking. It came out afterwards he had a dictaphone in his pocket.'

'A dictaphone?' I said. 'What kind of a pocket was that?'

'Well, something of the kind,' he said, sheepishly. 'Can't say for sure. Anyway, they nabbed him for it.'

'I'm going to tell the C.O. about it,' said Cobbett.

We saw the C.O. after breakfast. I felt it was going a bit too far, but I couldn't back out. Brent felt the same, I know, but he hardly ever said anything.

The C.O. was a fat man, with smooth puffy cheeks. He had a wonderful country house air about him which won most of the fellows over immediately, except for a few intellectuals, and even they had to admit that he was justice itself in his dealings with the men. He listened quietly and sympathetically as Cobbett told his story.

When he had finished, the C.O. sat quiet for a moment, looking at the floor. Then he got up and said, 'Good work, Cobbett. I agree, this must be looked into immediately. I'll investigate it myself, personally. You four had better come along with me.'

He told us to be ready in a quarter of an hour's time. When it was up he led us out and we crossed the road in a bunch, Cobbett at the captain's side. It was like a ridiculous expedition, from one side of the road to the other. We went up the steps and stood in the porch. We all looked at the door and at the columns on each side. The house was so quiet, so dead, the peeling stucco on the columns was so suggestive of decay, it seemed a shame to disturb anyone.

The captain pressed the button. We stood still, holding

our breath. 'Did you hear anything, Cobbett?' said the captain.

'No, sir. Maybe the bell don't work.'

The captain pressed the button again, not very hopefully but rather from politeness.

'They never mend their bells,' said Chambers.

The captain knocked. It sounded like the blows on an empty box. The sound ran round the house and up the walls, seeking an exit, and died away above our heads.

'Empty,' said Chambers. 'No one in there.'

'How do you know?' said the captain.

'I always know an empty house. I was in the furniture trade before this lot began. Removals. An empty house always rings hollow.'

'But you know there's someone there yourself,' said Cobbett.

'We're not sure, are we? And an old woman don't fill a house in any case,' said Chambers.

The captain didn't know what to do. 'Perhaps we'd better force it,' he said, obviously hating the idea.

Then Brent surprised us. He never says anything usually. He said, 'Perhaps it's open.' He stepped forward, turned the handle, and pushed the door in.

He stepped back, looking rather frightened. The captain grunted, and walked in, followed by Cobbett, who glared at Brent.

It was certainly a nice house, though rather old-fashioned. A thick green carpet ran up the hall and was continued on the staircase. The banisters were gleaming white, and had been cleaned recently. In fact, everything was pedantically clean and shining.

'We'll search the ground floor rooms first,' said the captain. He looked at Cobbett and Chambers. 'You come with me, and you two stand guard here.'

Brent and I gazed around us as the others began their

search. I was particularly interested in the pictures on the wall, which jostled each other and clambered up the staircase. They were the usual English wall decoration—portraits of ancestors, horses and the Doge's Palace.

Brent moved away and gazed at a full-length portrait at the foot of the stairs. It was an Army officer, in the dress of about the turn of the century. His features were certainly striking, apart from any methods the artist had used. He had a thin face with an extremely high forehead. His nose was a bit too long, and his eyes were nervous and agitated. The artist had taken particular care with them, and they provided a focal point for the spectator. I felt myself looking into his eyes, and had the absurd feeling that we were challenging each other.

I turned away with a shiver. I suddenly remembered how cold it was. 'About time this sort of junk was cleared away,' I said. 'How can we build our new world when people can't forget the old?'

'You don't see many faces like that now,' said Brent.

The others returned. 'No signs of habitation at all,' said the captain. He clapped his hands, and I noticed little clouds of dust shooting from them.

'Lot of good stuff going to waste in there,' said Chambers. 'Bloody shame. Think of all the people who can't get furniture!'

'We'll go upstairs,' said the captain.

He led the way, and we followed in single file; first Cobbett, then Chambers, and then myself, with Brent bringing up the rear. On our right the gloomy brown pictures seemed to march past us in procession.

Half-way up I heard a gasp behind me. I turned round and saw that Brent had stopped. He was gazing at the wall as though a masterpiece was nestling among all the other junk. I went back to see, and met those same eyes again. It was a very small head and shoulders portrait, but his features were so distinctive that there was no doubt about who it was. The paleness of his brow had been touched up to an absurd degree, and at first sight it seemed as though he wore a bandage.

I felt disgusted. 'Christ,' I said, 'what's the matter with you, Brent? Haven't you seen any portraits before?'

'Come along, you two!' called the captain. They were on the first landing now.

We ran up the remaining stairs. At that moment the door in front of us opened and a little girl came out. She was about nine years old, and wore a long white dress that reached from her muffled throat to her feet, the toes of which peeped out like mice. Her hair was long, and was gathered together at the back of her neck by some kind of brooch. She stood in front of us and looked at us gravely.

We all waited for the captain to say something. He touched his moustache and then said, 'Where's your mummy, little girl?'

Slowly her face broke into a smile, and then she began to chuckle. It was a rattling kind of laugh, which seemed to beat against her ribs. It became more and more uncontrolled, until at last her whole body was shaking. Her shoulders rose and fell, and her hands, clasped before her, danced together.

The captain and Cobbett looked at each other. Cobbett bent down and said, 'Is there anyone here? Anyone we can speak to?'

Her eyes opened wide, and she began to laugh more wildly than ever. Suddenly I felt someone grip my arm. It was Brent. Without looking at him I knew what he meant, as though mere physical contact had transferred a message. She was exhibiting all the symptoms of laughter, but her staring, accusing eyes were filled with terror and her wide-open mouth was trying to shout a warning at us.

Just as suddenly as she had appeared she turned and ran back into the room she had come from. Chambers tapped his forehead and said, 'I've seen 'em before, sir.'

The captain was more at ease with Brownings and grenades than with this sort of thing. He stroked his moustache, as he always did when faced with a problem, and mumbled something about trying to get some sense out of the little girl.

'She can't live here all alone,' he said.

Unwillingly he led the way into the room. Cobbett and Chambers crowded on his heels. It was almost impossible to see anything. After standing still for a few minutes we began to make out the lines of the furniture. The room was crammed with furniture; it was possible to make out the shapes of high-backed chairs, a sofa and a grand piano. Round the walls bulked what may have been sideboards and whatnots. I felt a strong sensation of claustrophobia creep over me, and at the same time I found myself breathing more deeply than normally, as though the air were rarified. After a little while I felt an irritation in my throat, which I am sure was due to the considerable amount of dust we were stirring up.

The captain groped for the light switch. 'I'm damned if I can find the switch,' he said. 'Perhaps one of you fellows . . .'

Cobbett brought out his lighter. The yellow flame cast its dim light on the wall, revealing a rich design of writhing plants, with stems and tendrils twining round each other and continuing endlessly—at least, to the boundaries of our flickering pool of light. But there was no switch.

'Extraordinary,' murmured the captain.

'This place gives me the creeps,' said Chambers.

Cobbett moved into the room, and we all kept close to him, as though our only safety lay in his shabby yellow circle of light. We threaded our way between the furniture until we had crossed the room. I found myself wondering why we were doing all this. There were no military objectives in this room. Then I remembered the little girl . . .

Cobbett stopped. He held the lighter in front of him, and dimly I saw her take shape. She was sitting primly on a high chair. On her lap was a book. Upside down I saw an illustration. It was in black and white, and the lines ran in curves and arabesques. I knew the style well—I had seen it before in old copies of the *Pall Mall Magazine*. She wasn't looking at the book, however, but was staring directly at us. Her face was in repose, and she showed not the slightest curiosity.

Cobbett began: 'Where's your —?' but the captain cut in. 'I think we'll go to the next floor,' he said.

I felt as though a band had been removed from my brow when I left that room. Perhaps it was that the air on the landing did at least circulate, if only very slightly, but in the room it had hung sullenly and clogged every movement and every thought.

We continued upstairs in the same order. Even Chambers was quiet now. We all felt that the top floor might provide a clue, but we had no idea what it could be. I for one was not looking forward to seeing the old woman, for now I was convinced that we would find her. This house might transform an old woman into a witch.

At the top of the stairs were two doors. We opened the first very slowly and peered in. To our surprise it was feebly lighted by a candle flame. The room was very bare, and seemed to have been converted into a kitchen. There was no one there, but a kettle stood on a lighted gas ring.

The captain opened the second door. It led into a room rather like the one below, but it was also lighted by a solitary candle in the middle of the mantelpiece. To one side sat an old woman. She seemed of medium stature, and was dressed in a plain, old-fashioned costume. A large white brooch at her throat was the only ornament she wore. She looked up as we came in, but she did not appear to be surprised.

We, on the other hand, were at a loss. After a moment's hesitation the captain took a step forward and said, 'Er, excuse me, madam, but could I speak to you for a few moments?'

She looked up at him and said, 'Certainly, captain, but I don't think I shall be able to help.'

As she looked up I saw her features for the first time. I shall never forget them. Although she must have been seventy her features seemed in some ways to be utterly boyish. Whether it was the clearness of her complexion, the lack of lines and the frankness of her eyes, or whether it was their physical structure which had remained untouched by time while everything else had become old and warped, I don't know. But as she looked up at the captain her patience seemed to be that of a boy when matched by the ignorance and arrogance of an adult.

'Won't you sit down?' she asked. 'It is a very cold morning. Perhaps you would have some tea with me.'

From the start she had imposed her personality on us, and not even the captain, to whom we all naturally looked for leadership, seemed capable of bringing up the subject that had brought us here. We sat down in that cold, fireless room and waited.

She rose, and walked slowly across the room. As she passed Brent she touched him lightly with her hand and said, 'Will you help me make it?'

We sat uncomfortably where we were, waiting for them to return. None of us said a word. My eyes wandered round the room, and were suddenly held by a portrait standing on the mantelpiece behind the candlestick. It was the same face.

I got up and went over to examine it. It was a photograph, and in the bottom left-hand corner was some writing in a round, flamboyant hand. After some time I managed to spell out, 'Died on the morning of Jan. 15, 1903, after seven days in great agony.' That was all. What surprises me now, in looking back, is that there was no name—usually the first thing to go on a photograph. But I suppose the inhabitants of that house were too familiar to need to carry their names as badges.

The old lady returned with Brent and the tea. She had been talking to him, for as they came in she was saying '. . . the door was usually locked.' Brent slumped into his chair. I moved away from the mantelpiece carefully and quietly and pretended to be examining a slender vase that stood on a small table. But she was paying no attention to me; instead the old lady began to pour out tea and hand round the cups. I caught Brent's eye and tried to draw his attention to the photograph, but he looked away and seemed almost consciously to keep his eyes from the mantelpiece.

'I have something that will interest you, captain,' said the old woman pleasantly. She went to a cabinet and came back with a long wooden box. The initials WM were engraved on the lid.

She opened the box, handling it as though it were a lover's gift. Inside lay a revolver on a plush bed.

'Do you recognise it, captain?' she asked.

'Er, no, I'm afraid not . . .' he began.

'Take it out and look at it,' she said, almost imperiously.

The captain took the revolver, but immediately replaced it. 'It's cocked,' he said.

'That's right,' she said, pleasantly once more, and with a slow smile coming to her face. 'Cocked and loaded. One bullet has been fired.'

She closed the box, and replaced it in the cabinet. As she came back she said, 'It's an old Army revolver. It belonged to my husband.'

She sat down again and appeared to forget about us. We all expected the captain to make a move of some kind, but he appeared to have lost all initiative. We sat in silence for several minutes.

Then she said, 'I was sitting here at the time. I daren't go in the downstairs rooms now. I'm always afraid Katherine will be there.'

I remember all this clearly. I cannot vouch for what happened afterwards. All I know is that we all suddenly jumped to our feet. I haven't the slightest idea why. Afterwards Brent said he distinctly heard a report, as though a shot had been fired. There may have been a noise of some kind which startled us, but it seems unlikely that none of us except Brent should have remembered it. I think it far more likely that Brent, who is a very highly-strung boy, fancied he heard something and jumped to his feet, and that we automatically did the same. Only the old lady remained where she was—at least, I don't remember seeing her again.

It was certainly Brent who led the procession from the room and downstairs. We had cleared the first flight of stairs and were just passing the landing when Brent, who now seemed to be our self-appointed leader, stopped dead, and we did the same. He turned round, and we turned round with him. But before we turned I heard the beginnings of that metallic, inhuman chuckle. She was standing on the landing in exactly the same place and attitude as when we had first seen her. And, just as then, her chuckle grew in volume until it became a laugh of hysterical terror. I suddenly felt lonely and isolated as I heard that wail and watched the contorted face of a little child.

And now I hardly dare to steal even a glance at that house when I pass it. Even more extraordinary is that the four of us only once discussed the subject afterwards, even when the passage of a few days and the open light of day had turned the episode into a bad dream. But when we mentioned it, and tried to revive, as a self-torturing exercise, the impression of the foetid air and the mad girl, we found that Brent had not been looking at the same thing as the rest of us; *he swore that she held a smoking revolver in her hand.*

The C.O. never followed the case up. He never even mentioned it to us. We even felt that he intentionally kept from contact with us, as though even the very sight of us revived associations too painful to bear. Not long after he was transferred.

THE EVICTION

CHRISTOPHER raised his arms above his head and yawned noisily. Then he closed his mouth and remained with his arms still outstretched and his head raised slightly from the pillow. The doorbell had rung.

He tore the bedclothes aside and felt with his feet for his slippers. Only a dim diffused light entered the room through the chinks between the blind and the window frame and he could see nothing clearly. The doorbell rang again.

He got to his feet quickly and ran through his sitting room to the front door. He pulled the door open wide, and then refrained from complaining, as he had intended. On the doorstep stood a thin drab woman with a little boy. Her lips were severe and tightly closed, and Christopher noticed that her bony fingers were playing round the bell-push like overgrown spider's legs.

'What do you want?' he said.

She smiled suddenly, and then said monotonously, 'Would you like a flag for the unemployed ostlers?'

'I have great sympathy with the unemployed,' said Christopher, 'but I've never heard of the unemployed ostlers. Have they a Union?'

She didn't answer, and Christopher was about to turn into his sitting room when he felt a tug at his pyjama girdle. He looked down and saw that the little boy was pulling it gently, with a curious smile on his face. He was very pale, like his mother, and the oversize school cap he wore made him look rather grotesque, but what Christopher noticed particularly was the long light brown lock of hair which fell down over each ear and rested on his shoulder.

His mother laid her hand gently on the boy's head and

said, almost in a whisper, 'Now Cyril, don't play with the gentleman's girdle.'

The sweetness of her tone checked the anger that was rising and Christopher said with a smile, and almost as gently, 'No, little man, that's not the thing to do.' Then he reached out with his thumb and forefinger and playfully tugged one of the little boy's locks. He did it very gently because he did not want to hurt the little fellow, but it was sufficient to unbalance his cap, which fell at Christopher's feet. The little boy turned with a sob and hid his face against his mother's stomach.

She drew herself up until her slight frame seemed to be strung at a fearful tension, and said, controlling her anger with an effort, 'Will you kindly keep your hands off my son? Isn't it enough that he is afflicted with a terrible disease that baffles the best medical brains in the country!'

Christopher struggled between shame and anger. 'I—I didn't understand —' he began, but couldn't finish.

'Perhaps not,' she said, looking him in the face very coldly, 'but that is no excuse for personal abuse.'

'He pulled my girdle,' said Christopher sullenly.

'Maybe. And isn't that what you'd expect a little boy to do? Don't all little boys pull things when they see them? But one hardly expects an adult to behave in the same way.'

The little boy's sobbing was becoming more and more violent, and she patted his head and smoothed his back, crooning, 'There, there, Cyril, there's no harm done, I'm sure. Nasty mans,' she added viciously.

Christopher was feeling cold, and was anxiously considering what he could do to make amends for his hasty action. 'Come,' he said, 'I'll make you a cup of tea, I'm sure he'll feel better then.'

She immediately pushed past Christopher, moving the little boy in front of her with her knees. 'Not for Cyril,' she said, 'he's on a diet, but I'll have one.'

'Perhaps I could get something else for Cyril,' Christopher called after her as he closed the door.

Her reply was scornful, yet triumphant. 'Not a hope. There's only a few nursing homes and sanatoriums in the country that can give Cyril what he needs—and they're very exclusive and extremely expensive, I can assure you. My husband works at least sixteen hours a day, and on piece rates too—and very often he works the whole clock round—and then we can't always afford to buy all the foods the little lamb should have. Why, I frequently go out to work to supplement my husband's income, otherwise I shouldn't be collecting now. It's not the kind of work I'd choose, but we can't always choose and they certainly pay very generously. But I daren't go out too often, because it tires Cyril so, and I couldn't be so heartless as to leave him at home. Besides, who could I trust to look after him?'

When Christopher returned from the kitchen with the tray he found that the woman had dragged his bed into the sitting room and placed it in front of the gas fire, which was full on. Cyril was lying at full length on the bed, his head on one pillow and his feet on another. His mother was stroking his forehead and crooning softly to him:

> Blow wind, blow rain,
> And come again.
> The night is steeped in witchery
> And the trees are asleep in the lane.

He put the tray on the table and went through to the bedroom without a word. He returned with his dressing gown and was about to put it on, when the woman turned quickly and smiled at him in the dazzling way she seemed to command at will. 'Oh, that is kind of you!' she said. 'Look, Cyril, what the kind man has brought for you!' She laid it over the boy's slender body, and began to chant to him a catalogue of the gown's qualities: 'Red and green and blue and white a lovely gown a lovely gown for little Cyril warm and snug warm and snug, snug as a bug as a bug in a rug.' Then she stopped and looked thoughtfully into the fire.

'What time is it?' she asked.

'Good God!' said Christopher in alarm, 'it's gone nine, and here I am not dressed!'

'Nine!' the woman almost screamed, 'nine, did you say? Why, you—you animal! Quick, help me with Cyril—he should have been massaged ages ago.'

She began to undress the little boy, and none too gently, it seemed to Christopher. She pulled him into a sitting position and tugged at the collar of his jacket so that his arms were pinned behind him and he began to cry again. At last the jacket ripped down a seam and she fell backwards into a chair, holding the remnant in her hands. Suddenly realising how urgent the case must be, but without understanding its urgency, Christopher strode to the foot of the bed and began to untie Cyril's shoe laces. His mother screamed, jumped up and violently pushed him away. 'You fool!' she cried, in a furious choking voice, 'anyone'd think you wanted to kill him. The very idea, taking his shoes off! Why that's just the place where the infection enters. Dr. Hardy' (at mention of the name her voice dropped to a low, even luxurious note, and she no longer appeared angry) 'Doctor Hardy said that if once his feet were exposed it would be fatal.'

She stopped, and became very quiet, playing with the boy's shirt which she had pulled off, and looking straight ahead of her with a curious glassy stare. 'It's a bacillus, some dreadful kind of bacillus, that eats through the soft skin between the toes and works its way up to the heart. Very few people are susceptible to it—I suppose it's a blessing, they have to be peculiarly sensitive, like Cyril.' As she mentioned her son's name her voice broke and she dropped into the chair again, and laid her head on her arms. 'Sometimes,' she said between sobs, 'I wonder why Cyril should have been chosen, but then I know I'm being wicked and I put the thought out of my mind. All's for the best, in some inexplicable way, only He knows. It's a great honour really, and one has to put up with the disadvantages.'

She sat up, very upright, and composed her face. Christopher noticed that her eyes were quite dry. 'They say Shelley had it,' she said. 'Only the best are afflicted, and it's up to us lesser people to make sacrifices.'

Christopher was now very alarmed, for in her grief she had forgotten the little boy, who still sat on the bed, absolutely still, wearing nothing but his trousers, socks and shoes. Christopher pointed to him, afraid that he might die or might even be dead, and said awkwardly, 'Hadn't we better —?'

'My gracious, yes!' she cried and jumped up. Putting her hand on Cyril's chest she knocked him backwards, yanked his legs up by the feet, deftly undid his fly-buttons and pulled off the trousers. Once again she seemed to have given way to hysteria, and she abused Christopher constantly, accusing him of interfering with her duty, of exposing the boy to great danger, and caring for nobody but himself.

The boy lay back naked on the bed, except for his shoes and socks. As soon as she looked down at him she forgot her anger again and her expression of gentleness and love returned. 'Ah, the darling!' she said, almost inaudibly, 'and that I should have borne him! Feel his skin, how deliciously cool and tender it is, softer than any baby's. Can you doubt that the bacillus should be tempted?'

Unwillingly Christopher laid his finger tips on the boy's chest and gently moved them back and forwards, while the woman bent down so that her nose was within an inch of his fingers, to see that he didn't pinch or bruise the white flesh. Then she grabbed a hand and started rubbing the palm vigorously with her fist, and shouted at Christopher to do the same with the other hand. Although the massaging made only a slight hissing noise, she appeared to think it was a roar, for when she spoke to Christopher she leant over the child's body and shouted in his ear.

'This is the only known method of annoying the bacillus, apart from certain foods and drinks containing certain properties. It sets up a howling noise within the body, something like the wind rushing through the veins and arteries. The bacillus, which is very sensitive, can't bear it and has to retreat. We have to do this several times a day, otherwise the bacillus would be at his heart in no time. The last X-ray showed that it has already reached the knee, which is very serious, for it means it's gaining ground. Last June it was only at the ankle, so as you can see, it's made considerable headway in only three months.'

There was a timid tap at the door, so quiet and unobtrusive that Christopher wondered whether there had been previous ones, drowned by the woman's voice. He got up and walked to the door on tiptoe, feeling that any vibration might affect Cyril's nerves or aid the bacillus. When he opened the door he saw a very short, weedy little man, dressed in an old navy blue jacket and filthy brown trousers, standing obsequiously in the passage, apparently very ill at ease. He held a rough tweed cap in his hands which he twiddled round so fast that it looked like a gramophone record. He coughed nervously as Christopher stared at him and said, in little more than a whisper, 'Sorry to trouble you, sir, but is me wife 'ere?'

Before Christopher could answer the woman had bustled past him and almost collapsed on the little man's neck. In fact, his knees bent and Christopher put out his hand to prevent a crash, but the thin legs straightened with an effort and the whole edifice remained standing, though quite miraculously, for now nothing could be seen of its support save the man's toe caps. Meanwhile the woman had succumbed to another wave of hysteria, and in between loud, smacking hisses and tremendous sobs and sighs, she cried,

'Herbert, dear dear Herbert, I was beginning to think you were never coming, oh how I've missed you, and you poor darling, you must be famished and *so* tired, poor thing, come in and have a nice cup of tea. When must you get back, oh how terrible to think of getting back in your condition, but what can we do, there's Cyril.' At the mention of Cyril's name she broke down completely. It seemed that the little man was unable to stand the combined weight of her body and emotion any longer, for he began to sag, or that's how it appeared to Christopher, for the woman slowly began to sink, lower and lower. He ran to her aid, and only just in time, for the little man suddenly gasped and collapsed. The woman screamed and ran back into the room, while Christopher picked up the frail body and laid it gently in the armchair, where Herbert immediately fell asleep.

'Oh, the trouble I have to bear,' sighed the woman, 'but quick, get Herbert some tea, and some for me too, I haven't had a chance to have any at all, and now it's cold.'

Quite dazed, uncertain whether to object to what seemed an imposition or try and help in every way he could (for the little boy's condition seemed really dangerous, and it was this that finally decided him), Christopher went into the kitchen to make another pot of tea. When he returned he was amazed at the change in the woman's appearance. She had put some rouge on her cheeks, some lipstick on her mouth, powdered her nose and rearranged her hair. She sat up very straight, smiling freshly and charmingly, and slightly opened her lips when Christopher came in and tilted her head. For the first time he saw that she was really a young girl and extraordinarily handsome. He put the tray on the table and squatted on the floor beside her. She laid her hand on his head, and lightly ran her fingers through his hair.

'You're quite young, aren't you?' she said.

He looked up at her, and suddenly felt weak because of the elegance of her throat, which he could see properly for the first time because she had unbuttoned her dress. He put up his hand and pulled her head down and shuddered as he felt her lips, no longer thin and tight, on his own. Then he pulled with his hand and pressed with his mouth so violently that she fell off her chair and tumbled on top of him, screaming with laughter. She screamed so loudly that Herbert woke up for a moment, looked bewilderedly about him, and then let his head fall back again and started snoring. Christopher jumped up in embarrassment and began pouring out the tea, while the woman lay full length on the floor and laughed more and more loudly.

Christopher turned to her and said quietly, 'Here's your tea.' She scrambled to her feet and took it from him. Then she looked at Herbert and said scornfully, 'Look at him! To think that I have to live with that pig of a man. One thing, no one would ever imagine the bacillus came from *him*.'

They drank in silence, while the snoring became louder and louder. At last she could stand it no longer, put down her cup and shook the poor man roughly by the shoulders. He stopped snoring with a tremendous snort, shot out his legs and then slowly opened his eyes. They had barely had time to take anything in than they began to close again, but the woman pinched him on the thigh and pulled his hair, shouting, 'Wake up, Herbert, it's time to go back! Come on, you fat thing' (which seemed a most inapt description, and certainly seemed to have no affect on Herbert), 'get on with you, it's time to go back to work, do you hear?' She sighed, and said bitterly, 'I don't think you care a rap for Cyril!'

All this time Herbert had shown no signs of life, except for his head which rolled from side to side as she pulled his hair and ears, but at mention of the boy's name he jumped up, snatched his cap, which lay on the floor, muttered, 'Cyril! Ah yes, Cyril!' and was out of the room in a jiffy.

The woman turned her back to Christopher and hugged

her arms against her chest, hunching her shoulders. 'This continual nagging,' she muttered, 'I hate having to do it, but how else can I get anything out of him?'

'He seems overworked to me,' said Christopher.

She turned round and almost screamed, 'Overworked! Him! He's the laziest devil on God's earth.'

He had never seen anyone so beautiful. Her eyes glistened, and her nostrils seemed to open and close like angry snapdragons. He rushed to her and flung his arms round her. He could scarcely control his breathing, and his desire grew as he felt her resistance lessening. Then he let her head fall back, and gazed at it with an anticipating smile—a delicious miniature framed in her black hair which flowed away to the floor. It seemed that there was nothing more to do but to lie down with her when she said in a very weak voice, 'How unkind you are! Taking advantage of me in my overwrought state!'

All his energy seemed to ebb away, and he was no longer holding a warm, beautiful woman but a bundle of straw. He pulled her upright and walked over to the furthest corner of the room. He wanted to answer her, but could think of no way of expressing his thoughts. At last he said lamely, 'Me unkind! You accuse *me* of being unkind!'

He watched her as she wearily walked to the armchair and almost fell in it. 'Those affairs exhaust me,' she said, more to herself than to him.

Christopher looked away in consternation, biting his lip, and then he saw something that made his teeth bring blood. The little boy was blue! Suddenly Christopher began to shudder, feeling the cold of the Spring morning and realising that he was still in his pyjamas. He ran to the bed and began to pummel some circulation back into the little fellow's body, shouting, 'For God's sake, look! He'll die of exposure!'

The woman languidly lifted her head and stared at him uncomprehendingly. 'What do you mean?' she said dully.

'Mean? What do I mean? Look! Look at him!' Christopher

could think of nothing more to say, but it seemed sufficiently explanatory, and he moved aside to let her see the child's body, now a bruised purple and mauve where he had been massaging.

She glanced at him, and then smiled faintly at Christopher. Then she spread her lap, patted it and said, 'You dear fellow, come and sit here.' He hesitated and then did as he was told. She ran her hand up and down his back and began to feather his lips, eyes, ears and neck with kisses, and all the time she talked to him cooingly as if he were the child and Cyril was something remote and unimportant. 'You don't understand at all, do you? But you do try, I can see that, and I love you for it. If it weren't that I felt a little unwell I would show you, I'd prove it to you, but I'm hardly up to it now. But you see, dear, it's not a chill or the danger of a chill that's important to Cyril. He might catch a chill, of course, like anyone else and if he did we'd all be very sorry and do our best to help him, I'm sure. But there's nothing much about a chill, not even 'flu would be important though it might be unpleasant. The trouble with Cyril is the bacillus and I don't know much about it myself, I couldn't describe it, though I understand it's something like an ant or a beetle. But anyway, it's some kind of insect, very small, but it has a tremendous appetite and that's the danger. If it didn't eat so much no one would mind, it would be no more harmful than a worm or a T.B. germ. But it never stops eating—flesh, bone, blood, tissue, cells of every kind. The doctors tell me Cyril's foot is quite hollow owing to the creature's activity, and you could see how disastrous it would be if the bacillus had all it's own way. Sooner or later Cyril would be just a hollow shell and—oh, it's too, too horrible.'

She laid her hand on his shoulder. Christopher patted her hair and felt the back of her skull, so tiny in his hand. 'I'm sorry if I've been tiresome,' he said. 'I didn't understand. I want to help, I really do.'

She flung her head up sharply, buffeting his nose and making it numb. She looked radiantly happy, and the tears in her eyes seemed to be lit from within. 'But you can help, darling, you can, only you must listen to me. The doctors tell me what to do, and I tell you and Herbert what to do.'

He slipped off her lap and knelt before her, gazing earnestly into her eyes. 'How can I help?' he asked in hushed tones, 'tell me how I can help. I'll do anything.'

'You can help in the same way as Herbert,' she said happily.

'Herbert?' He was puzzled. 'How does he help? He seems to be out all the time.'

'Exactly!' she laughed. Someone has to earn the money to buy Cyril's medicines and special diets. But the bills are getting bigger and Herbert's falling behind,' she added sadly. 'He's lazy, he sleeps too much—I so much need help.'

Christopher stood up and began to take off his pyjamas. 'I'll go straight away,' he said. He hastily dressed, while she watched him admiringly.

Before he went he kissed her lightly and said, 'I'm going to the factory. When I come back I'll have something for you—and Cyril.'

She took his hand, squeezed it and then laid it against her breast. He tore it away, because he could not bear such hopeless contact. 'I will never forget this,' she said simply.

After working 26 hours continuously Christopher began to feel faint, and the ache in his back and thighs were becoming unbearable. Herbert had gone three hours ago, and had to be carried to the door, so weak had he become. Christopher put down his hammer, walked out of the shop and asked for a sub.

When he got to the door of the flat he heard a strange whirring noise which rose and fell with a consistant, unchanging rhythm. He wearily let himself in and before he could take in the scene he was pounced on by the woman who cried and laughed into his shoulder. 'It's come at last,' she told him wildly, it's come at last. Now everything will be all right.'

He was so tired he leant against her, so that they supported each other like two propped cards. He looked round the room and saw an enormous machine in the corner, which hummed and vibrated and produced the sound he had heard before he came in. It was a giant steel structure, reaching almost to the ceiling, painted grey and red, and covered with dials, levers, nozzles, caps, and a number of other gadgets. One dial, much larger than the others, showed a needle which flickered agitatedly, and a thin flex ran from it to Cyril's knee, which was tightly bandaged with a broad rubber band. Beside the machine stood three men, all dressed in black and wearing neat bow ties. One of these pumped a handle, and was responsible for the rising-falling rhythm of the engine's roar. Another peered intently at the dial and from time to time jotted something in a notebook. The third man was beaming delightedly, and constantly slapped his colleagues on the shoulder and uttered remarks of satisfaction.

Christopher passed his hand wearily over his forehead. 'What is it?' he said, barely able to simulate interest.

'The bacillometer,' shrieked the woman, pounding his chest with her fists. 'It's what we've been waiting for for years and now it's arrived. It was specially made for Cyril, specially made in America!'

Christopher shifted his feet and stumbled over something on the floor. He steadied himself against the table. Looking down he saw Herbert, stretched out on the floor and wrapped in a blanket, with his mouth wide open.

'Is he dead?' he asked.

'Oh don't be silly. Come, look at the bacillometer, isn't it a beauty?'

Christopher stared hard at it, struggling to keep his eyes

open. The senior doctor, or at least the one who appeared to be supervising the other two, looked at him suspiciously and said, 'Who's this?'

'This?' said the woman. 'Oh, he's my assistant. He comes in to help. But explain it to him.'

The doctor coughed and said pompously, 'I should be more prepared to go through another explanation if he appeared to be more impressed. However' (with a fearful sigh) 'the principle is this. The bacillometer injects a serum into the child's leg, which agitates the bacillus to a frenzy. To tell you the truth, no one really understands how it works, but as you can see for yourself, it's a very impressive piece of work. All we know is that this needle measures the reaction of the bacillus to his treatment, and as you can see, the little fellow's quite upset.'

The other doctors stopped what they were doing for a moment and laughed boisterously. The senior doctor smirked and went on. 'Of course, it's incomplete as yet, but even this is a scientific miracle—if scientists accepted miracles.' (The other doctors guffawed.) 'With this apparatus we can discover that the bacillus is being kept busy, but we don't know the quality of his reaction. We don't know whether he's retreating or whether he's been spurred on to greater effort, which is possible. But that will be settled in time, have no doubt of that. And now, gentlemen, we have a particularly interesting case of gout round the corner, so I must interrupt you for the time being.'

The other doctors straightened up and the row died away to a wheeze and silence. They picked up their gladstones, which they had laid neatly in a row at the foot of the machine, snapped them open, took out sandwiches and left the flat, munching happily.

The woman turned to Christopher, her eyes streaming but her features transfigured to the beauty she seemed to assume at will. 'Oh, I'm so happy,' she gasped. 'Isn't it wonderful?'

Christopher said nothing, but merely took his pay packet from his pocket and handed it to her.

As she took it she yawned, saying indistinctly, 'Oh, I'm tired—absolutely exhausted.' Then she looked at what he had given her and her features straightened into gratitude. 'How kind of you,' she murmured, 'how very very kind!'

'It's for you,' he said simply. He looked round for somewhere to rest. 'I must sleep,' he yawned. 'I must sleep.'

She was bustling round him again, full of concern. 'Oh, my poor poor darling, how tired you must be! Of course, you must sleep! How thoughtless of me to detain you!'

She went to the door and opened it wide. 'You have a good rest,' she said, 'then see me again.'

Incapable of initiation or resistance, he dragged his feet to the door. He made a last effort. 'I must go?' he said.

'Why, surely, you need a rest so badly! And besides, I'm tired, I must tuck up too.' She winked and said roguishly, 'It would never do to have a stranger in the flat, with Herbert there, would it?'

He didn't answer, but walked out. He heard the door closing, and then, glancing behind, saw her face peering round the corner at him. She flashed one of her brilliant smiles and said, 'Don't forget what I said—I'll never forget your kindness. Never!'

MUSIC HATH POWER

THE Colonel glanced moodily at Jane and went on with his soup. He knew that everyone regarded him as a back number. He didn't mind that particularly, for they were wrong, but for the first time he wondered if his wife also shared their views. But he had a very good reason for feeling his isolation more acutely than usual this evening. He had suddenly realised, with a strong sense of conviction, something that had lain half-hidden in his mind for years. It had happened this afternoon, still only a very few hours back. It was the regimental march. It was ridiculous to make excuses to himself, even if he still made them to others. It was damn bad. It sounded like one of those musical comedy marches—Ruritanian, brassy-fiddly, something of the nursery about it. Dum dum de dum *dum*—bloody awful noise. That final *dum*, with its emphasis and vulgarity, was sufficient to make the regiment a laughing-stock. And then, to have it paraded through the streets of Stonefield, with the breezy Middlesex melody ahead and the bracing Duke of Wellington's behind!

'You're upset, dear,' said Jane. 'What is it?'

He lowered his head and scowled across at her, thinking what a damn fine figure of a woman she was for a wife. She was twenty years younger than him, in the fullness of maturity, with breasts like gentle Yorkshire hills and a darkness about her that fluctuated like the county of her birth—now menacing, now strikingly soft and sympathetic.

'I can't bear that damn march,' he growled. 'Dum dum de dum *dum*—och!' In times of stress he tended to lapse into a slight Scotchness, inherited from his mother.

'I've been thinking about it too,' she said. 'It's most depressing, though I suppose it's intended to be jolly. Why not change it?'

'Change it?' It sounded like a snort, and did in fact come through his nose. 'You can't change things like that. Once you've got a march you've got it. Nothing can be done about it.'

'It would be a wonderful idea to break away from all that— be the first to introduce a new, up-to-date march. After all, Mark, the soldiers who march to it are a bit different from those who originally marched to that piece of inferior ragtime. Everyone loathes it. Have you seen the face the bandmaster makes when they strike up? Poor fellow, he looks as though he's really trying hard not to be sick. It would certainly be an innovation.'

'Innovation!' The Colonel was against innovation.

'Well, of course, it's up to you. But just think of the effect it would have on Sandwich if you were suddenly to introduce a brand new march by a first-class contemporary composer!'

'Oh, Jane! Sandwich! Who cares about that foppish little squirt? Regiments have histories and traditions, eternal ones, whereas Sandwich'll be out on his neck at the next General Election.'

It sounded as though, despite his vehemence, the Colonel did care about Sandwich.

It was impossible to say whether Sir Irving Sandwich was popular or not. But he was a curiosity and he was always news. The new Government, unused to administration and at a loss to know how to fill the comparatively unimportant War Department now there was no war on, offered it to Sandwich because he was the only person among the Party high-ups who was not certain to be offended. And Sandwich played up. He didn't waste any time in accepting the office and immediately showed his enthusiasm by insisting that all Army vehicles should have overhead valves installed. Both the Government and the public were then prepared to see Sandwich decline into a quite harmless state of insignificance, while other and more powerful interests wrangled over civil aviation and proportional representation. That's when Sandwich caught them all bending.

This is not the place to go into all the reforms which Sandwich bustled through his Department and presented to an amazed and sometimes shocked Parliament and to an equally amazed and usually amused public. No one could do anything about it, as Sandwich made full use of the machinery afforded him by a democratic constitution and delegated all his legislation. It was, in fact, as a mild-mannered, small-boned Professor of Constitutional History that he had originally attracted attention. He had claimed, in a quiet voice and with a shy smile, that the citizens of a democratic state were never bound *in perpetuo* by existing law if a majority were not in agreement with the law. 'If a majority of citizens,' he said, 'believe that a law, either civil, criminal, constitutional or military—' (He paused here and smiled)— 'does not coincide with their interests, and constitutional redress is barred to them, they have an undeniable right to resort to other, unconstitutional means.'

When he attained office Sandwich showed that he was determined to make the constitution work to full capacity, thus relieving malcontents of their legal right to what used to be termed illegal action. He issued an A.B.7943 which was issued to every serving soldier and was distributed to the press and Members of Parliament, and quoted several times daily for a whole year before the novelty wore off. The first clause is worthy of quotation here, especially as it is the 'first cause' on which the whole structure rested.

(1) 'In a democratic state those citizens who voluntarily forego the chances of preferment and the physical comfort of civilian life, i.e., serving members of the Army, the Navy, and the Royal Air Force, should *by right* have a prior claim to the recognition and attention of a grateful public relating to all matters outside the scope of military custom and discipline.'

(The Admiralty and the Air Ministry were very annoyed by their implication, but it was too late to do anything but send a note.) Like all general principles, it was necessarily vague, but Sandwich developed it fully in the 153 clauses that followed.

It was inevitable that a young and vigorous man like Sandwich, still under the influence of the psycho-analysts and with a sentimental hankering after the philosophy of the Epicureans, should get rid of a lot of dead wood. They went, fast and protesting, bemused and threatening, mostly in the shape of old blimps in the 50-60 age group (the 1900 class, as the comic weeklies referred to them). They were replaced by young men from the military academies and even from the Universities and various professions, men who thought a sten was a film star but did not think a temperament was a non-military perquisite. This is the reason why Colonel Mark Slade was so irritated by the mere mention of Sandwich's name. He was like an undersized dinosaur in the new Army, a rare fossil sticking its thick skull through a crust of youthful intelligence. No one knew why he had been allowed to remain in charge of the Don Yeomanry, except that it was hardly worth Sandwich's while to discharge him when he was due very shortly for retirement. And possibly Sandwich gloated over the discomfiture Slade must feel when he met his fellow commanders of the Middlesex Regiment and the Duke of Wellington's—one the science master at a minor public school but a few months back and the other a poet who had substituted poetry readings for Church Parade!

Jane was therefore not surprised when, a few days later, after much coughing and clearing of his throat, Mark brought up the subject of the regimental march again, said he'd been thinking about it, been turning it over in his mind, had come to the conclusion, etc., etc.—in short, that he favoured a new march and to hell with what people thought! He never did care what people thought, anyway, and he was damned if he'd let an insignificant fish like Sandwich deter him.

'I think you're very wise,' said Jane, softly.

'I don't know much about music —' began the Colonel.

'I know, dear,' said Jane, and she said it so sympathetically that even Mark had to chuckle.

'I don't know much about music, but we want a damn fine rousing chorus—something like that thing, what was it, you know, we saw it some years ago—*Merrie England*. Now if we could get that fellow—who was it?'

'German, dear, but —'

'Eh? No, not that, you're thinking of Eastbourne or one of those places—Wagner, we don't want him, and he's dead, anyway.'

'No, his name was German, Edward German, but he's dead too.'

'Dead, is he? Damn shame. Well, aren't there any other composers alive to-day? Damn shame, the way we English leave these things to foreigners.'

'Now you leave it to me, dear.' She was most persuasive now, and had her arm round his neck. 'I'll fix it up. I'll find someone.'

'How? You don't know any musicians, do you?' There was a slight threat in his tone.

'No, silly, but I'll ask Edwin. He knows all those things.'

'Yes, he would,' sniffed the colonel. He didn't approve of Edwin either.

'He says he's got a letter from you, ordering 'im to report, sir. I seen it,' said the R.S.M.

'A letter? Why the hell should I send a letter to him? He must be crazy.' All kinds of men had tried to get through to the Colonel before now (usually to explain why they had to have leave) and they had tried to work all kinds of dodges, but never this one before.

'Is it likely I'd send him a letter, anyway?' the Colonel went on, because the R.S.M. did not appear to have anything to say. He was now constrained to say, 'No, sir, it isn't.'

'What did you say his name was?'

'Raveningham, sir. 1576226, Pte Raveningham of F Coy.'

'Well, tell him to clear off and warn him not to try such a trick again, else he'll be on a charge.'

'Yessir,' and the R.S.M. withdrew.

At half past twelve the Colonel was smoking a pipe and wondering what was for dinner. Then there was a knock on the door, and he snapped, 'Come in'; he did not snap because he was angry, but because it was customary and experience had warned him to expect the worst.

The door opened and something outrageous happened. A mere private walked into the room and gently closed the door, and *he was unescorted!* He was also very nervous, but privates were always nervous, even when escorted. At first the Colonel stared at him blankly and uncomprehendingly. For a moment the mad idea that this was a trick staged by Sandwich presented itself. He searched for a crown on the right arm, thinking he had created a new sergeant-major and forgotten about it. Then he looked for stripes and found none. There weren't even any service chevrons or proficiency badges. In fact, the sleeve was bare save for a little device that looked like a lyre and which the Colonel had never seen before and did not understand now he saw it. When, having examined these important parts of the creature's anatomy the Colonel transferred his gaze to the man's face, he felt affronted. The head was long and extremely narrow, and stuck out of its collar on such a thin neck that it resembled a doorhandle more than anything else. In addition to this the intruder wore thick-lensed glasses and had very red and moist and somewhat bulbous lips, and the Colonel could stand neither of these things. And then his visitor, whoever it was, smiled.

'Who are you?' snorted the Colonel.

His visitor was genuinely taken aback. 'Private Ravening-ham, sir. You sent for me,' he added hastily, before he could be thrown out.

'Sent for you? Are you the fellow who tried to get in here this morning?'

'Yes, sir. You see —'

'I see nothing. This is impertinence. You'll get 14 days' C.B. for this!'

Private Raveningham was almost in tears. He whipped a piece of paper from behind his back, where he had been clutching it like a concealed dagger, and held it in front of the Colonel's nose. He tried to say something, but only gulped.

The Colonel snatched it, glanced at it and then suddenly arrested his fingers as they were preparing to close and crumple the letter into a ball. He read it, and read it as though it were a remarkable document which he had never even imagined could exist, which was nonsense, for he had written it. He put it down slowly, looked at Raveningham, then again at the letter and once more at the frightened private. He was pale, and his lips were moving soundlessly.

'Are you—Arnold Raveningham?' he said.

'Yes sir,' came the reply, eager and relieved.

'Well—well—I had no idea,' muttered the Colonel. 'Why are you in the Army?' he asked, and his voice was as soft as when he spoke to Jane just before bedtime.

Raveningham had recovered confidence. 'It is the only place where a composer can find the necessary security and encouragement these days, sir,' he said. 'Catesby himself is a Lance-Bombardier in the 53rd R.A.,' he added enthusias-tically.

It was not the kind of answer the Colonel appreciated, apart from the fact that he had never heard of Catesby and loathed the Royal Artillery. 'Yes, yes,' he said, as a signal that conversation should only be resumed when he thought fit. Time was needed for thought—what was this young man first, musician or private soldier? A moment later he was wondering how he could ever have been in doubt.

'Raveningham,' he said, 'you know what you have to do. You are excused duties for this afternoon so that you can produce a new march for the Regiment. You know what I want—something stirring, something with guts in it, something the fellows can hum and whistle—when they're marching easy, of course. I know nothing about your musical abilities, but I am assured by an authority on music that you are the man to do it. Hand the—er, what d'you call it, script?—anyway, you know what I mean—give it to the Bandmaster first thing after breakfast tomorrow. Fall out.'

But Raveningham didn't fall out at all. He just stood where he was, with his mouth slightly open.

'You may go,' said the Colonel irritably.

'But, sir, I can't do that!'

'You can't? What do you mean, you can't? It's an order!'

'Yes, but, sir, I can't do it in an afternoon. It would take a month at least. I'd have to read up the Regiment's history and traditions, study the countryside and the fellows who compose it, try and get a synthesis out of —'

'Rubbish, man! You can't fool me. It's only a few whad'yecallums, bars, are needed. I've seen 'em, too, two or three lines—half an hour's work!'

'But, sir!' was all that Raveningham could manage.

'Very well!' snapped the Colonel, thumping the desk top, 'if you can't do it I'll find someone who can. Now get out and don't waste my time any longer. You're lucky not to be on a charge. Now go!'

Raveningham shuddered, turned and quietly left the room. Not only was he late for parade, but the R.S.M. had told him to sweep the NAAFI out in the evening as punishment for trying to see the Colonel in the morning.

When the Colonel told Jane about it she was furious.
Genuinely furious. She often pretended to be severe with
him; it was a little game which she enjoyed, though not quite
as much as the Colonel enjoyed it, for what man's masculinity
is not flattered when a woman pretends to take charge of
him? But this time it was no play. Jane drew her lips back so
that her teeth showed right to the corners—a habit she had
which made her appear really ferocious, transformed her into
a storm of a woman.

'Oh, you are a fool, Mark!' she snapped. Then she realised
the uselessness of abusing him, and sighed as she said, 'You
always blunder so.'

The Colonel bit his lip and said rather mildly, 'But he
said a month, Jane!'

'Of course he said a month! I'm surprised he mentioned
such a short period. Just you try and sit down and produce
a worth-while melody in a couple of hours. You don't expect
Jack Hollis to write his novels in an afternoon.'

'Now you're being ridiculous. The fellow's only got to
write a couple of whaddyecallums—you know what I mean—
those things with lines running through them. And besides,
he's trained to do it.'

Jane left it at that because she always won her victories in
her own absence. This time it was difficult for the Colonel
and took more courage than normally to reverse an earlier
decision. He couldn't very well call Raveningham and tell
him he'd changed his mind. He'd look a fool, and he wasn't
that, even if Sandwich was driving him crazy. He even called
on his old friend Sir Joseph Martin, who had once composed
the music for a pageant. He had to introduce the subject
somewhat circumspectly, for it would never do to allow Sir
Joseph to know a new regimental march was required. After
an hour spent in gossip over whiskeys the Colonel had
heavily manœuvred himself into the vantage point he had
been coveting for so long, and he put the question.

'Tell me, Joe, just as a matter of interest, how long did it take you to compose that merry little song, *When Buxom Girls*, tra la la, we heard in the pageant?'

'Well,' answered Sir Joseph leisurely, 'I first got the idea when I was still a lad living on my father's farm at Eastcote. I couldn't have been more than sixteen, and I was passing across a meadow when what did I see . . .' It went on for a good ten minutes. The Colonel really didn't hear the details, but he got the general import—that Sir Joseph had been turning the melody over in his head or mind or wherever he kept his working parts for close on twenty years.

The next few days were uneasy ones. Jane never mentioned the subject, which was terrifying. He knew she was really very excited about the new march, and the Regimental Ball they would be sure to hold after it got its baptism in the streets of Stonefield. Her silence seemed to say, 'If you insist on behaving like a fool, then count me out.'

At last, in desperation, the Colonel decided to adopt frontal tactics. Private Raveningham was summoned and the Colonel said, brusquely, but also a little benignly, 'Well, my boy, I only want to know how you're getting on.'

'G-getting on?' gasped Raveningham, forgetting to address the Colonel properly.

'Yes. How's the old tune going? Swinging along, I hope.'

'But, sir, you told me not to do it.'

'Told you not to do it? What on earth are you saying?'

'You wouldn't allow me the time I needed.'

The Colonel put on a horribly phoney laugh which vibrated in mock heartiness. 'You didn't take me seriously now, did you, Raveningham?'

'But I thought –'

'Why, you ass, I was joking. I thought you were aware of that! Well, you've been wasting time; you'd better get on with it!'

'Do you mean I can take time off to study the regiment's history and —?'

'Yes, of course, and to tramp its moors and dells.' (He'd got that from Jane.) 'Go ahead in your own way and don't trouble me again till you're finished.'

Eventually Raveningham reeled out, not knowing whether he was really an ass, as the Colonel had suggested, or the Colonel an idiot. As for the Colonel, he sat stiffly in his chair for a moment, muttering about the time that had been wasted. Then he relaxed and laughed his worst, because he really thought he'd been rather cute. But after all, he ought to know something about man-management after all these years.

Raveningham spent the next week going through the Regimental Records, or that part of them that the Colonel had had installed in his own library. He discovered many interesting things, most of them details that were never mentioned in the lectures on Regimental History and Tradition that he had heard from the Colonel during his first week as a recruit. There was a full account of the battle of Tarracourt, of course, when the Dons had forded a river in the face of firepower twice their own, and successfully stormed a hilltop fort (though the discrepancy in numbers was less great than the Colonel had claimed). Tarracourt was a battle honour, inscribed on banner and badge. St Mieux was not. At St Mieux a drunken major had led 2,000 gallant Dons into the wine-cellars of the town, and a surprise attack had resulted in the enemy's recapture of a strategic point and the enforced inaction for the remainder of the campaign of the same 2,000 Dons. That must go in, of course, as well as Tarracourt—the personality of a regiment rested as much on its defeats as on its victories.

On the third morning he raised his head with a laugh, and then sniggered quietly as he saw a rather handsome woman standing over him.

'I didn't think the Regimental History could be so amusing,' said Jane, with a little mocking smile.

'Didn't you? Then listen to this,' said Raveningham enthusiastically. ' "Coming home unexpectedly at 12.30 Major de Grasse found Colonel Perkins, his superior officer, sharing his own bed with his (de Grasse's) wife. De Grasse drew his sword, and Colonel Perkins barely escaped with his life, and completely without his trousers, which he had not had time to recover. Major de Grasse was the subject of disciplinary action for behaviour prejudicial to military discipline, and Colonel Perkins was transferred, at his own request, to another command." '

Raveningham looked up triumphantly. 'That's wonderful! said Jane, her eyes gleaming excitedly. Could you imagine dear Mark running through Stonefield for his life, minus his trousers?'

'Who are you?' asked Raveningham abruptly.

'The Colonel's wife,' she said.

After that she brought him coffee in the morning and tea in the afternoon. She spent more and more time listening to him as he read out passages that appealed to him. Her behaviour and reactions were somewhat eccentric. When he read to her an account of the siege of Tianopolis, she sighed, as was proper, and announced, 'How awful! What beasts we all are!' But when he came to the affair of the Sugar Mutiny (1847) she suddenly and inexplicably said, 'How old are you?'

He said he was twenty-seven. At other times he said his name was Arnold, that he came from Canterbury, that he couldn't bear the theatre, that he'd once spent a month in the Vosges, that his grandfather had written a book on squirrels, that he was unmarried, that his favourite authors were Conan Doyle and John Buchan, that he wasn't a communist, that he wasn't engaged to be married, that he was subject to bronchial catarrh, that he couldn't swim but could ride a bike, that his earliest memory was of being kissed by his uncle Harry and pinched by his waxed moustache, that he never intended to marry, that he ranked Dvorak above

Beethoven, that he was passionately fond of ice-cream and that cigars made him sick. She also told him a few things, but not so many. Chief among them were her name, her age (less five years), her frequent boredom, her delight in Dvorak, and her impressions of America.

Just before he left the library on the Saturday morning he mentioned casually that he had finished the traditions and was about to start on the environment. Oh, she said, a little subduedly, and what did that mean? That meant, he said, a tour of the country around Stonefield, whence the Regiment drew most of its personnel and which the Colonel was gallantly financing out of the Regimental funds. He would start with the old and immemorial Ilkley Moor and Shipley Glen, the ghylls, dales and valleys, with an eye open for gnomes, dwarfs, elves and kobolds. Then he would come to the contemporary and industrial—Wakefield and Dewsbury, Leeds and Halifax. Finally he'd try and put his impressions in musical form.

Whether by chance or accident, she met him next morning on the edge of Slagbury Moor. Together they sat on the ruined wall of an old shooting box, skirted round a desolate water-tower where a beautiful lady had once been incarcerated by her jealous husband, lay breathlessly in the grass waiting for a lark to descend, sheltered together in a huddle under his greatcoat when a rainstorm caught them trudging through a quarry. And when they lay full-length under an oak tree, both exhausted by the heat and the exercise, she suddenly rolled on to her side and kissed him. When she drew her head back she looked right into his eyes, with her lips tight and an almost frantic curiosity within her to know, now and definitely, what his reaction would be. At first he returned the gaze very soberly, then he slowly smiled and laughed out, 'The Colonel's wife!'

She let her head fall on his chest, and he picked and sucked a grass.

Stonefield was a mass of bunting, streamers, flags, crowds and pickpockets. The crowd grew more dense as you proceeded up the High Street (and so did the pickpockets in all probability, though we have no statistics with which to back this claim) until a portion of it packed itself into a remarkably small area around the limits of the Square, opposite the Town Hall. (Indeed, the proportion that fainted was quite considerable.) For beneath the balcony of the Town Hall was a rostrum, which at the moment I write of seemed to be the support of nothing more imposing than a microphone, pertly rearing its head on a stem of extreme slenderness.

This was the occasion when the new march of the Don Yeomanry was to be given its first performance.

The last two days had been anxious ones. Private Raveningham had undertaken to supply the completed score on the Wednesday, so that both the band and the ceremonial parade could rehearse it fully before the public turn-out. But Raveningham was not ready. Orderlies visited him two or three times every hour, but nothing was forthcoming. On the Thursday the R.S.M. visited him in person and started to scream. Raveningham looked pale and washed out. He said he was not satisfied with the march in its present form. He had stayed up all night trying to perfect it, and he certainly would not go to bed again until he was satisfied. The R.S.M. nodded dubiously and left the little room that had been reserved for Raveningham's labours, feeling both impressed and mystified. During seventeen years' service in the Army he had only endeavoured to get men out of bed; he had never known one to stay out voluntarily. The Colonel swore and shouted at the R.S.M., who agreed with everything he said. At one moment the Colonel gave an order to put Raveningham under close arrest, until he remembered that Sandwich had made close arrest almost a luxury. Then he had an idea which he thought was brilliant; he would promote Raveningham to the rank of Lance-Corporal. The promotion was immediately posted, and an Orderly delivered six stripes to the cause of all the flap. He absent-mindedly took them and stuffed them in his breast pocket.

The Colonel was convinced that it was this stroke that brought the march into the world. On the Saturday morning the Bandmaster phoned through to say that he had received the score, and they would rehearse it intensively till within half an hour of the parade, even eating sandwiches in the bandroom instead of queueing for the usual dinner. (Sandwich had forbidden queues, but he couldn't keep his eyes on everything, and the Colonel delighted in creating new and smaller bottlenecks wherever possible.) The bandmaster added that the score had only just arrived and he couldn't yet give his opinion of it.

The arrangements were as follows. At 14.25 hours the parade would issue from the High Street at the slope, preceded by the band which would start up the new march as they passed the corner. At the same moment the Colonel and Eric Naseby, Sandwich's personal friend and adviser at the War Office, would mount the rostrum and take the salute. The parade would march round the square, finally coming to a halt before the rostrum at precisely 14.30 hours. Then Naseby, followed by the Colonel, would address the parade and the citizens of Stonefield.

A minute before the parade was due to reach the Square, the Colonel and Naseby had their noses pressed against neighbouring panes of glass, gazing at the crowd. Behind them stood Jane, glancing over their shoulders, smiling and occasionally humming snatches of melody so softly that neither of the men was aware of it. Without turning his head Naseby said, 'I'm surprised you're not letting Raveningham come up, Slade. He's the man who's done the job, and I'm sure everyone would be more interested in what he had to say than anything we can do. But perhaps he's in the parade, which is quite a good idea in its way.'

The Colonel gritted his teeth, wondering if it was worth while being polite to this miserable civilian with all his Sandwich associations.

'I disagree. You can't maintain discipline if you invite any and everyone to get up and say his piece. That kind of thing's gone too far already. And Raveningham isn't in the parade simply because he's one of the most slovenly soldiers we've got. He'd make a laughing-stock of himself and all of us.'

'He's a fine musician,' sighed Naseby. 'Thank God for the Army! Someone's got to look after English culture.'

'You know his work?' asked Jane.

'Very well. It was only about a month ago that I heard his First Symphony. It was quite an achievement.'

Jane suddenly poked her head forward and said, rather too excitedly, 'There he is! Look, in the crowd. That fair-haired boy.'

The Colonel peered and swore. 'He hasn't got his stripes up,' he roared.

At that moment a thin skirl of sound floated into the room, gathered in volume and suddenly burst into a clap of thunder. A slow smile crept over Naseby's face, and he cocked his head on one side. But the Colonel was standing stiff, as though with horror, and his voice was like a child's wail when he cried, 'My God! It's the band!'

The next moment they were out on the rostrum. A ripple ran through the crowd, uncertain whether to maintain silence for the march or applaud the personages for whose benefit they had been herded into the Square. Naseby smiled wanly to the left, the centre and the right, then raised his hand and assumed an attitude of deep concentration. The Colonel stood on his right, as rigid as the microphone support but more bulky, staring blankly ahead yet seeing nothing—and hearing what he considered to be a devil of a noise. Every now and again he shook like a sturdy tree in a high wind,

every muscle resisting the power that threatened to over-
come him.

Everyone could now see the band, which was wheeling into
the Square like a Roman victory procession. First of all came
the bandmaster, standing on the platform of a specially
designed automobile (the driver was completely obscured
from view by the sign of the lyre which rose in grandeur
above the bonnet), and facing his musicians. First came the
fiddlers, mounted on little trolleys which were drawn by the
bandmaster's truck. Behind and marching under their own
power as had been the tradition for centuries, came the brass,
the woodwind, and the percussion. In the rear came two
harpists, seated in vehicles resembling bath-chairs, and
propelled from behind by lance-corporals.

Music is admittedly difficult to describe in words. It must
either be done technically, which is dull and meaningless to
most people, or it must be done romantically and ex-
pressionistically. All I can say is that Private (now Lance-
Corporal) Raveningham had somehow contrived to put the
essence of the Yorkshire scene, life, customs and ideals into
music. The march was a constant contrast between a
commonsensical ease of life, and a sinister, almost murderous
denial of it. One moment there was conflict, strained and
tense, the walls of the wool merchants pitted against the
primeval sweep of the moors. The next moment they would
click into harmony like gears engaging (Raveningham had
introduced a striking motif for this, one which succeeded in
combining fear and relief in the nervous responses of the
audience). And underneath, sometimes almost inaudible
against the swirl of the musical mist and the defiant laughter
of the human comedy, ran the march rhythm, insistent and
unvanquishable, like the theme of a Berber ritual dance, until
it seemed to gather and swell like a wave and pour its notes
on the eccentric strand, momentarily engulfing it. The
chuckle of the saxophone was succeeded by the ripple of a

harp, and the crescendo was a torrent of trumpet and drum.

At last it ceased, the parade came to a halt and the men were stood at ease. There was no sound from the crowd, which had its eyes directed towards the rostrum, where Naseby stood in a half-drooping posture, supporting his cheek in the hollow of his hand, and the Colonel stood to attention with his eyes closed so tightly that wrinkles radiated from the corners all over his face. Naseby slowly gripped the stem of the microphone and said without any introduction, 'We have been privileged to hear a piece of music which I am convinced is a masterpiece. To congratulate its author would be a hopelessly inadequate gesture. I confess that I can say nothing that would not appear banal. Silence alone can vindicate my judgment. I was prepared to discuss it in the conventional way, and at first I found myself searching for influences. The knitting of the parts into a pattern, I thought, was pure Bartok. The utilisation of the march rhythm, I thought, was a derivative of Holst. I even considered referring the unashamed, extrovert melody to Saint-Saëns. But then I stopped. For none of these was true. It was not Bartok, it was not Holst, it was not Saint-Saëns, it was something entirely new, a new creation as was the Purgatory by Dante and this universe by God.'

Naseby stepped back, indicating that he had finished. The crowd maintained a respectful silence, as though it were performing its devotions. Now, according to the programme, Naseby should have been followed by the Colonel. But the Colonel was still locked in his attitude of suffering and attention. Nevertheless, I do not think it was this that caused Naseby to act as he did—indeed, I am certain that Naseby was no longer aware of the Colonel's presence. However that may be, he stepped back to the microphone, and said in a hushed voice, 'Bandmaster, please play it through again.'

The Bandmaster bowed gravely, turned to face his

musicians, lifted his eyebrows at one of the harpists who was discussing a piece of counterpoint with an oboe, and flicked his baton. Once again the skirl of notes seemed to rise from an abyss, and mounted to a clap of thunder.

Now after this dramatic introduction there was a pause, during which the ear involuntarily strained to catch the sough of the wind or the flapping of wings. And then began the new theme of the Don Yeomanry, confident and even a little puritanical. But on this occasion another instrument wove its way into the pattern, one for which no orchestration had been supplied. It began among the soldiers, who stood to attention with their rifles still at the slope. Quietly at first, and only among a few of them, was heard a weird and barbarous chanting. It was rapidly taken up by the remainder, then it broke ranks and infected the crowd, until every man, woman and child in the square was singing loudly yet soberly. For it was a ritual of arcane significance, where a smile would have been out of place. Another strange feature of this affair was that although everyone articulated sounds and syllables in complete accord with one another and without any hesitation, the whole amounted to no known language. It was what the sceptic called mumbo-jumbo and the scholar hieratic. The music had plunged so deep into every heart that it had uncovered a language native and expressive, possibly the language of these moors, just as drink has been known to release the buried speech of the Fen tigers. (But that is a comparatively recent matter.) And the dominant points of all this fabulous song fell regularly and precisely on the off-beat, so that the effect of men marching was real and undeniable, but the men were not marching here and now, rather were they marching on the other side of Althorpe Hill and possibly the sound of their feet had drifted for many, many years.

This will sound incredible to most and preposterous to some, but few will believe my testation to what followed.

The soldiers, unbidden, began to move, but not in the mad, violent way in which they move after falling out nor in the tired, listless way which follows battle drill. They moved in some kind of formation, abnormal certainly and unknown to the officers, yet just as certainly the product of a unified will. After manœuvring themselves into a formation resembling an oval, they suddenly kick-stepped to the right and the oval was seen to be moving along the axis made by its points—a drill so delightful and so exquisitely performed that Naseby clapped his hands for joy. But the Colonel was gripping the rail of the dais with both hands, which supported him on the failure of his legs, which were bent beneath him. His head was bent on to his chest.

Naturally, the events I have described were sufficient in themselves to bring on the partial collapse, yet it was not this that had sapped the Colonel's strength, but the figure that formed, as it were, the crown to the oval's majesty. For the Lance-Corporal had been hoisted up on to the shoulders of his comrades, and was now being carried triumphantly from the Square. He sat there, hatless and bemused, a tiny smile flickering round his lips and his N.C.O.'s tapes still dangling from his breast pocket. And in this fashion he left the Square with a retinue of several thousand.

We need waste no time in describing the events that followed. History will honour the composer and his march, Yorkshire and its people, whereas the private affairs of Lance-Corporal Raveningham, Colonel Slade and his lady are matters of impermanance. The oval (which was later adopted by Sandwich as a drill formation on Naseby's advice, though never was it handled so expertly as on this occasion) proceeded down Kirkgate Street, left into Market Street, and then left again into a little alley with the stupendous name of Drury Lane. There was only just room for the oval, the two flanking men brushing the housefronts with their sleeves. The band had remained in the square and could only be heard faintly now, and it is noteworthy that the soldiers were once more acting under military orders, for they halted on a word of command (though it will always remain a mystery who gave the word). They were now humming the theme very softly, and Raveningham appeared to be clambering over their heads on his toes and finger tips. He made straight for an open window, the sill of which was little higher than his waist, and clambered through. Before disappearing he turned and waved his hand to the men below.

In the room he found a key on the table. He turned the key in the lock and entered a room which was in absolute darkness. He felt something soft and silky waving against his face and ears, and tried to sweep it away with his hands. Then he felt arms about him and a mouth moving over his face where the web had brushed him. He shuddered and said, 'Darling, it's been agony. The trumpeter was off beat. But it seemed to go well, didn't it? I don't think anyone noticed it.'

NAMES

Names swim from mud:
like bubbles from the seat
of knowledge smouldering in the voiceless dark
they rise to steer the craft
alone and cheerless on the grey waters
of a sunless continent.

Each name transferred with blood
labels the unknown self
with a symbol of its true constancy.
No chance, no measured plan
can score this flesh with any errant lines
asserting novelty in each foundation.

Names given at birth
dance, like butterflies,
nipping the sulky bubbles
of knowledge as they rise;
sipping the oily scales
upon the brooding waters.

Not only built by lines,
the maps of new Atlantis:
the human mind stacking its queer corners
with shackled crates of faith and noisy arts.
But also names, exotic Amazons,
sleeping in plains and cracking wide the sea.

RULES OF ACTION

Silence is not the emptiness of nature,
the absence of sound;
silence is the spirit driven to perplexity,
with ears indrawn, the sense of hearing drowned
    by the undiscerning flood
      of events outlined in blood.

Emptiness is rarely the classic void,
the exceptional vacuum;
emptiness is the satisfying order
dispersed and surprised out of the form
    that men have accepted
      and accidents rejected.

Silence and emptiness we dream in towers,
ugly and tottering,
foundations rotting in the yellow clay
and windows lit by candles guttering.
    Symbols of death
      to cloak the fervent breath.

When hermits spit in silence look behind
for vast magnetic orchestras;
when worlds are emptied of their dramas
raise spiral arms against the sly assassins.
    Entice opposites
      from their homogeneous chariots.

ON RETURNING TO POETRY

Today, after many months, I twist my wrist
for the action that yesterday denied
its passage from my hidden, questing corner.
Today I screw my nerve cells to a fist
of ardour, leap across the corpse that died
and sail my wits on a mutilated schooner.
Protect my sense, and give my hand free passage,
allow my distant genius his discharge
from stables furnished by our modern warder.
Give me the grace to set my croaking message
in canzonet. Today I ride my barge
of faultless cruelty to the clinical border.

INQUEST

The inquest will never end.
On every tactless morning comes the gaoler
And scours my limbs with litmus paper,
Hoping to find the new guilt
Distilled from my last night's dream.

Stabbed with cartridges, I totter
From one cell to another palace,
Caught by the hair in a bent machine,
Whose patent was taken out last year—
Designed to fell a tree or scar a soul.

Six men, in robes of gorse, the yellow flowers
Climbing their arms and singing of the world,
Sit at their desks; I try
To discover from their features whether
I am meant to cringe or die.

The sentence never varies; perfect ease
In a suit of lavender, fed by naked girls
With curls of love upon their shabby breasts
And smiles recorded on their blatant skin,
Telling me tales of Araby and sin.

The food is good; the wine goes to my head;
I spend my nights upon a ribald bed.
And yet I sick my ransome, plead my cause
Before my heart, before my lingering faith
In a world of hardship, breathing out sensation.

MY FUTURE LIFE

Here in this land of broken testament,
Of rhymes on toilet rolls,
Of cherished excrement,
I lie with my head in my arms.
The telephone rings.

I feel myself descend slowly,
Hung by a wire,
Clean, dry, ready to burst,
And tomorrow I shall meet my son,
Who crawls from time.

Give me a word,
A piece of broken pardon.
Salve my intention,
Allow me a century of continence.
Multiply my intention.

And now I am here,
Freed from a liaison,
That offered degradation!
All they can give me
Is a finite tombstone.

CHAPTER ONE

WHEN John Gibson came out of the army in 1915, he had a limp which made him stick out at the hips and bend forward like an old man. He hobbled into the house to meet his wife, Ada, and sat at the fire with difficulty.

'They've made a fine job o' me,' he said.

'Aye.'

'I'm no' able for much noo.'

'No,' she said. Her hands were busy with the teapot, and her back was towards him.

There was little else for him to say. Somehow, he felt he owed Ada an apology for coming back so maimed and helpless, but he was not good at putting his thoughts into words. The language of the trenches was still fresh on his lips, but Ada would not like that kind of talk. She had always been so proper, so down on him when he said anything out of place. Now she was like a stranger, masking the tea in stiff silence.

He propped his stick against the armchair, and laughed nervously.

'If you'll just help me aff with my jacket, Ada . . . I'll feel mair at hame, like.'

She helped him to his feet, and folded the coat on the bed.

'Well, sit in,' she said, speaking directly for the first time. 'There's your tea.'

He caught at her as she set the chairs and rearranged the teacups. 'Ada—ye'll no' mind ower much, will ye? I mean, me bein' like this. I ken I'm a bonny like ticket, but—I'll try an' get a job somewhere . . .'

'Aye,' she said, 'that's a'right, Johnny.'

'An' you're glad I'm back?'

'Aye, I'm glad. What d'you think? Sit in now, afore your tea's cold. Can you manage now?'

'Aye, I'll manage,' he said.

Afterwards, he thought that he might have had a worse motto than this. 'Aye, I'll manage.' It was easy enough to say.

*

The Gibsons' house was adequate. To some Glaswegians, it might have seemed opulent. It was a two room and kitchen, three stairs up, and the lavatory was on the same landing. That was something. Ada had resolutely refused to go into a house with an outside lavatory. 'It's hopeless if you've illness in the house,' she had said, and their marriage had been delayed a year while they searched for a suitable place. Now, they were better off than many who had married before them. The rooms were fairly large, and if they were crowded and difficult to keep tidy, that was only because they had so much furniture, heavy, solid stuff, bought piece by piece from second hand shops, and carted up the three stairs by cursing, sweating removal men. There was a three piece suite in green plush; a piano which had grooved parallel scores all along the close walls; a black horsehair sofa; a sewing machine; a double bed with bashed brass knobs, and an assortment of stools and chairs and other encumbrances. It had seemed a rich, cosy assortment when they first set up house, but now, after six years, it looked shabby, like the whole locality. Ada had often complained about the district, but John had seen no cause to grumble. 'It's no' bad for the wage I'm gettin',' he said. 'It'll dae the noo.'

He had looked forward to being at his own fireside, all through the horror of the trenches and the long weeks in hospital. He had pictured the kitchen as a snug retreat from the grey fogs and drizzle of Glasgow, and the greater chilliness of the war in Europe. It had never occurred to him that he might be disappointed.

And yet, he was disappointed. Everything looked depressingly familiar. The grate was not shiny enough. Couldn't Ada have polished the place up a bit for his return? The curtains were faded, and the rugs were losing their colour, askew on the dingy linoleum. Outside, the same purply-grey slates loomed through the fog, the same kids yelled in the backyard. The very smell was the same, the smell of cooking gone stale, and air too seldom changed.

Suddenly, he realised that Ada was looking at him furtively. He saw her lower her eyes to her plate, and pretend to be going on with her meal. Boldly, he stared at her, but she did not look up. Well, at least she hadn't changed. She was a big woman, a massive, rather brassy blonde, with fair hair piled above her brow in a puffed-out heap. Her white blouse was open at the neck, and she had a certain square arrogance which gave her a slightly masculine appearance. He had always felt insignificant beside her. Now, with his height diminished by his deformity, he would look almost ridiculous.

'Ada,' he said, harping on the same string, seeking for reassurance.

'What?'

'You havenie said you're glad to see me back.'

She laughed uncomfortably. 'Well, that's a daft thing to say, Johnny. You know I said I was glad when you asked me. Look at the nice tea I got ready for you! And I put on my new blouse . . .'

'Aye, but—where's Willie? I thought you might have had him in.'

'He's out playing. I thought we'd be better ourselves, for the first.'

'Aye, well, mebbe you're right. He'll no' ken his daddy like this. Ada . . . *you* dinnie mind? Do you?'

'Och no, Johnny; you're awfie morbid the day! You're not to say such things!'

'Mebbe you'd be morbid if you'd come through what I've been through. Ocht, I'm fair sick of it a'! I was daft ever tae volunteer. I'd have been as well here sittin' on my backside —and I'd have been just as much thought of!'

'Never heed, Johnny. You're home now. That's aye something. We can start where we left off, eh?'

'No, we cannie. I'll have nae job, an' no' much o' a pension. It's a good job we've got a hoose an' the furniture. It's aboot a' we're likely tae hae for a Hell o'a long time!'

'Och, Johnny —!'

She put down her teacup unevenly, and the tea splashed over the clean cloth in a long fawn stain. Her hands were over her face, her big shoulders shaking with sobs. 'Here, here, dinnie greet, Ada!' said Johnny, gripping the table, pulling himself round till he was able to stand beside her. 'We're no' that bad!' he consoled her. 'We've aye got each other, haven't we, Ada? Eh?'

'Aye,' she sobbed.

'Ada, you've never —' He was going to say that she had not kissed him, but suddenly he caught sight of himself in the mirror over the mantelpiece, a crooked wee man in shirt-sleeves, one hip sticking out ridiculously. 'Well . . .' He patted her on the shoulder, and limped back to the fire. Perhaps, after all, he couldn't expect anything else. For a moment, rage seized him, and he looked around for something to damage. Throw the teapot into the fire, hurl his stick through the window, kick the cat against the wall— no, it wouldn't do any good. Stiffly, he put on his jacket, and fumbled in the pockets for his pipe.

When his wife got up to wash the dishes, he realised that, so far as she was concerned, the subject was closed. There would be no protestations of loyalty, no fervent promises that they would stick together through thick and thin. She had said all that was to be said on the matter. 'We can start where we left off, eh?' He would take his cue from that.

She had been bitterly hurt by what had happened to him; perhaps she would not be able to think of him in the same way as when he had been whole and healthy; but at least, she was willing to accept him as he was. It did not occur to him that this was her duty. Sometimes, at night in the hospital, when he had been unable to sleep, he had tortured himself with scenes where he gave Ada her freedom. 'I can't ask you to tie yersel' tae me now, Ada. I'm done. If you'd rather be free . . .' It had not come to that; he was a lucky man; but there was precious little warmth about the whole business.

The door banged. Willie came in, breathless, his hair over his eyes, his jersey torn. Ada stood with the kettle in her hand, watching. John cleared his throat.

'How are ye, Willie, son?'

The boy stared, and sniffed. He said nothing. His father eased himself in the chair, and leaned a little forward.

'Come on, man. Do you not know yer daddy, eh?'

'Leave him a minute,' said Ada. 'He's strange.'

'Aye, he hasnie seen me for a long time.' John tried to hide his disappointment. Had Ada not paved the way for this reunion? Willie would be five now; he was a big boy, big enough to be shy.

'Are you at the school now, son?' he asked, a bribe in his voice. 'Are you startit school yet, eh?'

'Aye,' said Willie, still staring.

'Willie, get your tea,' said his mother. 'Wash yourself first. You might have kept clean when you knew your father was coming back.'

The boy washed his hands and face, and dried himself on the towel hanging in the cupboard. Sitting at the table, he had his back to the fire. His father watched him, the dark head, the restless heels kicking the chair, the way in which he turned round to have another look at the stranger by the fire. His own hair was black like that. Willie was going to be like him. He smoked quietly, coughing from time to time.

It would take a wee while before he settled down, but after a day or two, things wouldn't be so bad.

It grew darker, and the gas was lit. The slates opposite disappeared, and the window panes reflected the kitchen table, cleared now, with the plant-pot dead in the centre. Ada ordered Willie off to bed. 'You've to get up in the morning, mind,' she said. 'You've played enough for one day. Away you go, now, and quick about it. Say goodnight to your father first.'

'Goodnight.' His tone was casual, but not cold. He was merely making up his mind before he gave his friendship. John clutched his wrist as he went past.

'Here, have you no' got a kiss for yer dad, eh? You're no' too big tae give us a kiss, are you?'

The boy grinned, and ducked behind the chair. It was a hint to be chased, to be pursued in a rare game which would defer bedtime. John sat where he was, and made no move. 'Away you go, now, Willie,' his mother said again, 'and not be bothering your father. He's tired the night.'

The child grinned and protested. 'Away you go, son,' said his father wearily. 'We'll have a game the morn, eh?'

He did not want to stand up while Willie was still in the room. He wondered whether Ada had prepared him for his father's lameness, but he did not like to ask her. It was enough for one night. Everything would have to be straightened out in the morning.

*

There was no great straightening out, of course. If a man comes back lamed from the wars, there is little that can be done. Carry on as before; that is the best plan. In the old home, the old routine, gaps are easily filled, and if money is scarce, the problem is not a new one.

At first, John was self-conscious about his lameness. He stayed in the house, moping at the fireside, and getting in the way of the cleaning; but after a while, he grew used to his altered appearance. A man must have company. He had always liked his drink, and soon he began to limp down to the pub at the corner, leaning on his Harry Lauder stick, and grunting a little as he managed the stairs. He could not spend much, but a man can make a little go a long way, if he is an old soldier, and the company means more than the drink. He would sit there all morning, and often in the evening, too, discussing the war. He grew dogmatic, after a certain stage. 'I ken what I'm talkin' aboot. I've been there. Have *you* ever been in France? Have you been *in* the blasted Army? Well, then, whit are ye arguin' aboot? Ye dinnie need tae tell me onything aboot the war. I *ken!*'

It was in the pub that he met Alex Smart, a smooth, fair young man in a suit newer than was usually seen in the district. Smart was a conscientious objector—so he said. Johnny had had an argument with him, and at closing time, had asked him up to the house to finish it off. He liked the man, though he disapproved of his views. Sitting in front of the fire, they went at it hell for leather while Ada prepared the supper.

'What good has fighting done *you*.' asked Smart, his voice good-humoured and tolerant.

'Me? I'd have been as well at hame.'

'Well, then.'

'But we cannie *a'* stey at hame. Somebody's got tae dae the fightin'.'

'Why?'

'Well—well, somebody's got tae, that's *a'*.'

'Why should it be you?'

'It didnae *have* tae be me. I just went voluntary, see? If it comes tae that, whit wey should it no' be you?'

'It's none of my business. I don't want to kill a lot of poor blighters I've never seen in my life, and who've never done me any harm. Probably they don't want to fight either. If everybody adopted the same attitude, if all the common people refused to fight —'

'Ocht, yer granny.' Johnny had put forward the same arguments himself, when grumbling about the scanty pension he was allowed for his disability, but he would not pose as a pacifist. He had no interest in the war, and no desire to reason things out, but the Germans were the enemy; the Germans had to be beaten. If he had a quarrel with the British government, let it be a separate and distinct quarrel. He would not lose his status as an ex-serviceman and a martyr.

For all that, he liked Alex Smart. He was an educated man, by the standards of the neighbourhood. He did not speak so broad as the others in the pub. His accent was something like Ada's had been before she married, as it still was when she had anybody in for tea. And Alex was a good sort, too. He might be a C.O., but at least he lived up to it, not even losing his temper when girls handed him white feathers. Ada seemed to approve of him; he was lucky.

'You'll be back again, then?' she said, when he rose to go. 'My husband will always be glad to bring you, any time you feel like it.'

'Delighted,' said Alex. 'Goodnight, everybody. Thanks for a nice evening.'

'Well, he's certainly obliging,' said Ada. 'I mebbe don't agree with all he says, but I must say he couldn't have made himself more agreeable if he'd tried. Mind and keep in with him, John. He's better than the usual class of men you get in with down there.'

★

Next year there was another child, a girl. John had always wanted a girl, but poverty took the edge off the pleasure. It took them all their time to keep Willie decent, without having a new baby to care for. Food was scarce, and the only way to buy clothes was to get them on the instalment system, leaving a deposit, and paying up so much every week.

The weeks they paid the rent, they couldn't afford to pay the clothing club. Knocks at the door were classified; no one dared answer until the knocker was identified. Once, Willie had pretended to be the rent-collector, and given his parents such a turn that he had his ears boxed, and was sent to bed. Grocery bills were beginning to mount. Existence was such a strain that Ada sometimes forgot her forbearance and railed against her husband for being unable to support her. 'I know it's not your fault,' she said, 'but surely there's *some* job you can do? Can you not try?'

'My God, woman,' he would say, 'dae ye no' see me tryin'? I've tried till I'm sick tired, but naebody wants an auld crock that has tae walk wi' a stick an' cannie staun' ony length o' time. Dae ye think I like seein' you like this? God, it's enough tae sicken you . . .!'

Just after Jean was born, Alex Smart came up to see them. 'I've got a wee present for the baby,' he said. 'Now, you've not to say no. I'll be angry if you do.' He pressed ten pounds into Johnny's hand. 'It's all right, I can afford it. I made a packet on the races today. Don't thank me, or I won't come to see you again.'

John flushed. Ada did not look up. 'Well, we're much obliged tae ye, man,' said John, crumpling the notes up in his fingers, 'Mebbe we'll be able tae repay ye some time.'

'Och, away,' said Alex. 'That's all right.'

The ten pounds seemed to set things straight. For a little while, there was no fear of debt. The baby was healthy, as dark as Willie, and fatter than most of the babies born about that time. 'If we can only keep her that way . . .' said her mother.

It was a hard struggle. After the ten pounds were gone, there was only the pension again. No wonder tempers were lost easily. Johnny lived in a perpetual swing between anger and remorse.

One day, he saw Ada slip a pound note into her purse.

He could not understand how she had saved it. When he asked her, she blushed, but answered him candidly, with a touch of spite.

'I got it from Alex Smart last time he was up, if you want to know.'

'Alex Smart! My God, wait till I get him, giein' money tae my wife behind my back! The dirty —!'

'John Gibson, will you hold your tongue and listen? I'll not have you castin' out with Alex Smart. That money was given to me in a certain spirit, and I took it in the same spirit. No harm in that, surely, to get a gift from a friend?'

'He's no friend if he's goin' on like that behind my back.'

'It was not behind your back. He knew fine you'd never take it, so he gave it to me. It was to help the both of us. He knows we're bound to get into debt. If you cannie help us, somebody'll have to.'

'Ada, that's no' fair.'

'Well, it's no' my fault. I'm not blamin' you, Johnny, but I can't work miracles. Do you know I'm going to have another baby?'

'You're no'?'

'Aye, I am. Now can you blame me if I take a gift when it's offered? Alex Smart's an old enough friend by this time, surely to goodness. He's been coming about us long enough. Things were hard last time, I don't know what they'll be like now, with another mouth to feed —'

Johnny said nothing. He was angry at himself, angry at his wife, angry with everybody. Another child! Where in Heaven's name was the money to come from?

The baby, another girl, was born on Armistice Day. They christened her Isa. She was like her mother, fair, with her mother's square chin and broad shoulders. Alex Smart was godfather, and insisted on giving a christening gift of twenty pounds. Under the circumstances, they could not refuse. The man seemed to have money to burn. They had never learned his trade, or the source of his income, other than horses; they would never have dared to ask. He was a good companion, and seemed to be glad of an occasional evening at their fireside. Besides, he helped to keep the peace many a night when, but for his presence, tempers would have flared through sheer worry.

The year after the war was a hard one. There was a great deal of illness about. Coal was scarce, food was dear, and money would not stretch to the length required of it. John Gibson aged quickly. There were grey specks in his hair, and his limp was more pronounced. He had had all his teeth out, and could not afford to buy dentures. Day after day, he tramped the streets, offering himself for all kinds of work, but there were too many young men returning from the army, all looking for something to do. What chance had an elderly cripple? He began to lose pride in himself. His overcoat lost its buttons, and Ada either could not or would not find time to sew them on. His face had a wizened look, and he developed a nervous habit of blowing out his cheeks as he walked, bent forward, leaning on his Harry Lauder stick. One day he sang a song in the gutter. He had to do it; it was the only thing left to him. That night, he went home with two shillings and ninepence. It was better than nothing. After that, there seemed no point in doing anything else.

When Isa was one year old, Ada ran away with Alex Smart. Johnny came back to find the house in darkness, and the baby crying. There was a note on the table, fixed down by the milk bottle.

Dear Johnny,

I have gone away with Alex. I can't stand this any longer. You will be better off without me. We have been thinking about this for a long time, but put it off for the sake of the children. Don't be too angry, there was nothing else for it. Have left a sum of money to carry on with.

Yours, Ada.

He looked at the money—Smart's money. Ten pounds. For a moment, he thought of tearing it up, but changed his mind. There were the children. What in God's name could he do with them? The baby's cries were going right through his head, and Willie was pestering him for a piece. Slowly, carefully, he heated some milk in a saucepan. He was too numbed to be angry with Ada. Perhaps, after all, he couldn't blame her. If she was as sick of it as he was, she had every excuse.

Next morning, he went to see the minister. He had not been to church for years, but Willie had been sent to Sunday school—another of his mother's fads. The minister advised sending the children to a home. 'It's all you can do in the meantime, Mr Gibson,' he said sympathetically. 'At present, you're not in a position to give them proper attention, are you?'

'No,' said Johnny. 'No, sir, you're right.' Within a week, the children were gone, and the house was as quiet as a grave. Johnny sold the furniture, banked the money, and took a room in a different district. It was cheaper, and it was somewhere where he was not known. He wanted to go as far away from his home as he could. He wanted to forget his wife. He wanted to forget everything.

CHAPTER TWO

JOHN GIBSON's parents had been matter of fact people, working class folk whose imagination went no farther than the desperate gropings into next week's financial problems. No one bothers about imagination in the miners' rows, when the family comes in dirty from the pit, and the bairns get in the way, always making work in a kitchen too wee to keep tidy.

Still, the gesture had been made. It was not until John's sister went to school that she realised the implications of her name. When the teacher rapped out 'Next?' she said, shyly, 'Flora Gibson.' 'Any middle name?' queried the teacher again, and, after much looking at the ceiling, the child muttered, 'MacDonald?' making a question of it, her head on one side, waiting to see if the answer was correct. The teacher rose to the occasion. 'Oh, Flora *MacDonald!*' she said. 'Why, that's a very special name! Now can any of you children tell me who Flora MacDonald was?'

There was no answer. The children stared dumb and wooden. 'Well, as soon as I've made out the register, children, remind me to tell you the beautiful story of Flora MacDonald and the handsome prince. You'd like that, wouldn't you?'

'Yes, Miss,' droned the class.

So Flora learned about her namesake, and spent the rest of the day in the limelight. All through her schooldays, this scene was to be enacted. Whenever she was registered in a new class, the teacher always looked up with a smile of interest, and, in history lessons, the Jacobite period led to blushes and bantering. 'So we've got a real Flora MacDonald in the class today!' the teacher would say, and Flora would giggle and enjoy it. She liked to see the other girls turn round and nudge each other and smile at her.

She was able to pass as a pretty child. She had red cheeks, and her hair curled naturally. Even when she was very young, she had a strong sense of her own importance. At parties, when the adult in charge called for volunteers to sing or dance, Flora was always first, blushing, but eager to begin. At school, before she became too buxom and self-conscious, she was in great demand for tableaux and costume dances. Sometimes, she was asked to appear in little shows in aid of local charities, and then her mother, grumbling at the extra work, would iron her frocks and brush her hair and see that she had clean white stockings to wear. All this acting and parading on the stage was not at all the thing for poor folk's bairns; they couldn't be expected to keep up with all the expense; but in spite of it all, Mrs Gibson was proud of her child, and fully expected to see her an accomplished actress before long. 'Our Flora's different from the rest of us,' she would say. 'I don't know who she takes it off of, but she's got it born in her. From ever she was a wee thing, she was the same. It's just a pity we cannie give her a better chance.'

Perhaps, however, it was as well that the better chance was not forthcoming, for Flora had neither the brains nor the ability for a dramatic education. As she grew older, she lagged behind her classmates, and left school at fourteen, remembering very little of what she had learned. She went to work as a servant, but was never satisfactory because she was hopelessly slow in the uptake. At sixteen she was fat, at eighteen, she was enormous, her ankles large and ungainly. She became a joke among the young men who loitered at the street corners. 'Haw, Flora MacDonald!' they would call after her, with memory of their school days. 'Where's Prince Charlie the day?'

She took their teasing in good part, grinning back as she had done in class, though she was self-conscious about her size. She was twenty before her figure settled down to a semblance of shapeliness, and by that time she was courting Dick Gavin, whose father kept the pub at the corner.

They were married, and lived together for fifteen years, having only one still-born child. At the end of that time, Dick died, leaving a fat and mournful widow with nothing but her pension. Her mother was unable to help her, and her husband's people had moved from the district, and showed little interest. She had always felt that they looked down on her, thinking her a poor catch for a publican's son; now she knew.

The obvious thing to do was to look for work, and the only work for which she was qualified was charring. At first, she had no difficulty in finding people to employ her. She was a hefty woman, still under forty, and her cheeks were still red, her kinky hair full of life. There was an air of lethargy about her, a characteristic heaviness of movement, but, looking at her huge frame, housewives thought of the boon she would be at spring-cleaning, the reach and thrust of those brawny arms, the strength of her slow muscles. She was in great demand, for a time; but, by nature, she was lazy, and she found that, if she was to keep up such an energetic life, she must have some kind of stimulant.

This was not her only reason for taking to drink. Her existence was sad. Coming in at night, the house was cold and untidy, the breakfast cup and saucer on the sink, the slops in the saucer as cold as the empty kettle. She seldom had time to buy in meat and vegetables, and anyway, it was a bother to start cooking for one after a hard day's work. She dined off buns and tea and occasional fish suppers, eaten at the littered table; and because the house was so cold, and she was so sorry for herself, so lonely in her loss, so ill done by, she had to take a little glass of something to cheer her up. She became a familiar figure, slipping home with a bottle under her coat, but, at first, nobody blamed her. 'Poor soul,' they said, 'it would drive onybody tae drink, her livin' by hersel' like yon.'

Flora had little money to spare, after the rent was paid, and she spent most of it in the Red Crow. If there was not enough left for food, then food must go. Every week, the scraping together of the rent became more difficult. One day, she told the rent collector to go to hell. The woman next door, a kindly person, paid the sum, with the intention of getting it back when Flora was sober. She lost her money. The morning that the factor gave her notice to quit, Flora collapsed in the street. Her face was a curious purply colour, and she was snoring, and breathing with difficulty, her mouth twisted, and one arm stiff at her side. The doctor said she

had taken a stroke, and a solemn gloating crowd watched
her being lifted into the ambulance. 'Nae wunner, the way
she was goin' on!' said the gossips, forgetting their pity.

While she was in the infirmary, they enquired about her
relations. Her mother, it seemed, was dead, her brother
could not be traced at all. Her husband's people were in
England. They had heard of her drinking, and had cast her
off altogether. No need to look to them for help; it was one
thing to sell drink, another to die of it. Flora, therefore, was
removed to the poorhouse hospital, and put to bed in a
corner of the ward.

Eventually, she got back the use of her arm, and the power
of speech. She was quite content, lying there in the sunshine,
well fed, with nothing to worry her. She was hazy about
her illness, but she remembered things that had happened
a long time ago, the tableaux at school, her first job in
service, her brother, dapper and neat, going out with his hair
brushed and his shoes shining. What had happened to him?
He had passed out of her life a long time ago. Perhaps he
had been killed in the war. Whatever it was, she did not
worry overmuch. It was enough to lie without thinking, and
watch the other women working about in their neat blue
overalls. Fat and inarticulate, she was glad that no one
suggested that she should work.

In her own dull way, she was happy. Before going to sleep,
she would recite her name to herself, the name she had had
before she was married, Flora MacDonald Gibson, Flora
MacDonald Gibson . . . at first, nobody knew what she was
saying, but one day one of the nurses heard her, and repeated
it after her. 'Yes, yes,' said Flora, laughing and chuckling
like a child, 'Flora MacDonald . . .'

'That's a nice name!' said the nurse, and the woman in
the bed chuckled still more. Now she was happy, right back
in her childhood, where she had always wished to be.

That was in 1931. She did not know that her brother was

crippled, and that his wife had deserted him. She did not know that he led a vagrant life all round Glasgow, renting beds by the night, sleeping wherever it was cheapest, working when he could, and singing in the street when all else failed. She knew nothing, and John knew nothing about her. He had enough to worry him without pondering about the sister whom he had not seen for so many years.

CHAPTER THREE

JOHN GIBSON was fifty-five, and looked his age. His clothes, given to him at back doors, were shabby and not over-clean, and always he carried his Harry Lauder stick, leaning on it more heavily now, and dragging his lame leg with more of a limp. When he sang in the gutter, blowing out his cheeks at the end of a verse, and keeking sideways at passers by, grudging hands would rake into purses. 'Sly auld deevil!' they said. 'I wouldnie trust him as far as I could see him.' But they gave him the money, and that was all that mattered.

His abode was unsettled. Long ago, he had given up hope of getting another home together. At first, he had tried to save a little week by week, but it had been impossible. All that was left of his capital from the sale of the furniture was twenty pounds, and if he had ten shillings in his pocket, he considered himself rich.

Thirteen years of poverty gives a man a new outlook on life. He had ceased to regret his wife's desertion; if he were to meet Alex Smart, he would just look at him and turn away. Nothing mattered, except the essentials of food, warmth and clothing.

Then, one day, in spring, when tramps take the road again, he felt a curious urge to go back to his boyhood, to see his old house, and to enquire about his family. His parents, he knew, would be dead by this time, but perhaps Flora would be nearby. Last time he had heard of her, she had been married. Perhaps she would be glad to see him, perhaps not; it didn't matter very much, but at least it was worth trying.

Ten miles, in some cases, may be as great a distance as ten hundred. John took the bus, sitting doggedly in the front seat by the window, his eyes glued on the road ahead, his ticket tight between finger and thumb. It was years since he had rode anywhere, other than a penny journey by tram. The conductress had promised to put him off at the right stop, but he had no faith in her, and he fidgetted and dumped his stick on the floor with nervousness. 'Could you tell us when we come tae Ferniegair?' he said to the woman behind him, and every two or three minutes he would turn round to see if she was still there. Once or twice he thought he remembered the road, but there were so many new buildings that he could not be sure.

When he came to the cottages, however, he recognised them, the long brick rows, the tufted grass patches before the door, the slag heaps behind, like grey ashy mountains, and the chimneys of Motherwell poking to the sky without a curl of smoke between them. Time was when they had been alive, night and day, with the glow of furnaces staining the sky murky red. Never heed Motherwell, though. He stood at the bus stop, half afraid to venture down the shabby rows. Suppose they thought him a beggar? Suppose he had come all this way for nothing? He turned away, and had a pint to nerve him for the ordeal.

At last, leaning on his stick, his overcoat flapping wide open, he limped to the door of the house where he had been born. A broad, untidy woman in a skirt and jumper came out to meet him, one hand holding back a struggling toddler. 'Keep in, noo!' she said. 'Keep in when you're tellt. What was you wantin'?'

'I—I was wonderin' if you kent onybody the name o'

Gibson,' said Johnny. 'There was a Mrs Gibson used tae live here, my mother. She'll be dead by this, but I wondered if onybody had mind o' her, or my sister. Flora, her name was; Flora MacDonald Gibson.'

'Gibson, Gibson . . .' said the woman. 'No, I hinnie mind o' that name, but I'm only here fower years. Gang doon tae the end an' ax auld Leezie Murphy. Ye'll mind auld Leezie, if you was born here?'

'Oh aye, auld Leezie! I didnie think she'd aye be here. Thank ye then, thank ye.' His hand over his jutting hip, he hirpled along to the end of the row. At every window, hands held back the curtain so that wives could gape at him. He could recognise none of the faces. It was wrong of him to have come. A man returning to the rows, enquiring for relations, should have something to bring with him, wealth or position or a car to take him away again. It was daft to come back a beggar, an old man in search of a happier past.

Leezie Murphy was older than anyone he had ever seen. She had hardly any hair, and her scalp shone through like a baby's head. Her face was yellow, wrinkled like cold custard skin, and she had a wee thin voice, like the mewing of a cat. Johnny had to shout to make her hear.

'I was lookin' for a Mrs Gibson.'

'Eh? Eh? What's that?'

'Mrs Gibson. Do you mind of a Mrs Gibson?'

'Gibson? Would that be the woman in 39?'

'Aye, that's right!' He nodded his head in vigorous encouragement. 'Do you mind o' her?'

'Aye, course I mind o' her!' Leezie was angered that anyone should question her memory. 'Had she no' a son an' a dochter? The lassie had a gey fancy name, had she no'?'

'Aye, that's right. Flora MacDonald —'

'That's it. An' awfie-like name tae gie a lassie, an' her brother plain John. I dinnie ken whit happened tae him. I heard tell he went for a sodger . . .'

'What aboot Flora?'

'Who?'

'Flora. Flora Gibson.'

'Oh, her? She's in the poorhouse.'

'Is she? My —'

'Div ye ken her?'

'Aye, I'm connectit,' mumbled Johnny.

'Whit connection are ye? Ye're no' her brother, are ye?'

'Aye,' said John.

The old woman stared for a long time. 'Aye, man!' she said at last, 'An' you're Johnny Gibson? I wouldnie have kent ye, no I wouldnie. Has things no' been goin' weel wi' ye, Johnny?'

'No'—no' very weel.'

'Well—come in, come in the noo till I get a bit look at ye. Johnny Gibson! An' whit happent tae yer leg, John? Wis it the war?'

'Aye. What aboot my sister, noo?'

'Eh? Oh, yer sister. I never rightly got the way o' it, but I heard she broke doon wi' the drink, an' had a stroke o' some kind. They pit her in the poorhouse.'

'I'll need tae see what I can dae for her.'

'Well, I hope ye manage, I'm sure. Stey an' have a wee cup o' tea, Johnny. It's a long while since I had a crack wi' onybody that remembers the auld times. My, I cannie get ower it . . .'

Later, sitting in the bus for Glasgow, he crumpled his ticket and tried to sort out his thoughts. Flora was in the poorhouse. He had never thought that any of the family would sink so low as that. His own lodgings, in the past few years, had left much to be desired, but at least he had been independant. His three children had been sent to an orphanage, but they would come out when they were old enough, and they had their future before them. Flora, if he did not help her, would finish her life where she was. He left the bus with new cares on his shoulders, but with a new purpose in life. One drink, only one, to give him courage, and insight into his problem, and he would give up drinking for good. He would need all his money for other purposes. The idea of this new self-imposed severity was somehow exciting. There, that was better! He drained the last drop, licked the froth from his lips, and hobbled into the spring evening, his coat trailing on the sawdust of the floor.

*

Flora was allowed to get up now, to sit by the fire, or outside, when the weather was warm. The life was pleasant to her. All she wanted was affection, and this the other ladies in the ward were quite willing to give. She was an amiable, harmless body, like a great big baby, and they were all sorry for her. It was easy to see she was a wee bit simple, poor thing. The other eleven women had all had their troubles, but thank God, they still had their senses. Being now free of the said troubles, better fed, better clad, and cleaner than they had ever been in their lives, they could afford to be free with their pity.

They knew that Flora's middle name was MacDonald, and sometimes they used to tease her about it, with the old, rather obvious jokes which the street corner youths had bandied so long ago. Flora had a past, they said. Sometime or other, just you wait, a Bonny Prince would come and fetch her. Then, when she was rich, she would come back to the poorhouse and treat all the other women who were left. 'We'll have steak pie,' they used to plan, tormenting themselves with thoughts of past richness, 'an' trifle, an' jelly, an' tea an' chocolate biscuits. Aye, an' we'll a' get a new dress apiece, eh, Flora? You'll no' forget yer auld freens when your prince comes for ye?'

And Flora would giggle soundlessly, and shake her head. She loved it. She had developed a coy habit of rubbing her chin on her shoulder, her mouth gaping open. The authorities had supplied her with dentures, cheap yellow teeth like cubes of cheese, but she carried them about with her all day in her handkerchief, and showed her wet gums when she laughed.

Nobody could tell how much she remembered of her past life. Her speech was indistinct, and though the ladies were willing to tease and chaff her, they were not always willing to listen to long inarticulate stories. 'Aye, aye!' they would roar at her, when she showed an inclination to talk. 'We ken ye; we ken! Bonny Prince Chairlie!' and Flora would dissolve into giggles again, and show no regret at having been side-tracked.

Then, one day, it happened. The ward door opened, and the matron came in with a visitor, a small man leaning on a stick, his body bent so that his coat trailed on the floor. His blue eyes stared with embarrassment, and he kept blowing out his cheeks like a schoolboy who expects to be caned. All the women rose to their feet, except Flora, who was excused this mark of courtesy so long as her face showed proper respect.

'Mrs Gavin,' said the matron, 'Here is a visitor to see you—your brother. Do you remember him?'

'Yes,' said Flora, in a see-that-wet, see-that-dry tone of voice. She rubbed her chin on her shoulder, and sniggered. It was impossible to guess whether she recognised him or not.

John looked at her, his face perplexed. Flora looked well. She was fat and clean, with a nice coloured apron over her frock, and her hair was tidily done, with only a few gray streaks showing. He was shocked, however, to see her so stupid and helpless, the way her mouth puckered at one side when she said 'Yes.' That simper, too. God knows she had always been a silly bitch, but this was different. He stood by in silence, while the matron scolded her quietly and efficiently, with a professional smile in her tone.

'Come away now, Mrs Gavin, rouse yourself and take a little trouble when anyone comes to see you. Look at you, holding your dentures in your hand like that. They might as well be in your locker, for all the good they're doing you there. Come on, now, put them in and persevere. Fancy giving you nice new teeth, and you never wear them. I'm sure she looks much nicer with them in, doesn't she?'

'Yes, matron,' chorussed the women.

'Come along then, Mrs Gavin. You'll never get used to them like that. Careful now, don't drop them. False teeth cost money—a lot of money, Mrs Gavin. Press them in—*there* you are. Now, then.' She looked round the women, saw that they were all as respectable as soap and water could make them, and nodded twice in vague warning before sweeping out.

John did not know what to say, or what to do. The women watched with awful eagerness. It was a long time since they had seen a strange man, and even a little cripple like Johnny was welcome. He cleared his throat, and managed a husky 'Hoo are ye, Flora?'

'Fine,' giggled his sister. He did not know whether she would have said the same to any stranger. Lost for words, he blew out his cheeks and looked appealingly at the other inmates. They rose to the occasion. They told him all about Flora. They teased her, and made her parade her tricks for his benefit. Meaning to be kind, they hurt him more than they would ever know.

Before he left, he produced a poke of sweeties from his pocket. 'Here ye are, Flo,' he said, pressing it into her hand, 'ye can share thae wi' the rest o' them, see? Haun' them roon'.'

She kept them clutched in her hand.

'Here, come on,' bantered the women, 'share them oot, see? She's tae share them, eh, Mr Gibson?'

'Aye,' said Johnny. 'Haun' them roon, Flora. Gie them a' yin. There's plenty.'

'See, like this, hen.' One of them took her by the hand, and led her round the beds, the bag in her outstretched hand.

When she saw what was expected of her, she went round on her own, happy as a child. They had a job to persuade her to keep any for herself.

When Johnny left, he was more than ever resolved that she should leave the place as soon as possible. 'They're makin' a fair cod o' her,' he said to himself, 'treatin' her like a wean. If she's no' careful, it'll be the madhoose next. Aye, I'll need tae see what I can dae.'

Behind him, in the ward, Flora giggled nervously, over-excited and happy. It had happened, as the other women had always said; a man had come for her, and brought her sweeties. 'Aye, an' she had somebody up her sleeve efter a'!' teased the women. 'My, she's a fly yin! Jings, aye!' Greedily, they looked forward to the next visit.

*

If Flora was to come out of the workhouse, thought John, he must have a home to offer her, and enough money to keep her. He would have his own and his sister's pension, but he must have more. For three days he puzzled and worried, and then the idea came to him like a light. He had three children who ought to be old enough to help. He would write to the orphanage, to find out about them.

Slowly, methodically, he made his plans, one step at a time. He wrote to the Warden, his coat sleeve tucked up to avoid soiling the paper, his tongue hovering moist round his lips.

Dear sir,

Regards my three children placed with you, I was wondering if I could have the boy's address. He should be a good age now, and you will have found a job for him, for which I am grateful, but I would like him home now to help, so his address would oblige. I hope the other two are well, not having heard from them, I will write and arrange for them when things are settled.

Your humble servant,
John Gibson.

The address came with a short typed letter from the Warden. Willie, it appeared, had been a bright boy at school, and had shown a desire to study agriculture. He was now working at an up-to-date farm, and had been advised to save as much as he could towards a future course at some agricultural college. The girls were well. Jean was old enough now to leave, and accordingly, she would be placed in a situation, unless her father had any alternative plan.

John read the letter several times before making up his mind. Work in Glasgow was hard to find, and it seemed a pity to take Willie away from a good job. A boy with his heart in the land would never be happy in the city. Still, there was no reason why he should not help his father. Johnny wrote another letter, to Inverness-shire, this time, and told Willie that he would be obliged if he could send a little money each week.

'I am not able to work,' he said, 'and as I want to take your Aunt Flora out of the workhouse, I find myself in great need of ready cash. I wonder if you could oblige by sending on a little per week. If you were at home, I would have the benefit of you, but as it is, I have only my pension.'

Your loving father,
J. Gibson.

He waited a fortnight, and then the reply came, written neatly on blue ruled paper, the name signed with a flourish. He frowned as he read it. Willie was not a cheerful giver. 'I am afraid you have painted too rosy a picture of my future,' he said, words flowing easily, like the sentences in a book.

A farm labourer does not earn much, and education of any kind costs money. I have no one to turn to in this matter, and must depend on my own savings. Were I to do as you suggest, I should have to say goodbye to all my hopes. However, I have thought over your letter very carefully, and I do not want you to go short. I have therefore decided to send you ten shillings per month. It is a small amount, but it means a lot to me. Perhaps in a few years, when I have bettered my position, I may be able to give you further help, but in the meantime you will make it better for both of us if you do not ask for more.

Your faithful son,

William Gibson.

John was dashed by the letter. He read it at intervals, but the more he saw of the neat round writing, the angrier he felt. So Willie was going to act the Big Mick, was he? What right had he to put on airs? Him and his lordly ways '. . . you will make it better for both of us —' Hell, you'd think he was handing out gold, to hear him, instead of a meangy half-crown a week! Still, if he couldn't make it more, 2/6 would have to do. He wrote a stiff letter of thanks, and let the matter drop. Better to stand on your dignity . . .

The next thing now would be to get Jean home. It would be even better than having Willie. A girl would be handy about the house, to look after Flora, and keep the place clean. He wrote another letter to the orphanage, telling them his plans for the girl, and asking them to keep her until he sent for her.

At that time, he was living in a terrible little attic rented from a man called Nettleship. Every time he wrote a letter, he had to go downstairs and knock at the kitchen door and ask for the loan of pen and ink.

'Aye writin' yet?' asked Nettleship, when he went down yet again to borrow the pen. 'I'll be chairgin' ye for a new nib if ye go on at this rate. Whit are ye daein'? Writin' yer beeography?'

'Naw, letters,' said Gibson, limping in and helping himself to a chair. 'I doot I'll be leavin' ye soon, Archie.'

'Oh?' Archie Nettleship did not look dismayed. The attic

had never been a paying proposition. 'Where are ye goin',
then, Johnny?'

John grasped his stick firmly. 'I'm takin' a hoose,' he said.

'A hoose? A hale yin? Man, ye're no' thinkin' on gettin'
mairrit, are ye?'

'Naw, no me. Yince is enough. I'm gettin' my sister tae
come an' live wi' me, an' my dochter tae look efter us. She's
away at a schule just now.'

'A schule?' Nettleship was awed. 'My . . . an' whatna
hoose are ye gettin' . . .?'

'I dinnie ken. That's the trouble.'

'Well . . .' Nettleship was a tall man, and he stooped so
that his jacket always seemed too short. He hunched his
shoulders now almost to his ears, in the importance of his
proposition. 'I've a bit property in the Sooth Side, I'd gie ye
cheap. It's no' much, but ye'll no' want tae pey a great
deal?'

'I cannie,' said Gibson frankly. He thought over his assets,
the £20 he had saved from the sale of his furniture, not
daring to touch it lest he should ever need it desperately.
Out of that £20, he would have to buy a few necessities . . .
'I'll be glad tae get in onywhere,' he said, 'so long as it's a
hoose.'

The rent was low, but when he saw the place, he wondered
if, after all, it was not too dear. It was four stairs up, in a
dingy tenement off Clyde Street. The air was smoke, the
tired day smelt of cats and too many children. 'God,' said
Johnny, 'I thought oor street was bad!'

He was even more despondent when he got inside. It was
a two room and kitchen house, but the three rooms together
were so small that they seemed incapable of holding any
furniture. The floor boards were dusty and worn, the
windows cracked, and the cavity beds smelt close and shut
in. They looked up at the ceilings, stained with damp and
dirt. A gas bracket jutted out from the mantelshelf, and the

grate was red with rust, choked with ashes and half burnt papers.

'Christ!' said Johnny, 'It's terrible, eh?'

'Aye. You'll hae a bit bother pittin' it tae rights. It's kinna neglecktit.'

'D'you think it's worth it, Archie?'

'Well, I wouldnie like tae advise ye, either way. I ken it's gey bad, but it's like this: ye might wait long enough, an' no get the chance o' onything better. If ye've set yer mind on a hoose —'

'We'll just need tae,' said Johnny.

'Well, then, if you're prepared tae pit oot a bit expense— ye'll need tae spend a bittie on wallpaper, tae begin with.'

'Aye.' The paper was hanging in strips, and underneath flaked the stained plaster. Something round and brown fell from the ceiling, squirmed on the floor, and, righting itself, crawled slowly away. John looked from the ceiling to the walls, went closer, lifted a hanging strip, and dropped it again quickly.

'C'mere, Archie,' he said. 'Look at—that. The place is fair livin' wi' bugs!'

'Aye, they're a' the same, these auld lands,' said Archie calmly. 'I should have thocht, the way you've been livin', you wouldnie fuss much ower yin or twa creepers.'

'Yin or twa! God, man, there's aboot a hunner tae the square fit!'

It was no exaggeration. The most hardened slum-dweller would have shuddered at the thought of that house. The beltings, the panelling round the bed, the wood of the sink were all riddled, and the plaster housed nests of the stinking insects, brown and plump and always breeding. Even in broad daylight, they could be seen clustered in the cracks like lentils, or creeping slowly up and up out of reach. Johnny rubbed his neck under his collar, and blew out his cheeks. 'Makes you kinna itch, eh?' he said. 'I doot the lassies wouldnie like that.'

'I wouldnie like it masel',' said Nettleship honestly. 'You'd hae tae spray the place wi' paraffin, an' take doon a' that wood. After that, if ye gethered an' got some pent, we could dae the wa's ower.'

'Will ye gie's a haun'?'

'Och aye, shairly. I've got kinna interested in, Johnny. Forby, I couldnie see onybody go intae a hoose like this withoot giein' them a wee bit help.'

'It's awfie guid o' ye.'

'Och away.'

It was a long job, and sometimes they despaired of ever making any impression. At last, however, the walls were all painted a slimy and glossy green, and the floor reeked with lysol and paraffin and soft soap. 'God, but it's lookin' bonny,' said Nettleship, looking round when it was finished. 'I could just aboot live in it masel' noo.' The bugs still appeared at intervals, but Nettleship did not worry over them. 'Ye cannie get rid o' them a' at once,' he said comfortingly. 'They'll dee aff in time, if ye keep the place clean enough.'

Now there was only the furniture to buy. They combed the most wretched of the second hand shops, and bought chairs, a table, and three mattresses, with a few bedclothes. Johnny thought of the house he had had with Ada, the brass bed, the sofa, the piano. Well, no use grumbling. Things would have to right themselves in their own time.

*

The women teased Flora with jealous goodwill when she left them. 'My, is she no' lucky? Are ye glad ye're gaun, Flora?'

'Aye,' said Flora, grinning and mincing.

'Ye'll no' forget us, will ye no'?'

'No!' She rubbed her chin on her shoulder, and wriggled in her chair.

Her brother did not know how to cope with her when he had her at last in his charge. The workhouse doctor had warned him, 'I hope you know what you're doing, Gibson. It's no light charge, having a person like that on your hands, you know.'

'I ken fine, doctor,' he said. 'But I'll no' have a relation o' mine die in the poorhouse so long as I can help it.'

'How are you going to look after her?'

'I've my dochter coming frae school,' said Johnny. 'She's had a good training, an' she'll manage fine.'

'Well, I hope so,' said the doctor, dubious to the last.

Perhaps, thought Johnny now, perhaps after all he was right. Flora sat stiffly in the bus, a wooden look on her face, as if she was frightened of the country rushing past her. When he spoke to her, she would melt into giggles like a child. He was fairly ashamed of her. It was a job, too, getting her up the stairs. Nettleship, however, was there to meet him, slouching at the close mouth, and he shooed away the weans when they got in the way. He had laid the tea, in a last burst of generosity, and lit a fire from the few coals in the bunker.

Flora ate clumsily, very much on her best behaviour. 'Yes,' she said, when they asked her if she was all right. 'Yes,' very polite and bashful. John realised that there would be little conversation with her. She would sit by the fire, amiable and empty; her pension would help to pay the rent; for the future, they would have to depend on Jean, and the quicker she came, the better. Apart from the money she would earn, John suddenly realised that he wanted somebody young in the house. It would be gey dreary with only himself and Flora, neither of them so young as they had been; both of them old.

CHAPTER FOUR

JEAN GIBSON was small and dark, with a heavy bust and thick ankles. There was a coarseness, a thick healthiness about her, which told of plenty of porridge and pudding, vegetables, and country milk. Beside other Glasgow girls of her age, she was almost matronly, but her straight bobbed hair, her flat shoes, and her plain serge dress made her a child. She wore no make-up, and when she came off the train, she was carrying a sheaf of papers, the *Schoolgirl*, the *Schoolgirl's Weekly*, and the *Girls' Own Paper*.

Johnny met her at the barrier, and shook hands awkwardly, wondering if he ought to have kissed her. He would not have known her. Something in the smallness, the darkness of her, reminded him of himself, but he looked in vain for any resemblance to Ada. Ah well, it was better that she should not take after her mother.

Jean had little to say for herself, beyond agreeing, dutifully, that she was glad to leave the orphanage. Johnny wondered what she thought of him, her father, the first glimpse of the shabby clothes, the grey hair, the stick, the limp, and the blown-out cheeks. He had tried to drop this mannerism, but embarrassment always brought it back. His face was like a balloon as he took her up Adella Street. He was more than ever conscious of the cats, the papers flapping in the gutter, the chipped and shabby fronts of the buildings. 'We're just here temporary,' he explained, his voice saying, sorry, sorry. 'It's a kinna rough quarter, an' we've no' just got settled right in, but it'll dae meantime.'

'Yes,' said Jean.

He took her elbow, leading her through the dark lobby of the house. 'Aye, aye,' he said with forced cheerfulness, rubbing his hands together, his face round as a turnip. 'Well, here's Jean back. Jean, this is yer Auntie Flora. Speak kinna loud, she's a wee bittie deaf . . .'

Her aunt's hand was flabby, as she giggled and rubbed her chin on her shoulder. 'There, now,' said John, 'We'll hae some tea, I think . . .'

After the meal, with the fire made up, and the hearth swept, he plunged at the question he had been longing to ask.

'Well, an' do you think you're gonnie like it, Jeannie?'

'I don't know,' said Jean, in a doubtful, candid voice.

'I ken it's no' just what I'd like tae see,' said her father, 'but I've just got gethered thegither. Your auntie was in the poorhoose, an' I had a' the bother o' gettin' her oot. Then hooses are no' sae easy gotten nooadays.'

'It's awful wee,' said Jean. 'I've been used to big rooms, an' it makes you feel you can't breathe here. Is the rest o' the house as wee?'

'Aye . . . but you'll get used tae that. It's no' sae bad as some; an' when you get a job, there'll be a bit mair money comin' in, an' we'll be able to make some improvements.' He spoke as if he intended adding a wing or two, and knocking several rooms together to make a ballroom. 'We'll need tae see ye settled as quick as we can. I'll take ye roon tae the burroo the morn.'

'Have I tae start work already?'

'Well . . . as soon as possible. We havenie much money, lassie, an' ye're as well tae ken that now as later on. The sooner you work, the better for yersel'.'

'Will I get keeping my wages?' Jean's voice was sharp and grudging.

'Some o' them,' said her father reasonably. 'Some o' them. But mind, you'll no' earn enough tae keep ye for a while yet, an' ye cannie expect tae get runnin' oot spendin' whenever you like. We cannie afford it. But you'll get something tae yersel' each week, never heed.'

This questioning attitude shook him. He did not realise, or only half realised that Jean was suffering from acute disappointment. She had long looked forward to being home,

to being independent. Usually, it was only the more affluent
of orphanage girls who went to their own people; the others
were sent out to situations. Now she found herself in a dark
wee house with two old people who seemed to take it for
granted that she should just fit into their lives without
further ado. Her father, at least, seemed to think so. Her
Aunt Flora was a wee bit wrong in the head, and had no say
in the matter. Fancy having to live all your life with a couple
like that! Never mind, as soon as she could save up enough,
she would run away, even if it meant going back to the
orphanage. If the people up there had known the kind of
place she was going to, they would never have let her near
Glasgow.

'Who looks after this house?' she said suddenly.

'Well, it's like this,' explained her father. 'Your aunt an'
me's no' able for much. I'll dae what I can, but I thought
you could lend a hand at nights, like, wi' the wee odd things,
scrubbing an' washin' an' so on. It needs a lot o' cleanin',
this hoose, if ye're tae keep the vermin doon. It's a fair
scandal.'

'Vermin?'

'Aye. Oh, we're no' sae bothered wi' them as we were at
first; but they'll be back if ye dinnie keep at them.'

'Well—but if I'm to work all day, an' then come home
an' work at night . . . what time do I get to myself?'

Johnny said nothing, but blew out his cheeks and stared
at the fire. Things had gone wrong, damnably wrong.
Looking at it from Jean's point of view, he could see her
grievance, but what else could he do? It was going to be an
awful job if she was going to question everything and stand
on her dignity like that.

'I—I —' he stammered, and cast about for words. 'I dinnie
mean ye tae work a' the time, lassie,' he said, 'I ken you're
young, an' need yer fling, same as others. I'm easy pleased,
ye'll find that, but I just had tae get ye home for yer Auntie

Flo's sake. It'll be a wee bit rough at first, as I tellt ye, but we'll make through a' right. Mebbe a wee bit later on, we'll get Isa hame an' a'. We'll see. Noo dinnie greet, I didnie mean tae be hard on ye right away. We'll manage, you'll see.'

'I'm no' greetin'!' snapped Jean. Neither she was; but her face was dark, and her eyes smouldered as she kicked aimlessly at the fender. John Gibson, watching her, sighed to himself. 'God, there's aye something!' he was thinking. 'I can see there'll be a right rammy in this hoose afore long!'

*

Isa, though two years younger than her sister, was a head taller, and almost as stout. She took after her mother, with the same brassy yellow hair, the square chin, and the massive build.

The sisters did not correspond after they were parted. They had never been used to writing letters, Jean had no time, and Isa had no money for stamps. When it was time for Isa to go home, she saw her sister waiting for her at the station, and immediately noticed a difference. Jean was paler. Her straight hair wanted cutting, and she looked as if she was not too pleased with life.

'Well,' said Isa, full of delight at having reached home, 'How are you getting on?'

'All right,' said Jean curtly. 'Here, come on an' we'll get a tram. No use walking.'

'Is it far?'

'You'll see soon enough. The awfullest-like dump—I'd rather be back where I was, any day. Still, never let on I said anything. My father would be fair annoyed. He keeps saying he's done his best.'

'This is it,' she said briefly, when they came to Adella Street. 'I bet you never thought you'd land up in a slum.'

'It's a tinky sort of place, isn't it?'

'*Isn't it* ' mimicked Jean, thoroughly out of temper. 'You're surely speaking awful posh?'

'Me, speaking posh? I am not. That's the way I always speak.'

'You never used to.'

'Well, what's wrong with starting? You're not going to speak the same all your life, are you? You've got to try to improve yourself.'

'Fine chance you've got to improve here!' grumbled Jean.

In a minute more they would have quarrelled, but they came to the close mouth, and Isa was silent in shame at the sight of it, with it's randies standing in their shawls, and its smelling litter heaped in the dust. She saw now into the turmoil of her sister's feelings, the dismay of one forced into such conditions without warning. Without speaking, they climbed the stairs together.

Inside, it was not so bad as she had feared. The effect of the new paint had not yet dimmed, and the fire was bright in the grate. An old man sat at one side of the fire, blowing out his cheeks, and fidgetting with a Harry Lauder stick, and at the other sat a fat, heavy woman, beaming and smirking, with her feet stretched out over the hearthrug.

'Here ye are, Isa,' said the man—her father; and when he stood up, she saw that he was lame. Aunt Flora giggled, her tongue wet in her open mouth.

'Your Aunt Flora had a stroke,' explained Johnny, in a low voice. 'She's quite happy at the fireside, just hersel'.'

'Yes,' said Isa, staring round her, the tallest person in the room. 'Where'll I put my coat, Jean?'

'Here, ben the room. I'll come with you.' Jean led her into the poky little bedroom, and flung herself on the bed. 'Well, what d'you think of them?' she snapped.

'Give me a chance,' said Isa. Her voice, too, was edgy. 'You can't just judge by appearances.'

'You'll soon know, after you've lived with them a wee while. It's terrible. I've got to look after them and the house, and go out to work as well, and all I get is three shillings a week. They say that's all they can afford.'

'Three shillings! You should get more than that.'

'Course I should. And here—Auntie Flora—she's daft. She just sits an' sits till I could scream. My father wanted me to do her washing for her, but I refused. She's too dirty. I couldnie bring myself to touch her things.'

'Who does them, then?'

'I dunno. Herself, mebbe. Och, I'm fair fed up! An' my father's awful strict, far stricter than they were at the home.'

'What do you work at, Jeannie?'

'Oh, in a fruit shop, a terrible wee place where the lights are on all day. It's mostly tatties an' cabbages we sell. An' then, when I get home —'

'I know,' said Isa, 'you told me once. What about Willie? What's he doing?'

'He's at a farm, I think. My father never says much about him, because I think they cast out over my father wanting money off him. My, he's lucky, away on his own! If —'

'Are youse comin' through?' shouted Johnny from the kitchen. 'I'm aboot ready for my dinner, Jean. You should have had the tatties on by this.'

'Well, I was just puttin' them on,' said Jean.'

★

At night, undressing slowly, a small brown speck leaped and sprang from the whiteness of Isa's vest. A flea. Her skin was all red lumps, where, for a long time, she had been scratching herself uncomfortably. Her head itched, too. Shuddering, she turned down the bed, and sat waiting for her sister.

'It'll no' be so bad, now you're here,' said Jean, unlacing her shoes.

'I'll be away the minute I can get,' said Isa. 'I'm not staying here if I can help it!'

She did stay, however. It took longer than she expected to

find work, because she had to have something fairly near home, so as to be able to save tram fares, and be close at hand to help with the housework. At first, she had hoped for a domestic position, where she would be able to live away from Adella Street. Her father, however, had put his foot down, and an accident to Aunt Flora settled matters once and for all.

Flora had set herself on fire. She was in by herself at the time, and nobody was able to find out how it had happened. 'Did ye catch yer skirt in the bars?' said her brother. 'Did a cinder fa' oot an' singe ye? Was ye leanin' ower tae see something?' To every question, she answered 'No-o,' shaking her head in perplexed innocence. He could get nothing out of her, but there she was, with one side of her apron and skirt burnt clean away. It was a mystery how she had not been hurt, and how she had managed to keep the fire from spreading. However lucky the escape, the same thing must not be allowed to happen again. Someone must stay in the house all the time. After all, why keep two daughters if neither of them could help?

He put it to them, and they looked at each other warily. Neither of them wanted the job, but both, by this time, had learned the wisdom of giving in to their father. He was becoming more and more dogmatic these days.

'The way I look at it is this,' he said. 'Oor Jean's workin', bringin' money intae the hoose. You havenie got a job, Isa, an' though I dinnie grudge you yer keep, I cannie keep ye a' the time if you're no' earnin'. I've been on tae ye aboot takin' something for a while noo, but ye wullnie. Well, if ye're no' keen on the ootside work, you'll have tae try yer haun' at something else. Yer duty lies at home, Isa, an' yer aunt's in need o' watchin'. You bide an' see tae the hoose, an' Jean can bring in the money. You'll baith get the same pocket-money, so there need be nae rows ower the heid o' yin gettin' mair nor the ither.'

And so it was settled. Isa did not relish the prospect, but she knew that there was nothing else to do. She would just have to make the best of it. Where Jean would have sulked, Isa looked at the work around her, and determined to tackle it. She saw her father hirpling about in a frayed collar, with the wrists of his underwear dirty at the cuffs; she saw her aunt smirking at the fire, like a domestic witch, and knew that her hair was alive with head beasts. She knew from experience of the various parasites which infected the built-in beds, and she noted the drab grey fringe of the curtains, the smeared windows, the dust in the corners. These things could either be endured or abolished; Isa made up her mind to abolish them, but not because of love; merely because they stood in her way.

CHAPTER FIVE

Isa set herself to make a home out of the 'hoose' in Adella Street. Gradually, she brought small comforts into being, improvements so slight that they stressed the poverty of the family. Perhaps she crocheted a small d'oyley for the centre of the table; perhaps she retrieved from the ash-bucket a strip of linoleum, and nailed it down over a hole in the lino which had been left on the floor—rotten stuff, too done to lift. Nothing was too trivial for her to consider. She fought the bugs and the fleas, the soot and smuts and fogs of Glasgow; she forced her father to make her an extra allowance for polish and cleaning material, and at last she was able to say, with pride, that there was not a cleaner house in the building. The grate shone, the floor was scrubbed to the farthest corner, and the windows were spotless. Such curtains as there were were washed as soon as they showed the slightest trace of grime, and the bed was always covered with a clean spread, faded and patched, but whole.

She could do so little, however, against the overwhelming fact of poverty. It was a struggle all the time, an uphill struggle which seemed to have no ending. Plan as she would, work as she would, the house was still a slum dwelling, and they could not afford to live beyond their present careful budget.

Coal was a dear item. They could manage to keep a fire going, but one fire only, burning with a thin flame in the kitchen grate. The big room fire was never lit, but sometimes the room filled with backsmoke from the chimney next door, and a blue fog filtered as far as the passage. To the girls, who were used to centrally heated dormitories, the coldness of the room was a great hardship. 'If we had only a wee gas fire!' they grumbled. 'I'm sure it wouldn't cost that much!' But gas was as dear as coal, and it, too, must be rationed if they were to live within their means. The kitchen was lit by an incandescent gas mantle, a greeny-yellow light which hissed and dipped with a low looping noise. The other rooms were fitted with fish-tale burners, but these were never used. Instead, candles were carried through, anchored to old saucers in a bed of grease, and burned down to the last blue gutter.

In summer, there was no fuel problem, other than the getting in and storing of coal. They always bought what they could, but they had only a small bunker in the passage, and no outside cellar. They filled tin baths and old boxes, and kept them under the bed, but Ginger, the cat, used the coal as a lavatory, and the results were not pleasant. Often, after her end of the week cleaning, Isa had to drag the coal out, lump by lump, to clean up Ginger's carefully covered dirt. It was discouraging; everything about the place was discouraging. No matter how hard you tried, there was always something to pull you back again.

Household linen was a great trial. Isa had an almost maniacal desire to keep the curtains crisp and fresh, but the smoke and soot dirtied them so quickly that they were more often on the pulley than on the window. Every time she washed them, they tore, and ironing, no matter how carefully done, inflicted fresh ravages. There were so few sheets that they could not be changed sufficiently, and they had to take turn about with the pillowslips. They had two towels between the four of them, two towels which were always gray and damp, and sometimes spotted with blood where Johnny had cut himself shaving. The dish towels had to be washed after every meal, and dried in front of the fire. There was only one rug in the whole house, a mangy bit of runner laid in front of the kitchen fender. Johnny was doing his best, buying such necessities as he could afford, but it was taking a long time; a long, long time.

To give him his due, Johnny kept out of debt. He was eager to make a success of this new venture of his, and he derived a certain amount of pleasure from scraping and budgetting. Of the four, he was the most contented. Flora was happy with the little she had; it was a very little, for she was only a passenger in the household, and could expect nothing more; but Johnny had been dragged to the lowest depths of poverty, and now he had a home, a fire, and a bed. He was a householder, someone of consequence, and week by week, he grew more conscious of his position.

Some lingering feeling of inferiority, however, some defensive striving towards self-assertion, made him more and more censorious. *He* knew everything. He was a man who had suffered and seen life; let no one try to fool him with sermons and speeches! He read the paper every morning, finding fault with the country's foreign policy, its parliamentary decisions, and especially its stinginess. He bewailed his fate far louder than in the days when he had been homeless.

He was great against the upper classes. The working man, he insisted, was always trodden down. 'What for dae they no' a' get thegither an' protest?' he would grouse. 'The workin' man's no' gettin' a square deal at a'. Ye can see that wi' the taxes. It's a' the poor folk's pleasures that gets taxed, beer an' tobaccie an' things like that. The rich folks never kens the pinch, an' it's us that's workin' tae keep them in idleness. Aye, there's yin law for the rich, another for the poor. This is no' a democracy at a'. It's run by a monied parliament, an' it's us yins that peys tae keep them there.'

He was good on pensions. 'Aye, they make a great sang aboot naebuddy needs tae sterve nooadays, but I'd like tae ken what they think a man's gonnie dae wi' a' the pension the government allows them. Look at me; I've gied my health tae my country, an' what has the country done for me? Not a hate; not a bloody hate. Look at yer Auntie Flora.' (They looked at her, her eyes far away, her teeth, if she was wearing them, bulging her lips to a custard-coloured grin.) 'Aye, look at her! Hoo the Hell dae they think a weedow's pension'll keep a wumman in claes an' food an' rent? It wad cost mair tae keep her in the poorhoose, but dae ye think they'll make up tae me what I spent on her? No' bloomin' likely! An' us livin' in a hoose no' much bigger than a dug-kennel! I'm tellin' ye . . .'

And so it went on, nag, nag, nag, the gray Glasgow voice droning its complaints which none could remedy. He met with little sympathy. His sister did not understand what he was talking about, and his daughters had no interest in the problems of government. They wearied of his endless denunciations, and sometimes they groused at him, half laughing, in case he should fly at them in a rage. 'Och, shut up wi' your politics! We get them for breakfast, dinner, an' tea. I wouldnie be surprised if you blether in your sleep!'

Mostly, he paid no attention; but he was capable of turning on them if he happened to be in the mood. His rage was wild, surprising, even to himself. His temper and moods seemed to be erratic, as if his frozen emotions were slowly coming to life after his years of suffering.

What angered him most was when they mumbled with discontent about being poor. 'Och, I'm fed up!' said Jean one day, 'this is a right dreary place!' 'Fed up!' said her father, dumping the ground with his stick. 'Fine cause *you* have tae be fed up! You've a home here, an' freens aboot ye; what would ye be if ye had tae walk aboot in the snow an' beg afore ye could get the money for a bed? How would ye like if ye didnie ken where yer next bite was comin' frae? How would ye like tae be that desperate you could pawn onything ye had for a dinner, only you'd nothin' tae pawn? My God, when I hear that kinna talk, it makes me fair seeck! If you're no' satisfied, ye ken what tae dae. I'm no' keepin' ye. Ye can go as soon as ye like, an' good riddance, if that's a' ye think o' yer home. There's plenty worse off.'

He was never tired of telling them that, almost in self defence. At least, they were not overcrowded, like most of the other families on the stair. The Gillespies opposite had two families living in a room and kitchen, and the single end beside them had a man and woman and six children. Here, they could sleep in decency. John Gibson slept in the high kitchen bed, climbing into it with the aid of a chair, and lowering himself to the floor every morning, groaning as the rheumatics twinged his crippled hip. Flora had a room to herself, a wee cupboard of a place which held a bed and a chair, no more; and the two girls occupied the 'big' room, huddled together on a hard mattress, sharing the one pillow. It was not comfortable, but they need have no shame about it; not like the folks below, who all mucked in together, with no regard for age or sex.

And yet, the girls grumbled, if not for these reasons, then for others. They had no freedom. Certain streets and districts were out of bounds, and a very strict curfew was enforced. They were not encouraged to mix with the girls round about, so they remained practically friendless. 'You're no' needin' tae go oot,' said their father, when they pleaded for more liberty. 'Can ye no' amuse yersel's in the hoose? I'll see if I cannie get nothing tae break the monotony.'

'Break the monotony.' He bought games for them, halma, dominoes and ludo, and played himself, chuckling as he plied dice and counters. He seemed really to enjoy himself, but the girls were bored and disgruntled. What did they want with *games*. They were young; others had their freedom, and went out in gangs, boy and girl, up and down the street, with new clothes to wear, and money to treat each other to fish and chips in some steamy cafe. They did not ask for money; they knew the circumstances; but why should they not be allowed to come and go like the others? It was not fair.

'There's plenty places ye can go if ye like,' said Johnny. 'Can ye no' go tae some o' thae church clubs? I'm no' a kirk man masel', I've nae time for ministers, but I've nae objection tae ony o' youse goin'. Ye'll come tae nae herm, that's yin thing. Or what's tae hinder ye readin'? Ye get some quite nice stories out the free library; or spend some o' yer pocket money on pins an' wool, and dae some knittin'. There's plenty ye can dae withoot walkin' the streets like the lassies roon' aboot here.'

That was the real reason for his sternness, the fear of moral harm. Having been brought up in an orphanage, he reasoned, they could have no idea of the dangers of city life. He would never forgive himself, if, through neglect, either of his daughters came to harm.

'We're no' bairns,' said Isa, already saddled with the Glasgow accent. 'How is it other lassies can get oot, an' no us? We'll no' encourage strange men. We've mair sense.'

'Aye, have ye? It's no' sense that counts. Ye never ken what ye're up against. I was readin' in the paper aboot a case where a lassie was at the picters, an' turned faint. The fellie beside her cairrit her oot, an' she's never been seen since. It's that white slave traffic; they dope them . . .'

'Och, but that'll no' happen tae us. We'll stick thegither.'

'Aye, but ye'll stick tae the sooth side. Then I'll ken where ye are.'

It was no use arguing. Johnny would stand so much, and then he would flare up, 'Don't you be sae damnt cheeky!' At such times, he was really frightening, his cheeks blown out, his hands clawed round his stick, his head stuck forward arrogantly. Gradually, the girls came to believe much of what he himself believed. 'Aye, right enough,' they would agree, 'some o' thae streets is no' safe at night.' They could give instances where they had been followed over the suspension bridge, all along the foggy length of Carlton Place; they were ready to shriek if a street corner man so much as glanced at them; and once, when someone in a muffler, panting and dishevelled, stopped them and said, 'Here, did youse see a wee fullah jick doon ony o' thae closes?' they shook their heads, said, 'No, sorry,' and went straight home. They were well warned. It was best to be polite and know nothing. Gang fights were deadly affairs. Get yourself known with the gangs, and you were for it, from one side or the other.

They had fun, of a sort. One must accept one's life, and they prized the pleasures which came to them, stolen or otherwise, and, though they quarrelled, they always came together in bed, talking after the candle had gone out. All things seemed possible then. 'Never mind, we'll get mairrit some day, an' get oot o' here. The old folks cannie expect us tae gie up a' wir lives for them. They're just keepin' us here cos it suits them . . .'

Always the discontent behind the dreaming, always the resentment at what life expected of them. Why did others have youth, while here, their own youth was being drowned to keep old people in comfort? And why, in Heaven's name, did their father not *see* it, and be a little more understanding?

'It's easy to see who gets the best of it,' grumbled Isa. Jean had her job, a tram ride away every morning, fresh faces to see, fresh voices to hear. Life was easy for her. She got up in the morning, and her breakfast was ready for her; everything waited till she got out, scurrying all over the place, where's my overall, have you a penny for the tram, out the way an' let me get my hair done. She came back in a rush, and her dinner had to be ready for her to gulp and get away again. At night, she wouldn't lend a hand with the dishes; she wouldn't even wash her own overall. Isa began to wonder if she wasn't doing more than her share.

CHAPTER SIX

WHEN Jean was twenty, she met Bobby Coutts. One night, in bed, she made her confession.

'Isa, I've something tae tell ye.'

'What is it?'

'I've got a date on the morn, wi' a fellie.'

'What fellie?' Isa's voice squeaked in the darkness.

'His name's Bobby Coutts. He drives yin o' the fruit lorries, but just temporary. He's a builder tae trade.'

'How did ye . . .?'

'Och, I've been pally wi' him for a long while, but nothin' serious. We couldnie make up wir minds. It was atween me an' the ither lassie in the shop, but now he's decided on me. I think he's a decent enough sort. "When I go oot wi' a lassie," he says, "I like tae play fair wi' her, an' I expect her tae play fair wi' me." "Oh, that's a'right," I says, "I'm no' yin o' that kind. My father would half kill me if he thought I was runnin' aboot wi' different fellies." '

'What's he like?'

'He's a'right,' said Jean modestly.

'Does my father ken?'

'No' yet. I'll need tae kid on I'm goin' oot wi' you at first. You never can tell how he's gonnie take thae things.'

'But you're entitled —'

'Aye, but you never can tell.'

Isa kept the secret well, covering her sister's tracks, and arranging meetings. All this time, she had never met Bobby Coutts. Jean was possessive, and grudged spoiling an evening's pleasure with the presence of a third party. Isa's only reward lay in the bedtime confidences, and the feeling that she was helping to accomplish something against the narrowness of home.

'It was great the night,' Jean would say, curled up on her side, the blankets drawn round her neck. 'We went tae the Palais. He's a great dancer, Bobby. He was far mad at me because I had tae come away. "What wey can ye no' stey oot the same as the others?" he says. "Oh, I'd get intae trouble," I says. "You've nae idea what we've tae pit up wi' in oor hoose. I'm fair fed up." He says it's a right shame. He seem me right hame tae the close, an' we stood for ages. He was gettin' fair hot when I tellt him I'd need tae go in.'

Isa never tired of these tales. She envied her sister, but for the time being, her interest and loyalty rose above her envy. Jean was older; let her be served first. Her own turn would come in time.

With winter, however, difficulties arose. Johnny was over-solicitous about his daughters' health. It was no good mentioning the pictures when the rain was blashing on the window. 'You can go to the picters anither night,' he would say. 'Just take aff yer coat an' hae mair sense. I'm sure you can find plenty tae dae in the hoose, withoot goin' gaddin' in the rain every night. Can ye no' hae a game o' ludo or some-thin'? Get oot the board an' I'll play ye.'

Ludo! And Bobby Coutts standing at the corner, tapping his feet! And next morning, the reproach, the almost taunting rebuke—

'I waited over an hour for ye last night, Jeannie. Ye might've tellt me ye werenie comin'.'

'Aye, I'm sorry, Bob. My faither kept me in.'

'Jings, can ye no' jick oot withoot askin' him? Ye're auld enough, are ye no'?'

'Aye, well—I've tellt him, but you don't know what he's like. He had a bad time when he was younger, an' it's made him kinna feart for Isa an' me. That's what makes him so strict.'

She was always sorry, always apologetic. Sometimes, she thought she was too apologetic. It was Isa who brought things to a head.

'Bring him up tae meet the family. Make a clean breast tae my father; it's the only way.'

'Ocht, but —'

'It'll have tae come some time. I'll see the place is nice for you. It's no' such a bad wee hoose,' she said, in a mood of unusual affection. 'At any rate, it's clean. I'll have a nice tea ready, an' we'll see what happens.'

'A'right, then.' Jean was uneasy. She had always had less confidence than Isa, and there were so many potential drawbacks to the idea of an introduction. Her father might insist that she brought Bobby home instead of going out with him; in that case, life would lose much of its glamour. It was awful, this everlasting supervision. Why could she not have a life of her own? Then, she was not sure that she wanted Bobby to meet her people. Bobby's status was not much higher than her own, but . . . her father, blowing out his cheeks, hobbling with his hip sticking out . . . it was not his fault, and she felt ashamed of her shame, but suppose he started to rant about the Government, and Bobby was bored stiff? What if Aunt Flora showed her up? It was so embarrassing, and what girl could be doing with that when she had her boy friend up for the first time?

Her father, though, was more willing to co-operate than she had expected. 'Bring him up!' he said, 'bring him up!' He waved his hand magnanimously. 'I've nae objection tae ye takin' up wi' some chap, so long as he's decent. I'll soon tell ye what I think o' him. Just you bring him up, an' we'll see!'

The visit, on the whole, was a success. Isa, still in her co-operative mood, had scrubbed and polished the house, and bought in as many cakes and biscuits as the house-keeping expenses would allow. Aunt Flora's hair was fluffed and dressed for the occasion, and Johnny smoked by the fireside, very much the lordly host. At half past seven, Jeannie came in, and pushed in front of her Bobby Coutts, all stale cigarette smoke and embarrassment.

He was a likely enough fellow, broad, amiable, and without much intelligence. He grinned all round, and sat on the edge of a chair, staring into the fire, and dangling his hands between his knees. When Johnnie spoke, he listened respect-fully, and agreed with a great many nods and ayes. 'Aye, that's right, Mr Gibson—aye, aye, that's right. Aye.'

He made a great hit with Flora. In a sudden lull, she put forward a hand, and touched him on the knee. He looked up enquiringly. The woman was trying to speak.

'Flora MacDonald!' she mouthed, laughing and pointing to herself. 'Me, Flora—MacDonald Gibson!'

'She's tellin' you her name,' explained Jean. 'She's awful proud of it. She must have taken to you; it's no' often she speaks tae strangers.'

'Flora MacDonald . . .'

'Aye, aye!' roared Bob. 'That's a fine name; aye, it's a fine yin!'

'Sit in tae yer tea,' said Isa. 'Here, Bob, you'd better sit beside oor Jean. Wait an' I'll bring ben another chair . . .'

As the evening went on, Johnny grew more and more amiable. Jean was relieved. Seeing her boy down to the close mouth, she squeezed his hand ecstatically. 'It's a' right noo,' she said. 'I'll get oot onywhere, noo he kens ye. Youse got on a' right, did ye no'?'

'Och, aye,' said Bobby. 'I'll get on wi' onybody.'

★

Jean Gibson was now officially 'winchin' '. She and Bobby met several nights a week, and every Sunday Bobby came to tea at Adella Street. Once or twice, Isa managed to light a fire for them in the room, so that they could sit in privacy. From time to time, giggles were heard from the darkness, but the only time Isa showed her envy was when Jean returned, flushed and slightly dishevelled, from the embraces in the close. Sometimes they took as long as half an hour to say goodnight, and Isa could never settle for wondering what was going on down there in the dark. Why did they take so long? And why did Jean either giggle or go silent when she came back, humming to herself with a mysterious smile, or talking loudly on silly irrelevant topics? Isa would hang about, poking the fire, clearing the table, helping her Aunt Flora to bed. Trust Jean to stay away so long when she knew there was work to be done!

But, once in bed together, the whispering started, and Isa was as eager to hear as Jean was to divulge. 'You know this, when he kissed me the night, I thought I was gonnie faint! I got fair weak. Honest, it fair takes it oot o' ye! Bobby doesnie ken his ain strength, he had me fair beat. Did I look a'right when I came in?'

'You were a bit red,' said Isa curtly.

'Nae wunner. Wait till you're winchin', Isa, ye'll ken a' aboot it. Ye'll soon need tae be gettin' a man.'

'Ocht, a man! I'm no' in nae hurry!' she scoffed; and she really believed it. To have a boy friend to take you out, to give you presents and a certain amount of status—that was something; but a man . . . she thought of Jean's whispered descriptions, and felt slightly nauseated. She didn't want that. She tried to imagine herself kissing Bobby Coutts, and being kissed as Jean said he kissed, so hard that it hurt. It worked up her stomach, but it gave her no pleasure. 'No,' she said, with renewed assurance, 'I'm in nae hurry.' But a moment or two after, she was back on the subject again. 'Jeannie! Tell me what else. What else did he say . . .?'

★

The courtship was slow, by Glasgow standards, but at last they came to the point of marriage. The wedding was described by the family and the neighbours as 'fair posh'. With the aid of a clothing club, the subscription running on regularly week after week, they managed to buy new clothes all round. All the guests, as a point of honour, had rigged themselves out in the latest fashion, cheap and brilliant. With a crowd of kids sniffing and cheering at the close, they drove off in a taxi, to the church in the next street. It would never have done for them to have walked. Every custom, every tradition must be observed in detail, even to the scrambling of pennies at the close mouth. The Gibsons would never have held up their heads in Adella Street if they had been followed by shouts of 'Hush! Hush! Shabby weddin'! Cannie spare a bawbee!'

It was quiet in the empty church, the traffic noises muffled and faint. The whole wedding party were in strange surroundings; even the minister was strange to them. They never went to church in the ordinary way, but Jean had said she would not feel properly married in a registry office.

There were not many guests; a few relations of the bridegroom, a few of the neighbours from Adella Street, and Archie Nettleship, in a greenish black jacket which drooped from his shoulders. Everybody sat stiff and ill at ease. This was not the *real* part of the wedding. The part they understood was the time of feasting, of dances and songs and drink, with the bride and groom slinking off together, and a string of bawdy jokes flung with old shoes and bags of rice and pink and blue confetti.

There was much keeking over shoulders as the bridal party appeared at the door. Jeannie was dressed to the nines. 'The lassie doon the sterr,' a conciliatory person with an astonishing amount of clothes, had lent her a fox fur, and, with this draped over her shoulders, and a somewhat gaudy bouquet in her hand, the bride went slowly up the aisle. Her coat was a little too tight, strained across her waist and her plump hips, and her legs in their shiny silk seemed too short and fat for her body. She was smiling self-consciously, and a tilted hat sat over her right eye. Her elaborately curled hair was already beginning to fall.

Her father was to give her away. He kept himself as erect as he could, but still he limped, and his stick went thud, thud, all along the coconut matting. Isa, dressed in pale green, came behind, almost spitefully pleased with her own appearance. At the church door, as she came out of the car, someone had whispered, 'There's the bride.' She knew perfectly well that she looked better than her sister.

Taking it all together, it was a very creditable turn out. The Gibsons had not been shown up by the Coutts; that was something. Even Aunt Flora, gaping stupidly, refrained from causing any trouble. It had been an awful job getting her down the stair, but here she was now, staring at the ceremony with, as likely as not, no idea of its meaning. At least, she behaved herself. Isa had lectured her well when dressing her, pulling up her stockings, and bundling her into her new frock. Her head wagged loosely when her hair was combed. 'Och, keep *steady*, Aunt Flo!' Isa had grumbled. 'And put your teeth in, for God's sake!'

After the church service, they went to a studio to have their photographs taken, the bride's shoulders hunched under her borrowed fur, the bridegroom stiff and possessive, and Isa thrusting herself forward as well as she could. She loved being photographed. Back at the cafe, where the reception was being held, they went through a ritual of kisses, toasts and tea. As soon as the minister left, the jokes began, bawdy jokes about beds and young couples and 'nine months later'. Jeannie blushed, and looked frightened. Isa, though faintly disgusted, was somehow envious. Her sister was going through something she had yet to experience, and she wondered when the time for her own initiation would come.

Bobby had managed to get hold of a single end in Ballater Street, and, though not above reproach, it had at least been better than Johnnie's house when they looked it over for the first time. With the aid of the hire purchase system, they had furnished it sparsely with a table, three chairs, a chest of drawers and a dressing table. The walls were papered in green and fawn, the woodwork was still tacky with fresh paint, and they had lacquered the grate to save polishing. Directly after the wedding party, they moved in; and Isa went home to an untidy, cold house, with the two old people, and a deep sense of despondency.

*

Now, at Adella Street, there was a little less money; things were a little more drab, and Johnny was stricter than ever. Apart from this, the days went past to the same old routine, the same words spoken at the same times, the same faces, the same tasks, endlessly repeated.

The old people soon grew used to Jean's absence. They would have missed Isa more, because they were dependent on her for almost everything. As it was, Isa felt lost without her sister, the talks, the quarrels, the young company. The only consolation was that Jean's house in Ballater Street was near at hand, and always open to visitors.

In a week or two, Jean considered herself sufficiently experienced to advise Isa on the troubles of married life. 'I might as well tell you, seein' you're my sister. After a', ye've got tae learn. Ye ken this, I was awfie feart at first . . .' she went into a long rigmarole of somewhat unsavoury facts, whispered low by the fire. 'Aye, it's nae joke. You'd think a' yer troubles were over when ye get mairrit, but they're no'. You soon get the nonsense knocked oot o' ye. We've had mair than yin tiff a'ready . . . but ye wouldnie be natural if you didnie have a quarrel, would ye?'

'I don't know,' said Isa abstractedly.

'No, you wouldnie. A young mairrit lassie's no' aye in the mood for a man's cairry on. He didnie tell me he drank.'

'Does he?'

'No' much, but I fair hate the smell o' it. Right enough, it's an awfie business . . .'

So that was married life? Already, the kitchen was beginning to look dusty and shabby. Jean had never been a worker. Well, serve her right, now she would know what it was like, tied to the sink and the grate all the time. And yet, even now, she managed to escape a good deal. When she came to Adella Street, she took care to arrive at meal times, to save cooking for herself. Oh, she was fly, was our Jeannie!

Isa despised her for her slipshod attitude, but she envied her too. She, too, wanted a house of her own, a life of her own; but where Jean got her leisure at the expense of her home, Isa possessed more integrity. She might grumble, but she would not relax, till the old people were clean and fed. She scoured and polished with increased zeal, and almost convinced herself that she was accomplishing something.

CHAPTER SEVEN

AFTER their baby was born, it was obvious that the Coutts had given up the struggle against slum conditions. Bobby's job as a lorry driver had come to an end, and he was unable to find builder's work, or any other work at all. He grew more and more slovenly, standing at the corner with a muffler at his throat and a check 'bunnet'. Jean was down at heel, trailing along with the baby in a shawl, shushing it at the close mouth, and screeching with laughter at the women across the way. The single end was sour with clouded milk bottles and half dried woollies, and Jean's excuse was that she 'hadn't time'.

Often, looking in in the morning while shopping, Isa would find her sister still in bed, the baby asleep with a dummy tit in his mouth, and the table not cleared from last night's supper. 'My, some folk's is early!' Jean would say. 'You'll just need tae take us as you find us. I never got nae sleep wi' the wee one till five o'clock. He was that crabbit—aye, he's sleepin' noo. Mind an' no' wake him.'

'I think he's needin' changed,' said Isa, sniffing and drawing back.

'Aye, but I'll no' touch him till he wakes. He's as well tae get his sleep oot.'

Isa, of course, did the cleaning for her. It had been the same before the baby came. 'I'm no' able,' Jean whined, and Isa always obliged. Now she was growing tired of it, but she did what she could for the sake of the baby. Already, young as he was, he seemed to know her. 'You'll have that wean wasted,' said Jean. 'He's gettin' fonder o' his auntie than he is o' me.'

'Nae wonder,' thought Isa.

There is, of course, a certain consolation in playing the part of a martyr, and Isa played the part well. Mary Mochrie, 'The lassie doon the sterr,' with the fox fur, was her chief admirer. Isa had a stock of phrases to meet her sympathy. 'Right enough, I ken it's no' a life for a young lassie, but what can ye dae? My folks comes first. They'd be fair stuck withoot me.

'Right enough, my father does his best. He's had a hard life, that's what he tells us when we grumble. I couldnie leave him noo; still, it's no' fair it's me should get it a' tae dae. Jean's lucky that got mairrit.'

'Mebbe ye'll get mairrit yersel',' said Mary, who had been engaged twice.

'No, I'll no'. I never meet ony chaps. I never get oot.'

Her father thought differently. 'I dinnie ken what ye're grummlin' at,' he argued. 'Ye've been oot every night this week.'

'Just to Jean's.'

'Well, what mair dae ye want? There's plenty tae dae in yer ain hoose, if you'd only settle. There's dominoes, an' halma; ye havenie touched them for a long while —'

'Och, dominoes!' she stormed. 'After bein' cooped up here a' day, I want something mair excitin' than dominoes!'

Mary, who was genuinely impressed and sorry for her, did her best to introduce her to eligible males, but Isa scared them away before the friendship could develop. To them all, she told her hard-luck story, seeking to catch them by pity, if by nothing else. 'I havenie a very happy home life,' she said. 'I've got a couple o' invalids tae look after. Still, I manage. I'll no' always be single.' Then, lest this should be taken to mean that she had already had an offer, she would add, 'Mebbe some day I'll get a hoose o' ma ain, when I meet the right fellie . . .'

Twice, when the man had seemed impressed by her tale, she had asked him up 'to meet her folks'. On each occasion, he had been polite, but had never turned up again. With the second one, she had already started to knit him a scarf, and when he left her in the lurch, as she styled it, she behaved as

if she had been jilted. She added the tale to the long recital
of her woes. 'Aye, I had a fellie once, but he walked out on
me . . .'

'Well, ye're better withoot that kind,' said Johnny. 'Never
heed, you've plenty time yet.'

'Plenty time.' All life resolved itself into a race for a
husband; and day after day, Isa found herself being left
farther behind.

★

Everyone was surprised when Willie came to Adella Street.
Isa, opening the door, saw a short but handsome man with
a soft hat, and a mac over his arm. She did not know him.
It was only when he spoke that she realised who he was.

'My, you're a big stranger!' she drawled. 'Come on in.
Gosh, my father'll be surprised to see you!'

Johnny, startled, was half out of his chair when they came
into the kitchen. He stood petrified, gaping, bent almost
double, one hand on his crippled hip. 'How are you, dad?'
said Willie easily, putting out his hand.

'My—my, this is a surprise! I wouldnie have kent ye,
Willie. Ye were just aboot five when I seen ye last.'

'I wouldn't have known you wither.' The boy had a slight,
attractive trace of the North in his voice. 'I've a weekend's
holiday, so I thought I'd look you up.'

'Very kind o' ye,' said Johnny, rather dryly. Sit doon,
Willie, sit doon! Ye're just in time for yer dinner. My, I
cannie get used tae ye yet . . .'

He had certainly changed from the pale youngster he had
been in his Glasgow days. He was still lean, but his face was
brown with the sun, and full of vitality. Sitting at the fire,
he crossed his legs, and looked round the poky kitchen.

'What dae ye think o' the hoose?' said Johnny, still in the
same dry tone.

'The house? Oh, well—it's all right, but a bit wee, isn't

it? I'm used to plenty of space. To tell you the truth, I'm not keen on Glasgow at all.'

'I can tell that,' said his father. 'It's no' very often you look near us.'

'I'm kept busy,' said Willie quickly. 'You don't get much free time on a farm.'

Isa, pouring potatoes at the sink, clenched her teeth tightly. That was just like her father, to go at a person before they'd had time to get settled. She was going to change the subject, when the wee room door opened, and Aunt Flora came in half dressed, lurching forward precariously to wash herself.

'Here's yer Auntie Flora,' said Johnny. 'She bides wi' us noo. She's a wee bit—you know —'

As soon as she heard her name, Flora turned and saw the visitor. Half embarrassed, half pleased, she rubbed her chin on her shoulder, and sniggered. Willie's face grew red, and he half rose. Isa put down the pot, and gripped the woman by the shoulder.

'Auntie! Away an' dress yersel' right! You're no' decent, comin' ben like that when there's folks in!' Flushing, she steered her back to the bedroom, and shut the door.

'Isa!' Her father glared at her. 'Ye've nae right tae speak tae yer auntie like that. She's as much right here as you. Michty, ye'd think it was royalty was in, instead o' yer ain brother!'

Isa said nothing, but she muttered to herself as she mashed the potatoes with a fork.

During dinner, Willie answered questions about himself and his work. 'Well, I'm saving to go to a college,' he said, 'but it takes a long time. You don't get very much on a farm.'

To change the subject, which seemed to annoy him, as did any talk of money, he asked about Jean. 'I'll take you round after dinner,' said Isa. 'I bet you'll see a difference in her.'

On the way, she enlarged on this difference.

'Gosh, there's none o' them got any go in them! There's our Jean, she's got right slummy since she got mairrit. You'll see, her hoose'll be like a midden. She doesnie try. What do you think our place would be like if it wasnie for me? I'm fair fed up. I wish I was away frae Glasgow a' thegither.'

She kept on about it on the road home. 'You see what I said? Jean's got nae idea o' keepin' hersel' decent noo. An' the wean's no' gettin' a chance, either. What do you think o' it, Willie?'

'Think of what?' Willie had been only half listening.

'Oh, Jean, an'—an' everything.'

'Well, I'm sort of disappointed. You know, Isa, I—I sort of wish I hadn't come. My father does nothing but grumble about the government and his pension, and I know he's hinting at me for more money. Well, I can't afford it. I'm not mean, but I have to work hard for what I get, and I've other plans for it. Then Aunt Flora—wouldn't she be better in a home, where she could get proper attention? It must be an awful job looking after her.'

'Aye, you've nae idea the work I have wi' her. She —'

'And now Jean. She's not making much of herself. You and me are the only ones with any ambition.'

'What can I dae wi' ambition, stuck here —'

'Well, don't go on as if it was my fault, Isa! I'm trying to think what I can do for you. The trouble is, there's nothing, except mebbe have you at the farm for the week, if old Gammack would let me. If you saved up, could Jean see to the old folks for a week?'

'She'd have to,' said Isa indignantly. 'Gosh, if I could just get a wee bit of money! Fancy gettin' away for a whole week!'

★

After Willie had gone, Johnny gave his considered verdict. 'He's got swell-heidit,' he pronounced, sucking his pipe noisily. 'Thinks he's somebody, struttin' doon here wi' his coat ower his airm an' his "How are you, dad?" Fair stuck up wee puggy, that's what he is. "I'm not keen on Glasgow at all," he says. Aye, he kens tae stey as faur away as possible. He's feart he might need tae support his faither, that's what it is!'

Jean, too, had a lot to say. 'My, his accent! He speaks that proper, makin' on he's educated! I couldnie imagine it was my ain brother. He gied the wean a sixpence, as if it wad hurt him. It's a'right for him; he doesnie ken what it is tae live aff the burroo.'

'He doesnie need tae,' snapped Isa. 'He works for his livin'.'

'He's lucky that can,' said Johnny. No, I cannie say I'm pleased wi' Willie. He's mebbe gettin' on, an' advancin' himsel', by his wey o' it, but I'd like tae see a bit mair openness aboot him, a bit mair freedom wi' his money. He didnie even ask me if I wantit a drink.'

'He disnie drink himsel',' said Isa. 'I don't see why he should treat ither folk.'

'I didnie ken you an' Willie were as pally,' said Jean, rocking the baby to and fro in her arms.

'Och, shuttup,' said Isa. 'You'd think it was a crime tae get on a wee bit. I'd stey away mysel' if I got the chance.'

*

It was the following spring when Isa was able to go to Inverness-shire. She had bought a cheap camel coat, paying it up at a shilling a week, and she got her father to give her a hat and new shoes. Everything was accomplished with elaborate ceremony and ritual, the packing of the case, the sticking on of the label, the buying of the railway ticket, the enquiry about train connections, the reminders about sending a wire as soon as she arrived. She took a taxi to the station. It was an expense, but Johnny wanted to see her off, and it saved him all the bother of getting on and off trams. Besides, it impressed the neighbours.

The week was hardly long enough to get to know the place.

She enjoyed being with Willie, who was still almost a stranger to her. But her chief joy lay in her meeting with Andrew White. He was fully a head taller than Willie, with light brown hair, a lazy voice, and a slow smile which showed his large, square teeth. Isa, in her city clothes, watched him grin in sheepish admiration. He had never had a girl; the other men teased him about it, as they teased Willie, but Andrew just laughed at them.

That night he met her—by accident, it seemed, though afterwards he wondered if it had really been accidental. She was hanging round the byre, lifting her feet high as she walked, out of the glaur and the wet. 'Evenin', Miss,' he said shyly, with his slow, serious smile. Isa smiled back. Andrew White was different from the Glasgow keelies she met at home, a real man with an open-air look about him.

It was not long till he knew everything about her. 'I was brought up in the country,' she prattled. 'Me an' Willie are the same, we cannie stick the town, but I'm tied down wi' my folks. It's just through my married sister I was able to get away this week. I'm tryin' to get a' the fresh air I can. It's a wee break for me . . .'

Back in Glasgow, she babbled excitedly over her holiday. 'Oh, Jeannie, I got clicked! I got off wi' a farmer!'

'You never!'

'Aye, I did! I gave him a photie—yon yin o' me wi' the blue frock an' the fancy beads—an' he said I'd tae write tae him. His name's Andrew, but I ca' him Andie. Can ye imagine me mairrit tae a fairmer, eh?'

'Are ye that length a'ready?'

'Och, no', dinnie be daft! A' the same, I think he's quite keen on me. I used tae meet him at nights . . . at last Willie left us thegither . . .'

She wrote regularly, retiring into the 'big' room with pen and ink and Airmail writing pad. She was a good letter writer—that is, she wrote naturally, as she spoke. Her spelling was bad, her grammar imperfect, but she managed to tell all her troubles, what her father had said to her for coming in after ten o'clock, all about the fresh guy that had spoken to her in Crown Street, all about her housework. . . . 'Well, I'll have to close now, as I have to polish the room floor. I wonder sometimes where all the dirt comes from, but I must say I'd rather be clean than not take a pride in my house. My father says I'll make a good wife for some-one, but I say no, nobody ever gets a chance to see me, I'm that busy inside all the time, looking after him. Still, it's my duty, so I suppose I can't complain, though I wish I could be like other girls and get out a bit, it's wearisome always in the house and me just young . . .'

'Whit dae ye get tae say tae that fellie?' her father asked teasingly. 'I'm shair ye've writ enough tae fill a book.'

'Aye, ye'd like tae ken!' Isa licked the stamp as if she were kissing it. 'I find plenty once I get startit!'

She began to watch the post for letters, making a misery of herself six days out of the seven. 'I wonder if there'll be word frae Andie the day? I've wrote him three letters, an' there's nae reply.'

'He'll be busy,' said her father.

'He could write fine. There's nothing tae hinder him.'

When he did write, the letters were brief, but Isa made the most of them. She would go through to the room to read them, and return smiling mysteriously, fitting the sheets into the envelope with tantalising care. She asked for a photo-graph, but he ignored the request. When Mary down the stair asked about it, she explained that he hated being snapped. 'He runs a mile if he thinks you're gonnie take him,' she said. 'Still, he didnie refuse the yin I offered him!'

She invited him to Glasgow. He made excuses about work and the distance, but at last he gave in, and came for a long weekend. Isa scrubbed and polished the house, and spent her hoarded money on a cheap perm. Meeting Andrew at the

station, she kept very close to him on her way up Adella
Street, where everybody, she knew, would be watching. She
laughed up into his face, and put on a Kelvinside accent for
the occasion. Andrew said little. He had smiled slowly when
he shook hands with her, but after that he had been as grave
and correct as a funeral.

★

Andrew was worried. An inoffensive, easily led person, he
did not know what to do about Isa. He liked and admired
her brother, whom he thought a sensible person with an eye
to the future. He admired Isa, too, but she was a different
type, tallish, fair (queer how girls got their hair done into
all those frizzy curls!) and somehow hard. They weren't like
brother and sister at all.

The poor kid had to be hard, of course, to put up with her
home conditions. Now that he saw how she lived, he was
more than ever sorry for her; at the same time, he was somehow repelled. Adella Street was a revelation to him. He had
known poverty in the country, but there it had been healthy,
vagabond poverty, where the poor poached rabbits, and went
barefoot because they didn't like shoes, anyway. He had
seen what could have been called slums, but they had been
picturesque, the roses round the door drowning the smell of
bad drains, and a fine view from the ricketty front door.

Here, there was ugliness and sin. The place seemed peopled
with old women and men who looked as rotten as their
homes. This was where Isa lived. No wonder she had been
glad to get away from it all. The family, too, had been just
as bad as she said. No wonder Willie said so little about
them! The old man was a terror—was there anything of which
he approved? He wanted everything for nothing, and then
grumbled when he got it. Maybe he had had a rotten deal;
but he wasn't doing anything now to improve himself. He
was respectable now, he said, gloatingly; but how much of
his present respectability did he owe to Isa's industry?'

Andrew wanted to take her out, and let her forget her cares for a while. He wanted to take her away from the South side, with its dark mean streets, into the city where there were lights and broad roads and well dressed people. She dressed up as eagerly as a child, and he took her across the river, hurrying as if he were escaping from something.

He enjoyed that evening; but through everything, their walks in the park, their cinema shows and their high teas, he had the fear that this weekend might lead to something he had not intended. He liked Isa as a friend; nothing more. He laughed at himself; a hard-working girl like Isa would not go imagining things into his ordinary behaviour. It was just that he wasn't used to girls.

He had come to this conclusion when Johnny had his talk with him.

Isa was out, and Aunt Flora was dozing by the fire. Johnny lit his pipe, and eased himself in his chair. He was watching the young man carefully.

'She's a good lassie, our Isa,' he said.

'She is that,' said Andrew warily.

'She's been very careful brocht up. She hasnie been oot much wi' men, ye ken. I havenie encouraged her, knowin' the dangers a young wumman has tae face in Glasgow.'

'Aye.' Andrew could think of nothing else to say.

'I've often thought I'd like her tae take up wi' some nice young fellie. I ken she's been tied doon, an' I wouldnie like tae think either her auntie or me had spiled her chances. She diesnie say much tae me, but I can see she feels it sometimes, when she sees her sister mairrit an' wi' a wean. It's only natural she gets discontented, though I will say she's been a good dochter tae me. She's done mair than her brother has, onyway.'

Andrew said nothing.

'It's no' a subject I talk aboot very much,' went on Johnny, 'the only reason I'm openin' it the nicht is because it's been brocht tae my mind wi' seein' Isa openin' oot a wee bit wi' havin' a bit o' companionship. It does me good tae see it. I've always tellt them tae bring hame ony freens they take up wi'. "Bring them up here," I say. "If ye can bring them up tae meet yer folks, there's no' much wrang wi' them."'

'No,' said Andrew.

'You'll no'—I'm no' wantin' tae pry, ye ken, Andie, but I'm just askin' this in a matter o' general interest, dae ye see?—ye'll no' have said onything aboot marriage tae oor Isa?'

'Oh no,' said Andrew. 'I never—I wasn't thinking—it never —'

'That's a' right,' said Johnny, waving his pipe in the air. 'Say nae mair. I was just wantin' tae ask hoo things were. I just wantit tae say that whoever gets Isa's gettin' a rare wee wife, an' they neednie be feared o' bein' burdened wi' Flora an' me.'

'Well —'

'I've thought it a' oot mony a time,' he said. 'I kent fine I couldnie depend on her for ever, though I've nae doot she'd be willin' tae cairry on. But her ain man comes first. When Isa gets mairrit, I'll take steps tae get Flora an' me looked efter elsewhere. It's no' fair tae be a burden on the young, an' I ken Flora would say the same.'

Isa's key rattled in the lock, and Johnny made a sign to change the subject. 'Well?' he said, when she came into the kitchen, 'What are youse twae daein' noo? Away oot for a walk, the pair o' ye. I'll hae a read o' my paper when ye come back.'

Andrew did not want to go. He would have preferred to stay and tell Johnny the exact state of his feelings; but how could he do that when he didn't know himself? He hated the dark wee house, the perpetual feeling of age and decay, the narrowness of the people as expressed in their talk and their views. He wanted to escape from them as soon as

possible; but Isa . . . he hated the thought of leaving her here.
Looking at her, the sulky droop of her mouth when she was
arguing, the almost childish way she took her pleasures, he
convinced himself that she roused in him more than pity.
When he was near her, he found that he wanted to touch
her, to hold her tightly . . . sometime he might do it, and
then, what would happen . . .?

'You're awful quiet, Andie,' she said pertly.

'Aye, I'm thinkin'.'

What if he did? She was the sort of girl he had always
thought of marrying, big, strong and healthy, a wife who
was not afraid of work. Every man needed a wife, though he
had not really considered it until it had been brought to his
notice.

'Isa,' he said. 'Isa, did your father ever say anything to you
about—about getting married?'

'Me? Oh, no!' said Isa innocently.

CHAPTER EIGHT

'WHAT'LL ye dae aboot yer folks?' asked Mary Mochire,
when she heard about the engagement.

'Oh, I dunno. I cannie very well leave them.'

'How did they manage afore?'

'Och, that's different. They're no' gettin' ony younger.'

'Well, neither are you.'

'Aye, but I cannie see them stuck.'

To her sister, however, Isa was more outspoken.

'I'll no' let them doon, but I cannie manage them baith.
There's nothin' tae hinder you takin' yin o' them.'

'I've nae room. Besides, there's the wean —'

'An' what if I have a wean?'

'Och, for Heaven's sake, gie it a rest! You're no' mairrit

yet! Besides, I thought my father was goin' tae see himsel'
fixed up?'

'Aye, but . . .'

And so it went on. Isa was not sure, these days, whether
her consideration for the old folks was genuine, or just a
pose. Sometimes, when the sun shone, and the house was
clean, the grate glittering, and the dinner savoury on the
hob, she felt a slow stirring of something that almost ap-
proached happiness. With it was blended a genuine pity for
the invalids. These people, after all, were her own, and her
father had done what he could to keep them all respectable.
She knew that the other folk on the stair looked on the
Gibsons' as 'better class'. There was never any drunkenness
in their house, and they always rose to the occasion when
anything was wanted, a subscription for a wreath, or a
wedding present. All the conventions were observed. Yes,
they were respectable, and that meant a lot. Looking back on
the last seven years—my, had she been in Glasgow seven
years already?—she saw that things turned out all right. Jean
had got away, to live the life of her own choosing. Soon, she,
Isa, would get away too.

But the days were slow in passing. She wanted excitement
and life, not the mere promise of it. She had waited long
enough; her whole life seemed to have been spent in waiting;
and if Andrew kept her hanging much longer, she might—
well, you never know. A girl couldn't be expected to wait
forever!

*

When war broke out, Glasgow went dark, and the south
side drabber than ever. The long chains of gas lamps disappeared from the river streets, and now there were no lights
to wink in the Clyde, nothing but the dimmed out head-
lamps of trams and buses, and scurrying torches in the fog.
The tenements no longer brightened to the tartan of lighted

windows, chequered over the black stone; the greasy pavements were treacherous, and brick baffle walls and air raid shelters rose to make the streets even more confined. Ribbed with staring white, they squatted at intervals, tenanted by cats and courting couples, and the closes were all buttressed with great wooden joists, blocking up the narrow space, and tripping unaccustomed feet.

Isa seldom went out at night now. More often, Jean and the baby came down to Adella Street. It saved making supper, in their own house, and Bobby always seemed to be at his best in other people's company. He would laugh loudly, teasing Aunt Flora, and making violent love to Isa. 'Och, *stop* it, Bobby!' she would shriek, struggling with him, and laughing shrilly, 'I'm no' needin' you; I've got a man o' my ain!'

'Och, behave yersel', Bobby!' Jean would scream. 'D'ye ken, he has me fair affrontit when he's oot onywhere, but in his ain hoose I can hardly get a word oot o' him. If it wasnie for the wean, I'd be fair lonesome. The wean kens his mammy, divn't ye, hen? Oh, the braw!—' it went on and on in one long blare of sound.

Mary Mochrie's visits were perhaps more stimulating. She seemed to be having a grand time up in the city. 'I'm oot nearly every night wi' ma pals,' she would say. 'An' gosh, it's great!' She had tales to tell of the various 'clicks' she had had. The Central Station was swarming with Americans who spoke just like the films, and there were New Zealand airmen, black Africans, and gallant Aussies strange to Scotland. The Poles, however, were the darlings of every Glasgow girl, heel-clicking, romantic, with their pathetic ignorance of Scotch, and their willingness to learn. ('I buy you freesh-sup-pair, no?') Mary, of course, had a Pole. 'You ought tae get yin, Isa,' she said confidentially. 'There's nae herm in it. Just tae go oot for the night wi' —'

But Isa would not fall. 'I'm no' yin o' thae lassies,' she

said. 'I couldnie dae a thing like that, no' when my man's no' here tae stick up for himsel'.'

'Will he no' be ca'd up?'

'No, he's reserved. His employer'll get him off. Same wi' our Willie, he's reserved an' a'.'

It was good to see the war passing them by. Bobby was in the army, but there was no sign of him going abroad. He came home on leave every three months, causing Jean to clean furiously, then neglect her home worse than ever. She spent a great deal of time at Adella Street, reading out extracts from her letters, and watching Isa prepare meals. 'Aye, well, I'll mebbe just stay an' hae a wee bite. It's no' worth cookin' for just masel' an' the wee yin . . .'

Johnny enjoyed the war. It gave him fresh scope for his criticisms. He spent the mornings in bed, with his pipe and newspaper, reading out items, and providing an acid commentary. 'I see they're tryin' tae raise the pensions. No' afore time. Wait an' you'll see, they'll waste as long bletherin' aboot it, we'll a' be deid afore they're done. It's easy seen it's no' the man in the street that's runnin' this war. Thae big bugs in England just sits still, an' us common yins has tae go an' dae a' the fightin'. I ken; I was in the last lot.'

Even the measures for his own safety gave him cause for complaint. He resented the Air Raid Warden's visits, and he insisted on being fitted with a gas mask at his own home. 'I'm no' able tae walk a' that distance,' he protested. 'If they're wantin' me tae wear yin o' thae things, they can just come an' gie me yin. Hoo the Hell dae they expect ye tae breathe wi' yin o' thae?'

'It'll no' be that if you're gassed,' pointed out Isa.

'Ach, we'll no' be gassed. I ken as much aboot gas as ony o' thae A.R.P. yins. Look at yon Jimmy Brownlie doon the sterr—whit does he ken aboot it? Right enough, it's a funny war this—they gie ye a wee bit badge, an' a tin hat, an' ye kid yersel' ye're a sodger. I'm tellin' ye, we'll be just aboot as bad as the Jerries in a wee while. They're gaun the right way aboot it. A' this rationin'—I bet thae yins at the tap doesnie dae wi' half a pun' o' sugar!'

He was glad that Willie and Andrew were reserved. 'Oor Willie could dae wi' a taste o' the army,' he said, 'but he's right tae stey oot as long as he can. Ye'll be glad Andie's safe an' a'?'

It was then that Isa dropped her bombshell.

'Oh, Andie says he'll no' go, even if they ca' him up,' she said. 'He's gonnie register as a Conscientious Objector.'

Her father took the pipe out of his mouth, and the veins on his forehead zig-zagged down, throbbing and purple. 'A *What?*' he said, his voice all throaty and choked. 'What did ye say?'

'A conscientious objector,' said Isa, wondering if she had mispronounced it. 'How?'

'A—a bloody conchie! I'm tellin' ye, Isa, there's nae lassie o' mine gonnie marry a conchie. I'm tellin' ye, now! Mind, I'm tellin' ye!'

'Aye, but—he's no' exactly a conchie, yet. He's reserved. It's just if—he says he doesnie believe in wars. He's no' gonnie kill chaps he doesnie ken, that's what he says.'

'Och aye, the same auld stuff! Where wad we ha' been in the last war if we'd a' been conchies? Eh? Where wad we ha' been?'

Isa challenged him. 'I thought you said it was daft tae volunteer?'

'That's different. I cannie dae wi' a' this Pacifist stunt. They're no' pacifists at a', they're just feart. They should get the same as they get up the line for cowardice—pit against a wa' an' shot; nae bother.'

'You've nae business sayin' that aboot Andie!'

'I'll say what I like, an' don't you be sae damnt cheeky. I'll no' hae yin o' thae conchies for a son-in-law. I ken that crowd! Yin o' the dirtiest tricks I ever had played on me was wi' a conchie.'

'Well, I cannie help that. It wasnie Andie.'

'Doesnie maitter. I'm just tellin' ye.'

★

Isa was perturbed. She had never thought of Andrew as a coward, but her father's words had struck home. In her next letter, she mentioned the matter, telling him of her father's threats. 'Not that I mind,' she said, 'I'll marry you no matter what, but I would like the wedding to go off in harmony, and no quarrels regards our different opinions. If I knew how we stand, I could act according.'

Andrew's decision was a long time in coming.

Dear Isa, he wrote,

I feel you would be much happier if I was in the army. You have not said it, but I feel it in every word you write, as if you was trying not to be ashamed of me. At that rate, you must be ashamed of your own brother too, as him and me feel the same about not fighting, only he is more determined than me, and is going to stick to his views. I wish I had his courage, which I haven't. For my part, I still think the same, but do not think I could stand anyone despising me on that account, least of all you, Isa. I have therefore volunteered, and am expecting my papers any day now. I feel perhaps I have been wrong in doing this, but if you are pleased I will be quite happy. I am not sure about how I stand about getting my job back after the war, but if you like we will get married on my next leave, as things are very uncertain just now . . .

She was shocked, shamed, elated, she hardly knew what she felt. For the first time, now, she really felt she was engaged, with wedding arrangements on the way, and the date almost fixed. She wanted to be married in white, and once again, the affluent Mary Mochrie came to the rescue. 'I'll lend ye a frock, Isa. Ye deserve a nice weddin', efter a' ye've been through. My white yin's aboot your size—it was aye a bit big for me. You'll be needin' a veil, but I ken a lassie's got yin she'll lend ye. My, it's fair excitin' . . .'

'You're surely gonnie be awfie posh,' said Jean, her brows raised querulously. 'A white frock, an' a veil, an' a'—when I got mairrit, I had tae make do wi' a costume.'

'Well, it's no' as if I was buyin' the frock,' argued Isa.

'No, but ye're buyin' plenty besides. It's funny how you can manage tae get roon my faither. He didnie gie me a' that.'

'Well, I'm sure I've worked for it. I staun' plenty off him, maist o' the time.'

Johnny, indeed, did seem eager to please his younger daughter. Isa half suspected his motive, his desire to keep in with her lest he should find himself cast off when she became independent, but she did not let the thought worry her. You only get married once! Let everything be the best, then; have a cake, a car with ribbons, and let everybody see that the Gibsons are as good as their neighbours!

Everything went off well; rather better than at Jean's wedding, she thought triumphantly. Jean and her man sat rather dumped and disappointed, as if they were thinking of the day when they had made the same promises. Now wee Peter Coutts was walking, staggering about at the reception, amusing everyone. At least, thought his mother, she was still that much ahead. She made a great effort to assert herself, carrying the child about, telling everyone, 'Aye, it just seems yesterday I went the same road. Well, I've nae regrets. I only hope she's as happy as we've been, eh, Bobby?' Bobby grinned rather sheepishly, and said nothing.

The wedding couple went up to Inverness for three days, and then the war claimed Andrew again, and he put on his battledress, shouldered his kitbag, and kissed his wife good-bye. That night, Isa went round to her sister's, and they sat by the fire more amiably than they had done for a long time, bound by the mutual pain of separation. 'Aye, it's terrible,' said Jean. 'I'm glad I've got the wean. You've to go through a lot tae get them, but it's worth it in the end. Wait till ye've yin o' yer ain, Isa, an' you'll see.'

'Och, we're no' that length yet,' said Isa.

Taking stock of her position, she found that she had not advanced very far. She was still tied to Glasgow, with its fog, its mirk and its litter, and the old people still shuffled in front of her, tripping her up when she wanted to hurry on alone. At least, she could say she was married; her future was reasonably secure, and there was the present consolation of extra money. She had a soldier's wife's allowance, and, to her, thirty-five shillings a week was wealth. She bought a regimental brooch, and a locket to hold Andrew's photograph. She made a fetish of being photographed herself, and sending prints to her husband in return for the routine portraits in which every soldier invests as soon as he gets into uniform. She bought cheap flashy frames for these likenesses, and hung under them little texts in tartan, 'Bring Our Boys Safe Home,' and bunches of white heather and artificial forget-me-nots. She left no doubts in the mind of anyone that she had a man in the army. The fact blazed from every ornament, every corner of the kitchen. The top of the dresser looked like a shrine. 'Well,' protested Isa, 'it shows I appreciate my husband. You've got to show yer feelin's.'

CHAPTER NINE

AUNT FLORA died in the spring. She had been improving, by slow degrees, in everything but intellect and understanding, and Johnny was so pleased that he had made plans to take her out—or rather, for Isa to take her out. 'She's gettin' mair like hersel',' he said with delight. 'I'm tellin' ye, in yon place they treated her like a daftie. That's nae good tae onybody. This time next year she ought tae be able tae get oot by hersel'.'

And indeed, there was a difference in her. She seemed to move more easily, and her hands were more controlled, so that she did not need so much attention at the table. She could not carry on a conversation, other than by odd phrases, often unrelated to what was being discussed, but she was not so apt to giggle and grimace. The winter had passed without any serious ills; and now Isa was looking over her outdoor clothes, and trying to make them respectable.

'This is a terrible coat,' she grumbled. 'It's fair oot o' fashion. Naebuddy wears thae big cuffs nowadays.'

'Pit her wee fur on, an' it'll look a'right.'

'Och, the fur's no' much better. I fair hate tae take her oot lookin' like that. Is there nothin' else she can wear?'

'She's no' needin' nothin' else. It's no' as if she was oot every day. I'm sure naebuddy's gonnie worry what she's on.'

'No, but I worry.'

'Well, worry away. If you're wantin' tae get her a new coat, ye can pay for it yersel'.'

So Isa, grumbling, had to content herself with mending the frayed buttonholes, brushing and sponging at the stains, and pressing the baggy sleeves. The coat was a dingy brick colour, and the hat to match was of straw, deep and bucket-like. At the wedding she had had the loan of a coat . . . Johnny felt a sudden misgiving when he saw her dressed. She was a large woman, and years of sitting had added inches to her girth. The coat stretched over her big hips and bust, and the hat came down over her eyes, shading her fat, dull face. 'Put in your teeth, Auntie,' Isa insisted, and the poor woman stood mouthing at them, uncomfortable, with the great custard-coloured wedges square between her lips.

'Take care o' her noo,' said Johnny. 'See an' no' walk her too far.'

Flora grinned uneasily, and looked at her large feet.

'Take her intae the park,' said Johnny. 'She can sit an'
git the sun. If there's ony sweeties in the shop, ye can get
her some. See she enjoys hersel'.'

'O.K.' said Isa, without enthusiasm.

When they had gone, he limped through to the front room
to watch their progress. There they went, right down the
middle of Adella Street, keeping to the road to avoid the
brick baffle walls. The sun was red with mist, and at the end
of the street, like silver smudges in the dimness, the towers
and chimneys beyond the Clyde stretched with a curious
illusion of nobility. Towards the river went the two women,
arm in arm, slowly, swaying from side to side as they walked.
Johnny felt a sudden possessive love for them. The garbage
flapped and stank in the gutter, and old newspaper blew in
the spring wind, but, never heeding, the women went on
steadily, step by step away from him. He leaned on the sill
to watch them, the stone cold on his palms. On they went,
rock, rock, rock—did Flora stagger, or was it just his
imagination? The whole street seemed to be swaying, the
black tenements slanting outwards from the pavements, the
slits of light between the houses now broad, now narrowing,
and all the time the women going away from him . . . he drew in
his head and shut the window, holding on by the shutter till
the dizziness had passed. 'I doot I havenie a heid for heights,'
he said to himself. 'I was nearly a waster that time.'

Isa was unhappy. She wished she had thought of asking
Jean to come with her. She was acutely conscious of her aunt,
plodding along like a brick-red elephant, and she tried to
move faster, to escape from the people who must be
watching, wondering who the old dame could be. They
turned right, into Glasgow Green, past the iron gates and
the sparse rows of trees. Here, there were seats, where they
could rest until it was time to go home again. No use trying
to go farther.

From her handbag, Isa took a folded copy of the *Red Letter*. At least, it would help to pass the time. It was quiet in the green, and the sparrows, tame and impudent, cheeped and hopped in flocks in the tawny grass. Everything was bare and bleached, in the last deadness, before bursting into leaf. The coloured trams, gliding past, seemed silent and far away.

It was the silence which disturbed her at last. She had read through all the serials, and was about to start on the last story, when she heard the soft whirr at her feet. They had been sitting so still that the sparrows had come right up, and were playing within an inch of their toes. As Isa moved, they flew up in a brown cloud, and their wings made a draught in the air. It seemed suddenly cold. She looked at her aunt, and saw her sitting huddled up, her eyes screwed, her mouth tight and blue, and her hands in a knot in her lap.

'Aunt Flora!' said Isa.

The woman did not answer. Isa shook her arm.

'Aunt Flora, come on, we're goin' home now. Are ye comin'? That's a nice rest ye've had . . .' she began to panic, shaking her roughly, pulling at her coat, hitting her on the shoulders. A policeman passed, stared curiously, and returned.

'Anything wrong, Miss?'

'No—I just—she'll no' answer! She was out for the first time the day, an' now she'll no' speak. Auntie! Auntie Flora!'

'Easy, now. Don't get rough! Here, Missis!' He touched her lightly on the face, and she relaxed suddenly, as if his touch had been magic. Slowly, she grinned at him, rubbing her chin on her shoulder.

'All right, now?' he asked kindly. 'You gave the young lady a fright. Must have dropped off to sleep. Here, see if she's all right on her legs. She's mebbe a bit stiff with the sitting.'

Flora could stand; but, once out of the park, her walk became erratic. Sometimes she would give a great lurch

sideways, and when Isa pulled her up, she would look at her
indignantly. Once she stopped altogether, and Isa was shamed
almost to tears to see a trickle of water run down her
stockings and dribble away in the dust. 'Och, come on an'
hurry!' she snapped, and dragged her away. The stairs were
a nightmare, coiling round and round without a handrail,
but at last they were at the door, and she was dragging Flora
over the threshold. As soon as she was set into her chair, the
old woman began to cry.

'Whit's up wi' her?' asked Johnny, his cheeks puffed out
in dismay. 'Ye havenie tired her, takin' her too far?'

'I never!' Isa herself was almost in tears. 'We just went
as far as the green, an' we sat in the sun a' the time. She's
wet hersel', that's what's wrong. I'm no' takin' her oot again,
I'm no' carin'. I was fair affrontit, her wettin' hersel' like a
wean.'

'Well, never heed that the noo. Get her chinged an' intae
her bed. She's lookin' cauld. Here, hen, dinnie greet. Ye're
a' right, Flora. Gies a wee smile; come on, bonny Flora
MacDonald . . .'

He wheedled away while Isa changed her, washed her, and
did all the intimate tasks which so turned her stomach. They
put her to bed, and brought her hot tea before she went to
sleep; but when Isa went to call her in the morning, she
was dead.

Isa could not feel regret. Inside her, something was singing
at her release. No more dirty washing, no more searching in
the thick hair, no more guiding the heavy woman about,
resentful of her weight. And yet, through the relief, there
was also a sense of sorrow, the sorrow that was never far from
the atmosphere of the street, the sorrow of her father's
bereavement, the automatic pain of conventional mourning.
The sun half shone through the clouds, into the dust of the
backyard, and then melted away in a grey mist. Isa hushed
her voice, and met the neighbours on the stairhead. 'Aye, my

auntie Flora,' she said. 'She just slipped away in her sleep. She must have got a chill yesterday. Aye, my faither's takin' it awfie hard. He'll no' eat nor nothin'.'

Johnny went back and forward from the kitchen to the bedroom, touching the dead woman's face. 'Aye, Flora? Is that you away? I could have kept ye fine, tae. Bonny Flora . . .

The funeral was all that they could have wished. The 'Society' saw to that. Willie came to Glasgow, but would not stay the night. 'It wasnie very nice o' him goin' off like that,' said Jean afterwards. 'I'd have thought he might have stayed wi' my faither for a wee while. You can see he's had a shock.'

They whispered together all the evening. At nine o'clock, Johnny went to his bed. He had changed beds with Isa now, and slept in the big room. 'You'd better watch him,' said Jean. 'Ye never ken what might happen tae him when he's like that.'

'Ocht, there's always something,' grumbled Isa, putting on the kettle for another cup of tea. But as she laid the cups out, she saw her aunt's empty chair, and a laugh trembled inside her. No harm to the old woman, but she had been nothing but a nuisance. Now she was gone, and, sad as it was, it was a good riddance to her.

*

'There's always something.' The next thing was a War Office letter to say that Andrew had been wounded in Africa. Isa immediately went into a state. 'Oh, my man! My man's woundit! What'll I dae? Oh, Andie —!' Jean came round and hovered about the kitchen. 'Aye, I ken what you're feelin' like, hen. I ken what I'd be like if it was ma Bobby.'

'But it's no' your Bobby! It's always me that things happens tae. Whit wey is it always me?'

By next morning, however, she had calmed down, and rather enjoyed her position, the position of a woman whose husband had been wounded fighting for her and for his country. People stopped her in the street, or came up to her in the butcher's queue, and asked about him. Pale and restrained, she answered in a tired voice. She knew what they were saying about her, 'Aye, she's a brave lassie, Isa Gibson. You wouldnie think she'd had a' that bother, yon auld wumman deein' on her hands, an' her faither tae look efter, an' now her man woundit. Aye, some folks gets it hard . . .'

In time, she learned what had happened to him. One of his arms was riddled with shrapnel, and his jaw had been broken. The worst injury, however, was to his leg. It was feared that he might be crippled for life.

Isa kept the letter for a long time before she told her father. Somehow, she could not bear to break the news to him, with him hirpling around the house, crippled himself. Then there was the feeling that somehow, he was to blame. If he had not been so down on pacifists, Andrew would never have been driven to join up. After all, he had been reserved. If she thought too much about it, she might lose her temper, and say more than she intended. When at last she did tell him, briefly and coldly, his sympathy shamed her.

'Aye, it's a pity, a fine young fellie like that. Ye'll notice it's aye the best yins –' he paused, confused, and looked down at his own twisted hip. 'Ah well,' he finished, 'he'll mebbe staun' his chance yet. They can dae great things nooadays, ye ken.'

When Andrew was moved to a hospital in Scotland, Isa with much pomp and circumstance, set off to visit him. He came towards her on crutches, and she watched with the smile of welcome tight round her gums. Why, he—he was worse than her father! The thought of it made her faintly sick. Fancy having to live with an invalid all over again; she had never counted on that. Andie was her husband, and her own age; that was always something; and, at least, his treatment was not yet finished. There was still a chance of improvement; but . . .

'Isa,' he said, 'what is it? You knew, didn't you? You looked sort of funny.'

'It's all right,' she said. 'Just the shock. I've been that worried, Andie!'

'You don't need to worry about me. I'll be all right. I'm lucky to be alive, you know.'

'Aye.'

'And I'll get a pension. I'm sure we've a lot to be thankful for.' His lips were cold and sneering as he spoke. 'Aye,' said Isa again. She did not know what else to say.

CHAPTER TEN

AFTER the first shock of her husband's lameness, Isa began to look forward to having him home with her. When he was discharged, she decorated the house as if for a party. The kitchen shone with Brasso and furniture polish, and clean curtains hung stiff on the bed recess.

Andrew accepted all these attentions without pleasure. He seemed to want nothing more than quietness. Johnny stared and puffed his cheeks, and hobbled about trying to make him comfortable. 'No, dinnie get up, Andie, I'll get it for ye. Dinnie you move.' He dragged himself round and round the kitchen, till Andrew bit his lips to keep from screaming. He hated to see the old man, a cripple, attending to him; it rubbed into him his own fate, his own helplessness. Better to have had the leg off altogether; then, at least, he could have had a false one, and walked erect.

At night, he tried desperately to be frank with Isa.

'Isa, I'll never get work like this.'

'Och, never heed that the now. You're just new back, Andie.'

'But we might as well get it sorted out once and for all.

This is different to what we expected. I thought I'd be able to support you, and get you out of this dump; now I'm just another drag.'

'Och, no, you're no', Andie!'

'But I am! Look at your father; he had ideas, hadn't he? He told me all about them, before I joined up. Look at him now!'

'Well, he's kept himsel' respectable.'

'Och, respectable! If this is what you call respectability, livin' in a room the size of a pig sty, fighting bugs all the time, I've another name for it. Who the hell wants that sort of respectability?'

'Well, it's just that my folks —'

'Aye, your folks. They've dragged you down all their days, and now it's me. Well, I'm not asking you to —'

'Andie! What a like thing to say!'

'Well, it has to come some time. I'm no use to you, Isa, and the sooner you face it, the better.'

'Oh Andie!' She put her arms round his neck, sobbing desperately. 'Andie, stop it! We'll be a'right, Andie. We'll manage. We'll manage fine.'

'Well, I hope so,' he said glumly.

'And you're no' tae go on like that again. You get me fair scared. We'll manage, eh? Say it, Andie.'

'All right,' he said briefly. 'We'll manage.'

For the moment, she was comforted.

After that, they lived together amiably enough, but there was an undeniable gulf between them. At first, the difference had been merely that of environment, each life narrow in its own way; but now, Andrew had been abroad, met people, and shared experiences she would never know. He could not explain why he had drawn away from her, and she could not or would not understand. She thought that his injury was at the root of his moodiness, but she was only partly right. When at last he sank into uncomplaining resignation, she felt that she could expect no more. He was good to her, and he was her husband. Be thankful for small mercies.

*

Johnny was worried. He had been down to the lowest depths of poverty, and then had come the turning point of his life, the slow uphill climb, the striving towards betterment. He had raised his family, lifted his sister from degradation, and known the kingly feeling of being a householder, a man with a home of his own, and women to look after him. Well, they were settled now, and all provided for. Andrew had found a job addressing envelopes in a large store, and until he could find better work, and a home of his own, he and Isa had no intention of moving. It seemed that the future was secure for everybody; and yet, Johnny was worried.

There was a change in Isa. Now, more than ever, she was house-proud, mock-genteel in her ways. She worried over any spot on the floor, any smear on the grate or window. It was nag, nag, nag, morning, noon and night; and when he protested, she would toss her head, and say, 'Well, it's no' as if I needed tae stey here. Me an' Andie could easy go an' get a hoose o' wur ain. It's just that I'm no' wantin' tae see ye stuck that I'm bidin' here.'

'Ye're awfie independent all o' a sudden. Whae's hoose is it, eh? Dae ye realise I'm still boss here? The hoose is in my ain name, mind.'

'Well, look efter it yersel', then, an' see how ye get on.'

It had never been like this before. No matter how great their discontent, the girls had always deferred to him in the end. Now Isa went her own way, hoity-toity, sullen and perverse. It was nothing to do with Andie, who kept his own counsel, quiet-like, brooding a lot, though he never grumbled. Perhaps he was dreaming of fields and horses and harvesting, and what could you say to a man in that mood, when you knew he'd never follow a plough again?

Gradually, Johnnie's confidence and comfort seeped away. Everything he had built round him was slipping. He lost his sense of ownership, the almost patriarchal sense of dignity which he imagined he possessed. So far as he was concerned, he might have been nothing in the house, or just a burden. Had Flora felt like this, the wondered? But Flora had been witless, and therefore impervious to hurt.

He grew more and more silent and withdrawn. Sometimes he cringed when he was nagged at and his movements became furtive, always trying to conceal things, the drip of soup on his trousers, the tea stain on the cloth, the cut on his face when he was shaving. If he had had some money, if he had been younger, he would have gone away on his own, but where could he go now? Only to Jean's, and Jean had no room; besides, she might not want him; she probably wouldn't. There was only one alternative, and he put it away from him as soon as it entered his mind. It was a last ditch move, only to be used as a threat when things became desperate.

He mentioned it once during a quarrel. 'I'm gettin' fair sick o' this,' he blustered. 'I cannie get a bit o' consideration in my ain home. I'd be better off in the poor-hoose.'

There. It was out now the spectre which had been troubling him for so long. He had exorcised it by acknowledging its presence, and now it would go for ever. But, after tea, when the house was tidy and quiet, cosy, the way he liked it, Isa said, in a timid but unusually friendly tone, 'Mind you said yon about the poorhouse . . . did you really mean that— that —'

'How do you mean?' he said.

'Well—well —' Her face was red, and one of her knees trembled as she spoke. 'I—I'm going to have a baby, an' I—Andie an' me thought if you were somewhere—no' the poorhouse, nothing like that, but a sort of respectable home for men, it would . . . no' that we want rid o' you, but it's a job having *two* folk when you're no' just right . . . we thought . . .'

It had come at last. He looked at the warm kitchen, the crimson fire purring and sparking in the grate, the pictures on the walls, the bright American cloth along the dresser, the scrubbed sink, and the red cover on the table. It wasn't only the kitchen, there were the other two rooms—a two room and kitchen house. Outside, there was a wind, and a batter of rain on the black courtyards. His heart was beating like a wheel inside him, drawing the breath from his throat and the blood from his face, but he said in a calm, clear voice, strangely far away in his own hearing, 'Aye, Isa, that's what I've been thinkin' mysel' for a long time.'

The family, of course, had to be consulted about it. Willie came down to join in the discussion. Andrew was the only one who said nothing. The others went round and round the subject, with Isa on the defensive all the time.

'It's no' that I grudge it, but I'll never manage when I have my wean.'

'I'd take him,' said Jean, with great satisfaction, 'but I havenie room.'

Willie was restless and uneasy.

'You're all talking as if the two of you had done everything. You seem to forget I've been helping to keep him for years. I could have done with all that money I've given him.'

'Well, it's the least you could do.'

'I'm just telling you, that's all.'

'Well, you're going on as if we've no right tae suggest puttin' him away.'

'I am not. But . . . well, I don't like it, that's all. Still . . . even if he'd pots of money, he'd still need a woman to look after him.'

'Aye, a wumman. It's aye the weemen. Well, I'll have enough weeman's work in a wee while. I'm no' wantin' tae be habbled *a*' my days, as I've been in the past.'

'Did he *say* he wanted to go?' asked Willie.

'Aye. Well, he sort of hinted, an' then I asked him, an' told him how I was placed, an' he said aye, he'd been thinkin' aboot it for a long time.'

'Well . . .' Jean knit her dark brows. 'It's awfie like pittin' him oot his ain hoose . . . but what can ye dae?'

'Aye, what can ye dae?'

And so Johnnie's fate was decided.

*

The man's ward was warm and clean. As the Warden ushered Johnnie in, the other old men moved up and made room for him at the fire. They were very clean old men, smelling of disinfectant and tobacco. Johnny felt that he, too, had never been so clean in his life.

Gradually, as they grew used to his presence, they asked him questions, insinuating themselves gently into his private life. 'I came in voluntary,' insisted Johnny. 'Aye, I wasnie *pit* in. I had a hoose o' my ain, a two room an' kitchen, but I couldnie—well, I —'

'You couldnie keep it up, like?' A man with his nose eaten away scratched his head and nodded.

'Aye, I could keep it up! I'm tellin' ye I *gied* it up! I came in voluntary. They wouldnie have got me in if I hadnie wantit tae come; but my youngest dochter's no' long mairrit, an'—an' I gied her the hoose as a present. Me, I'm no' carin' where I bide. The hoose was in my name, but I gied it up voluntary.

There was a buzz of admiration and disbelief, the kind of sound heard in barracks when a soldier announced that he *likes* the army. Outside, through cold corridors, a bell rang. 'Come on,' said the noseless man eagerly, 'That's dinner. There's spicy duff the day.'

Johnny's eyes went dull. 'I'll no' heed dinner,' he said. 'I'M no' very hungry. I had a meal—a *good* meal afore I came oot.'

At home, Isa was remembering that last meal. Johnny had crumbled bread, and spilled his tea, and had attempted a fearful, ghastly gaiety as he went out. His Harry Lauder stick went scrape on the landing, his coat trailed on the floor. 'Well, cheerybye,' he said at the poorhouse gate, blowing out his cheeks bravely. Isa sat and thought of it all, restless, with no notion of working or anything.

'It seems queer withoot him,' said Andie, for the fifth time.

'Aye.' She scored a knife along the tablecloth. 'Still, I don't see what else I could dae. They cannie say I havenie done my bit.'

'No.' There was something despondent in the man's tone. Isa put her arms on his shoulders, and tried to smile.

'We'll get on better now, eh, Andie, just oursel's? We're no' bad off. We've got a hoose tae wursel's, an' a pansion. We'll manage fine, eh?'

'Oh, we'll manage,' said Andie. But he did not look at her as he said it.

This book is set in 12-pt. Centaur, a design based on punches cut in the fifteenth century by Nicolas Janson who was one of the earliest and most successful of Continental printers. Mr Bruce Rogers designed the Arrighi Italic which accompanies Centaur. The face was cut by the Monotype Corporation and is chosen to interpret and emphasize fine prose or poetry. Centaur was used for printing the Oxford Lectern Bible.

Illustrations by Ida Procter, typography by Henry Jacob.